"Fans of Avery Corman, age 50 or not, will take this gentle book to heart. In a way, Corman draws on two of his previous works, *Kramer vs. Kramer* and *The Old Neighborhood*, to create a story that resonates with nostalgia, pain, ambition and insight. . . . A novel of compelling sensitivity."

Chattanooga Times

"Sensitively, lovingly written . . . You come to care for the characters. . . . When the book is completed, you'll be angry with yourself for reading so quickly."

Grand Rapids Press

"With humor and tenderness Avery Corman treats his morose middle-class character with an affection that is touching. . . . The wonderful thing about Doug Gardner is his grit. He's got principles, he's got guts and he's got the will to persevere. Doug's a winner. And so's this book."

Wichita Falls Times

"Gardner's predicament lends itself to touching and witty storytelling. [Corman's] descriptions of Gardner's relationship with his children are poignant and priceless. . . . The novel is entertaining indeed."

Cosmopolitan

Also by Avery Corman:

OH, GOD!

KRAMER VERSUS KRAMER*

THE OLD NEIGHBORHOOD

*Published by Ivy Books

50

Avery Corman

IVY BOOKS • NEW YORK

FOR JUDY

Ivy Books
Published by Ballantine Books
Copyright © 1987 by Avery Corman, Inc.

Library of Congress Catalog Card Number: 87-4602

ISBN-0-8041-0300-3

This edition published by arrangement with Simon and Schuster, Inc.

Manufactured in the United States of America

This novel is a work of fiction. Names, characters, places and incidents are either the product of the author's imagination or are used fictitiously. Any resemblance to actual events or locales or persons, living or dead, is entirely coincidental.

First Ballantine Books Edition: December 1988

1

AFTER THE EYE EXAMINATION DOUG GARDNER SAT across from Dr. Jeffrey Weiss in an office so dark with its heavy leather furniture, murky brown wallpaper and dim lighting, the only good light a desk lamp on the doctor's desk, he thought it might have been a psychological ploy. Everyone leaves here thinking he's going blind and is, therefore, in desperate need of Dr. Weiss's ophthalmology. Weiss was trim, about six feet tall, with a full head of blond hair. He was probably one of those people who regularly passed Doug on the jogging track in Central Park while Doug slogged along. Everyone passed him. Doug loathed jogging and did it because of the articles, all that evidence about cardiovascular benefits that would keep you alive longer. Nobody gave you an actual number, though. Will one thousand miles of tedious jogging give you an extra six days, six weeks? And when do you get your jogger's bonus, he wondered. Now, when you're still able to eat a pastrami sandwich, or at the end when you're already on a life-support system?

"When was your last eye examination?" Dr. Weiss asked in a sharp tone.

Doug judged this dour man to be in his late 30s. The problem, suddenly, was not the headaches from eye strain or that he was holding his reading matter so far away he was running out of arm length—it was that he was getting older than the doctors.

"About five years ago," Doug said.

"Five years?" Dr. Weiss responded with disapproval. "You shouldn't wait five years at your age, Mr. Gardner."

"For anything?"

Dr. Weiss did not smile at Doug's remark. What does this mean? Does he have dire information on his pad?

"You have a typical diminution of focusing abilities for your age group," the doctor said charmlessly. "Middle-age eyes, I call it. You need reading glasses."

"Just for reading?"

"Yes. But I'd like to make a suggestion. If you engage in any sports involving a ball, racquetball, tennis, buy yourself a shatterproof eye guard. You'd be surprised at how many men your age I see with serious eye injuries. Let's face it, your eye-hand coordination starts to go, too."

"This is turning out to be more than I want to know on the subject."

"I'm just being factual, Mr. Gardner."

"Yes, I get that."

"I'll write you a prescription for the glasses. I suggest you make an appointment to come back in six months."

Did he have to add the part about eye-hand coordination? Doug had good eyes once, the Eddie Stanky of his day, with an ability to wait patiently and foul off pitches for walks. As he headed along crowded Forty-second Street in Manhattan, another of the people with poor posture, their faces drawn with New York tension, he

2

conceded that getting bases on balls was no longer a marketable skill for him. He hadn't prided himself on not wearing glasses, the idea of glasses never occurred to him one way or the other. Now that he had to wear them and would continue to have headaches if he did not, he felt as if he were starting to creak, a tin man needing oil. The left shoulder was stiff as well. "Adhesive capsulitis," the orthopedist had told him. Doug awoke one morning and couldn't put his left arm in his shirtsleeve. "It's a mystery sometimes how it gets started. Think of it as similar to tendonitis." He gave Doug arm exercises to do. Stiff shoulder. Fading vision. Am I becoming a hypochondriac? Or am I beginning to break down? And, frankly, is there any difference?

He entered Vision Opticians on Madison Avenue and was approached by an attractive Hispanic-looking woman in her 20s, almond-shaped eyes behind glasses lightly tinted blue, a wedding band on her finger.

"May I be of help?"

"My first pair of glasses. I have a prescription."

"What we need to do is select a frame that fits your personality. What *is* your personality?" she said coquettishly.

"Beats me."

"We have a thousand frames."

"I must be in there somewhere."

She guided him to a seat at a small table with a standup mirror and he looked at himself in the first glasses she suggested.

"This is very popular. The Urbanite," she said, showing him a frame that was similar to those of aviator glasses.

"The Urbanite?"

He looked in the mirror, barely noticing the glasses, scrutinizing himself. Doug Gardner had a sharp, angular face, as if he had been chipped out of wood by a primitive craftsman in a hurry, a wide nose broken several times in sports as a youth, brown eyes and receding brown hair. Five feet ten, slightly built, his weight was usually in the 150s. He had taken to weighing himself daily of late. Am I good-looking? Would this Hispanic lovely, married, who sees men in this place all day, go home with me? Of course not. But would it be her fantasy, too? I'd settle for that, for it to be her fleeting fantasy.

He appraised himself in the glasses. "These look like aviator glasses," he said.

"No, this is the Aviator." She produced a more extreme version of the first.

"Do you have the Bertolt Brecht, the Franz Kafka?"

"We don't carry that line."

"Glasses that say this is an intelligent man of character." She was confused. "Simple, round glasses with a thin wire frame," he explained.

"Oh, the Librarian!" she said triumphantly.

She found the glasses and he tried them on.

"You look very nice in those."

Doug checked himself against her salesmanship.

"I'll take them," he said, making a final appraisal in the mirror. He had considered himself passable-looking when he was single. Married to Susan, he had felt his best-looking. He loved to walk into public places with her. She was so pretty to him, slender, with large brown eyes, straight black hair, and dimples when she smiled, that is, when she was still smiling.

DOUG GARDNER LIVED ON WEST SEVENTY-EIGHTH Street in Manhattan in an old elevator building, three bedrooms, a living room and an eat-in kitchen. All the furniture had been purchased at Conran's on one frantic Saturday, a wild dash through the store for beds, a couch, chairs, end tables, dishes, glassware, so that he could create an instant environment. The wall hangings were purchased that same day from the Poster Gallery. He was not going to mope around like some recently divorced men, living in barren rooms out of cardboard boxes and mooning over their wives, the custodians of their personal taste. The children were with him that day to choose the pieces they wanted for their bedrooms. They could barely keep up with him as he raced through the store. When he moved in he had no illusions about the decor—not an antique on the premises, nothing with any depth. But it was done. He didn't need Susan and her eye. I can do this on my own, thank you. Susan had remained in their original apartment on West End Avenue. She had the furniture of the marriage. He theorized that he could have qualified for an article in the home furnishings section of *The New York Times*, "How I Expunged Any Trace of My Former Life and Former Mate in Just a Few Hours."

Sexual mores had changed since the first time he passed through as a single man. Under the new ground rules if the woman didn't want to go to bed with you by the second or third date she wasn't interested, or you shouldn't be, and if she did, that still didn't mean she was interested, or that you were. In the two years since the divorce, his longest relationship was three months with an advertising copywriter who announced one night she was leaving New York to become a creative director at an agency in Chicago. Nothing was to be negotiated between them. This was a career opportunity, she explained, he had children in New York and that was that. After the Sexual Revolution it was the woman as easily as the man who turned over first after sex and went to sleep. And now, following the Feminist Revolution, it was the woman as easily as the man who relocated.

FOR DOUG AND SUSAN GARDNER IT WAS AS THOUGH they had a grocery store where the partners didn't speak. Doug recalled such a relationship, J & S on Amsterdam Avenue, when he was growing up. Jimmy and Sal were brothers-in-law, separated by an ancient grievance, bound by the business. Like Jimmy and Sal, Doug and Susan dealt with the public and had little to say to each other. They kept a public face for teachers, the children's doctors, grandparents. When they spoke to each other on the phone, usually discussions of logistics, their tone had the vitality of air-traffic controllers. On some occasions it was required of them to meet each other, such as to look over material concerning the children. They had settled on "their" place, a coffee shop on Broadway and Seventieth Street, so hectic it dictated an abrupt, unromantic encounter. They conducted their business and they left.

Doug and Susan had joint custody of the children. At two-week intervals the children arrived by themselves or were dropped off by the relinquishing parent, who buzzed up on the intercom. Doug thought Larry Hart could have made a lyric out of it if he were still alive. How love becomes buzzing up.

HE WAS A COLUMNIST FOR *SPORTS DAY*, A NATIONAL daily sports newspaper with headquarters in Houston and bureaus in several cities. The New York office was located in the Chrysler Building, the staff consisting of Doug, who wrote a three-day-a-week column, an editor, a feature writer, and a secretary-receptionist. He had taken this job two years before when the newspaper began operations, leaving the *New York Post*, where he had covered sports events and had written features. Doug's office was a madhouse of clippings, photos of athletes, souvenirs, awards, luncheonette menus. He had a television set on a table for watching sports events, and he worked on a computer, his copy traveling electronically to Houston. He was paid more than at the *Post*, an important reason for his changing jobs; Doug had discovered that divorce was more expensive than an acrimonious marriage. His colleagues were Pat Lahey, the bureau editor, who edited and expanded wire-service copy of sports events in New York, and Brian Wilkes, who covered the major events on the sports calendar in the city. Wilkes, in his 20s, had a television-age Saturday-morning cartoon style, fast-cutting, nonverbal references, "SPLAT! Winfield thwacked the ball so hard the juice was running out of it, GLUGG!" The secretary-receptionist was Sally Cole, a thin 21-year-old with blue hair, one side of her head shaved in a buzz cut, who on this day was wearing a jump suit made of camouflage material as though the *Sports Day* offices had been placed on military alert.

"Good morning, Mr. Gardner."

She called him "Mr." She and the Chinese-laundry lady were the only ones. The Chinese-laundry lady was rather formal. Sally probably calls me "Mr." because I'm so incontestably ancient.

"Sally, how old am I?"

"Don't you know how old you are?"

"Do you know how old I am?"

"I never thought of it."

"Take a guess."

"Gee, I don't know. Fifty-something. Fifty-six."

I am going on a diet immediately.

"Fifty-six?"

"You look about as old as Mr. Lahey and that's what he is."

Lahey was a rummy-nosed, potbellied, rumple-suited man of 56.

"I'm forty-seven, Sally."

"Oh, forty-seven is not so bad."

Not so bad. Out of tension from this exchange with a 21-year-old, when the snack wagon came by he ordered a corn muffin and a hot chocolate. The diet would have to wait.

Doug was working on a column about hockey violence when Pat Lahey entered his office. On Doug's desk he placed a copy of the *Houston Chronicle* turned to the business section. Lahey had marked a paragraph of an article on National Communications, the Houston-based conglomerate that owned *Sports Day*. The chairman of the company was asked about the performance of the newspaper and said he was pleased, but was entertaining several offers for purchase, including one from a Houston group and another from a European syndicate.

"That's an outright invitation for a bidding war," Lahey said. "We might as well pack up and leave."

"Pat, I don't see any specific mention of my future in the article, or yours."

"New people come in, they don't want the old people."

"What does Doug think?" Brian Wilkes asked, joining them. Wilkes was a reminder to Doug to keep up his exercising. About Doug's height and slim, Wilkes brought his slim waist and his bicycle to the office every day.

"Doug is still absorbing it. Wait until he realizes there are maybe three jobs in the world where he has the autonomy he has here and two of them are taken and he's in the third."

"Pat has us making up resumes," Wilkes said.

"Pat was with the *Trib* when it closed and the *Mirror* when it closed. It's his doomsday background."

"This is good news to you?" Lahey responded. "The newspaper you work for is rumored to be up for sale."

"What can I do? I can't buy it," Doug said.

"Doug is right. We should worry about it when we have something to worry about. It's a rumor."

"Meantime, I'm still working. I've got a piece to get out," Doug said.

"Me too, Pat," Wilkes said, and walked out of the room.

Lahey picked up the article and handed it to Doug, obliging him to look at it again.

"Now that our young man is out of earshot, can we talk?"

"You don't necessarily lose your job in a sale, Pat."

"Ah, 'necessarily' finds its way into the conversation."

"Europeans?" Doug said, scanning the piece.

"Right. What do they know about American sports? They'll turn us into *Soccer News*."

"Please, Pat. I am over my quota on stress for this entire decade."

AMONG DOUG'S PHONE CALLS DURING THE DAY WAS ONE from Tony Rosselli, whom he had known since high school. Rosselli was a broker for commercial real estate, with dreams of being a sports promoter. Years before, he had the idea for a sports complex to be located in New Jersey near enough to New York City to draw on the New York population while tapping the New Jersey suburban areas. He failed in his attempt to finance the idea because he was not established as an entrepreneur, and shortly after, plans were announced for the successful Meadowlands Sports Complex. Another miss was his attempt to bring a minor-league baseball team to New York City, the team to play in one of the outer boroughs, an idea Doug thought had merit and had written about, but again Rosselli was not financially powerful enough to see it through.

Rosselli asked Doug if they could have a beer, and they met at the Blarney on East Forty-fifth Street, a long narrow place with two television sets on either end of the bar, a working-class hangout where a few journalists also gathered. In the rear was a room with ten booths. Others were known at the Four Seasons; Doug could always get a booth at the Blarney for a hamburger and a beer.

"I've got something special, Doug. I'm letting you in on it, exclusive, given the nature of our long-standing relationship."

"What are you promoting, Tony?"

"Not promoting. This you don't talk about like it needs promoting. This is a major event."

Rosselli looked around theatrically to see if any of the construction workers in the place were eavesdropping.

"Don't worry, Tony. Nobody here is in your field."

Rosselli was always in motion. A small, wiry man, he constantly tapped his feet, fiddled his fingers. He was given to wearing shiny suits and silk shirts open at the collar, and he continually adjusted the fit. His eyes never stopped darting in all directions as if life's parimutuel windows were going to slam shut before he could get his bet in.

"It's sensational, Doug. I have a deal for a wolf girl."

"Come again?"

"A wolf girl. Brought up in the wilds of Colombia by she-wolves. Twelve years old. She runs like a wolf."

"On all fours?"

"As fast. The fastest girl runner in the history of track. The fastest miler ever."

"She's a miler? The wolves—they have a measured mile?"

"I'm going to sell the rights to TV. A race against the clock. Maybe she'll break three minutes."

"Have you tried anybody else? Ringling Brothers?"

"You got to see for yourself. Come to the track outside

Yankee Stadium. Saturday morning, ten A.M. It's incredible, I'm telling you. From the wilds of Colombia.''

Three readable columns per week were not easy to produce, and in the hope that the alleged wolf girl would make good copy Doug decided to take his stopwatch to the quarter-mile track in the Bronx.

Rosselli was there when Doug arrived. He was dressed in a shiny brown suit, a white silk shirt, and brown loafers. The wolf girl had not yet made her appearance. A slumping old Buick cruised by on the street, and when it stopped, two Hispanic men emerged leading a slightly built teenage girl. Rosselli went over to them, money seemed to be exchanged, and they nudged the girl toward Rosselli, the men remaining near the entrance to the area. He walked with her to the running track where Doug was standing. The wolf girl was wearing gym shorts and a T-shirt and on her head was a wolf's skin that looked like it came from a costume shop.

"What is that, for her gestalt?" Doug asked.

"You understand English?" Rosselli said to her.

She grunted or growled, or something in between.

"You run the mile?" Rosselli ran in place to communicate. She gave no sign of understanding. Doug attempted to clarify, making a sweeping gesture toward the track indicating the number of laps she would have to run.

"*Cuatro*," Doug said. "I don't know what that is in wolf."

The girl nodded that she understood. She took a starting position. Doug set the stopwatch, gave her a tap on the arm and said, "Go!" She burst into a furious sprint at a record-breaking pace and Rosselli was yelling "Yahoo!" When she reached the far side of the track, suddenly she ran off the track in the direction of the two men, who began edging to the car. "Hey!" Rosselli called out. "What's going on?" They were all running

11

now, the two men and the wolf girl, Rosselli chasing after them shouting, "Hey, come back! Gimme back my three hundred bucks!" Rosselli was running and sliding in his loafers, chasing and groaning, the girl opening a gap between them. Doug remembered a so-called wolf boy once. He amused himself thinking this was a product of feminism, the first wolf girl scam. He was going to leave Rosselli's name out of it or Rosselli would never be taken seriously again, but Doug knew this had to be a column. Rosselli was still in pursuit as though his money were flying away from him on little wings. He had fallen far behind, and finally he gave up the chase, the wolf girl, meanwhile, losing her wolf's head, running out of the park and out of legend.

DOUG ANSWERED THE INTERCOM TO HIS APARTMENT. HIS children were downstairs, Andy, 15, Karen, 12, with Harry, part cocker spaniel, part beagle, the joint-custody dog. Doug opened the door and kissed Karen, who kissed him back. Andy lowered his head, allowing his father's lips to graze his hair. Andy no longer liked to be touched, no more hugs, no more holding hands with Doug while crossing the street, no more sitting in his father's lap. The boy held himself at a distance, encapsulated by his approaching manhood. Harry entered, giving Doug a token little wag of his tail. This dog, Doug was convinced, didn't know who the hell it belonged to.

The children looked like brother and sister. Doug doubted they looked like him, both having inherited Susan's soft features and striking dark eyes and hair. Andy was a sturdy boy with broad shoulders, Karen a petite, thin child. Ironically, given their physiques, Andy had little interest in athletics, while Karen was an excellent gymnast. Karen was also a young artist, and she was carrying some newly purchased art supplies. They brought their belongings into their rooms, suitcases and bookbags, and efficiently unpacked, having been on the road in this gypsy version of family life for two years. Doug had ordered pizza and they sat at the table as he received reports of the last two weeks.

"We had a project in school and we all took turns making believe we worked in city government," Karen said. "I was on the city council."

"Sounds like a good project."

"My first act was to get Halloween declared an official holiday. Schools closed."

"I like that," Doug said. "It's the best kids' holiday."

"The job I'd want in city government is taxi commissioner," Andy said.

"I think there are more important jobs than that," Doug responded.

"Uh-oh. He's worried. I might be serious."

"I'd like to be taxi commissioner, too," Karen said, teasing him.

"We're going to turn out fine, Dad," Andy said.

"All right. You got me. I was being too parental."

"And taxi commissioner isn't all that bad," Andy continued. "You can affect people's lives. How long they have to stand in the rain. How much leg room they have."

"I'd like to own the cabs. You could always get a cab that way," Karen said.

"Anything you want to be," he said, taking their teasing.

Karen's paintings, largely watercolors, were placed about the apartment, her work space an area in the kitchen. The children's rooms were adorned with various posters and flyers for social causes, Karen's interests tending toward animals, the saving of, the cessation of experiments upon, which she filtered through her child's innocence: "The dogs feel the pain." Andy, older, took the longer view, the saving of the planet, nuclear proliferation, environmental abuses. They were on mailing lists, sent small contributions, and promoted Doug's participation. He was the only New York sportswriter he knew who belonged to the New England Anti-Vivisection Society.

In the morning they were having breakfast together and Karen said suddenly, "Dad, if you got married again, that would make your new wife our stepmother, wouldn't it?"

The question appeared to be of interest to Andy, too, who turned to Doug.

"Yes. My wife would be a kind of mother and, technically, she'd be your stepmother."

"A girl in my class—her father got remarried and she calls her father's new wife her stepmother. But I used to think you only say 'stepmother' or 'stepfather' when somebody dies."

"No, if somebody remarries also."

"And the father and the mother of the new wife, do they become 'stepgrandparents'?" she asked.

"I suppose you can call them that."

They were both thinking about this information.

"There's something very important you have to know about all this," Doug said. "Your grandparents will always be your grandparents. And your Mom and I, we may be with other people, but we're your Mom and Dad forever." He touched Karen's face and reached out for Andy, who allowed him to grasp his hand. "I'm your Dad forever."

HAD HE BEEN TOLD WHEN HE STARTED AS A CUB REporter for fifty-five dollars a week that one day he would be a nationally known sportswriter earning over fifty thousand dollars a year he would have found it as unbelievable as the idea that fifty thousand a year was nearly the minimum in New York, for maintaining an apartment, expenditures for meals, clothing for work, social life, and the expenses of bringing up two children. The terms of the divorce had Doug and Susan dividing the costs of the children's needs *except* for school tuition. "Divorce agreements are the art of the payable," Doug's lawyer said at the time, and Susan could not afford to pay any more. So Doug paid their tuition, and he was looking at a letter announcing a tuition increase of six hundred dollars for each child. It cost him fifteen thousand a year to send them to private school, net, after tax dollars. Doug and Susan had tried the public school system in the early years with Andy, and he lasted until the third grade in a West Side elementary school. The class sizes kept increasing, the school became more run-down, special programs were eliminated. They enrolled him at the Bradley School on Riverside Drive, which Karen now also attended. Private school was no longer as elitist as in Doug's days in school, it had become the norm for children of families middle class and above. His brother, Marty, a dry-cleaning-store owner, sent his children to Bradley. It was the norm, but savagely expensive. He had made a mistake having the tuition bills come directly to him, he decided. He should have had them routed through Susan so she could see them. She probably doesn't even know how much the tuition is.

Doug lay awake at 1:12 A.M. You used to know the time vaguely if you hadn't fallen asleep yet from anxieties and knew if you didn't fall asleep soon you'd be tired all the next day. These digital clocks tell you to the minute how late it is, and if I don't fall asleep in the next three minutes I will be, as Wilkes would write, SPLAT tomorrow. Is Susan sleeping? Is she in bed with someone? How good was she in bed, he wondered, liberated from marital sex, liberated from him? What did she like now? Did she go down on everybody? He was caught by

15

that image, Susan taking men in her mouth, and he shuddered. This is perverse fantasy, she's long gone, let it go. He couldn't help it. He didn't want to stop himself. He went into the bathroom and on the rationale that the release of tension would help him sleep, he masturbated to Susan going down on him and then on top of him, her hands pulling his hair, so fevered and hot she was gasping.

They saw each other a few weeks later, and he was momentarily ill at ease, as if somehow she knew what he had done. They were at the school for parent-teacher conferences. Susan was wearing high heels, which made her about two inches shorter than Doug, and a stylish print dress with a design of geese in flight. Geese? She is the least outdoorsy person I know. Susan's idea of a brisk walk is to go through Bloomingdale's when the air-conditioning is on. No, that's unnecessary. It's a nice dress, you look good. Wearing your hair a little longer lately, but with the bangs you always had. You can't get away with that in your 40s unless you have a pretty face, and you do, still. Jesus, you're 42, Susan. You look younger. You look almost the way you did twenty years ago when we met. Clearly, he was having difficulty concentrating on the teachers' school reports, which were routine, the children were doing fine. Twenty years. That's before joint custody and modern divorces like this one where the parents show a smiling face and attend parent-teacher conferences just like any other couple.

After the meetings they stopped on the sidewalk in front of the school building.

"So they're okay," she said.

"They're good kids."

"How are you? What's going on?"

"The usual. Did you see the wolf girl column?"

"No."

"As you wish."

—16—

"It is not in the divorce agreement that I have to see everything you write."

"True. Maybe you should see the checks I write. Tuition is up. Six hundred dollars the child."

"That's fifteen thousand a year."

"I didn't think you'd know that."

"I know it. It's the least liberated thing about me, that you pay the tuition. But I'm working on it."

"Fine with me."

"Doug, I'm changing jobs. Maybe it will speed matters along. At first this is going to be a parallel move. Actually, it's a little decrease in pay."

"Oh—"

"Eventually I'd be making it up in bonuses."

"Well, I wish you luck—" and in awkwardness he extended his hand and they shook hands.

"Does Andy let you touch him anymore?" he asked.

"Not as often."

"What happened to those times when the children used to snuggle in our laps and we'd read them bedtime stories?"

"The children grew up, Doug."

"That's not exactly what I meant."

They looked in each other's eyes for a moment, then they both looked away.

"So—give me some time. I'm going to try to settle my bill," she said.

He reached out and touched her hair. I still love you. And I still hate you.

2

SPORTS DAY WAS SOLD, NOT TO EUROPEANS, TO Houston Enterprises, an innocuous name for the aggressive company run by Robby Reynolds, 36, who began with family money from oil, then moved on to acquire electronics firms, real estate and newspapers. A telegram was sent to staff members in the bureaus saying Reynolds would be coming to each of their cities to visit with them personally. He arrived punctually for his meeting in the New York office conference room: Reynolds with a broad Western smile, wearing an impeccable gray suit, cowboy boots, six feet two, slender, a handsome, narrow face, wavy black hair, capable of playing himself in the soap-opera version of his life and family. He unwound himself in a chair opposite Doug, Lahey, and Wilkes, placing his feet on the conference-room table. Doug noticed the soles of his boots were not only unscuffed, they were totally clean. How did he walk around with clean soles? Of course. If you were rich enough, you never had to walk in the street.

They were to call him Robby. He was going to take a

close interest in the newspaper and was naming himself publisher. Prior to purchase he had ordered an extensive market-research study, he told them.

"Circulation has been holding firm, but we're soft in some of the major metropolitan areas. I'd like to know why you think that is."

Doug did not like the challenge aspect. If Reynolds had the results of competent research, he probably knew the answer.

"Pat?"

"Maybe advertising hasn't been strong enough. It's expensive to advertise in large cities and maybe there hasn't been enough."

"Maybe."

Doug presumed Lahey had failed the little quiz. Reynolds turned next to Wilkes.

"Brian?"

"People watch more sports on TV in the big cities?"

"That wouldn't relate to our circulation discrepancies," he said with a slight tone of annoyance.

"Doug?"

"Why don't you just tell us, Robby?"

"I want to hear from you because I'm interested in your opinion."

"All right. My sense is that large cities have the strongest sports sections in their daily newspapers. The most loyal readership. And that would be the hardest competition for us."

"I would tend to agree with you."

So I passed, did I?

"We're going to have to develop some new strategies," Reynolds said. "With coverage the big-city papers aren't providing. Your other sports, like wrestling."

"Wrestling isn't a sport," Doug said.

"Let's not split hairs. We're going to initiate wrestling standings and run wrestling results."

Reynolds outlined his other plans, a new "Big Games" feature with writers from other bureaus coming to New York when necessary. Lahey was to minister to their needs. Wilkes was to concentrate on articles about personalities, such as "What is Hulk Hogan really like?" Doug's work was deemed by Reynolds "A good all-around feature." He added, "But I do expect you'll favor us with the occasional wrestling column." He talked a while about sports in general and ended by saying, "We're going to revise the layout, outplay the competition. We're going to win!"

After Reynolds left, Lahey commented, "Downright rousing. We're working for good old Knute Rockne."

"There's nothing old about him," Doug said. "This is strictly the new corporate bottom line. Do the research, check the demographics and produce the numbers. And if wrestling sells, give them wrestling."

ACCORDING TO A *WOMEN'S WEAR DAILY* CLIPPING SENT by Doug's friend Jeannie Martins, who owned a public relations firm in the fashion field, Susan was joining the newly formed Merchandising Unlimited as a "merchandising consultant to create in-store promotions for department stores nationwide." Her parallel move, her gamble for future bonuses. Men who have to pay for the tuition and for the extras that were not specifically covered in the divorce agreement, the costs of day camps and gymnastics sessions and painting classes, those men don't get to gamble with parallel moves. If a genie came and said, "What may I grant thee?" I would answer, "Parity." An even split. If you get a divorce and have joint custody of the children, of the *dog*, then you should also share the anxiety. The *Women's Wear Daily* piece referred to Susan as "Susan Brook." She had been using her marriage name until then. The reversion to her maiden name seemed to Doug as if she had suddenly found a last possession of his lying around the apartment and decided to ship it back.

ROBBY REYNOLDS SENT DOUG AN INTEROFFICE MEMO, modern communications style. A flashing indicator light on Doug's computer signified a message waiting for him and he brought it up on the screen.

"I notice wrestling matches in your area this week. You might want to check them out."

He showed the screen to Lahey. "Big Brother lives," Doug said.

"I got the same message. Only I'm supposed to see that you go. Maybe you should, then you can decide how you want to deal with it."

"Is this playing up to the new boss, Pat?"

"It won't be so bad. I've got a new friend dying to meet you. We'll have a few beers, a few laughs."

"I have a feeling *he's* listening. That the screen is going to flash, 'Right, Doug, it's just one night. What can you lose?' "

"I think you have to check it out, Doug."

Lahey had been either separated or divorced from his wife for many years, he was vague in telling Doug the details. He was the father of two married daughters who lived on Long Island, and he had a place in Queens. In a cab on the way to the wrestling matches at Madison Square Garden, they stopped at an apartment house in the Thirties for Lahey's friend, a middle-aged blonde with a substantial bosom.

"This is Rhonda. Rhonda, Doug."

"I can't believe I'm meeting you. I read you all the time."

"Thank you. You're a sports fan?"

"I used to live with a football player, but I can't tell

21

you his name on account of because he was married. You won't write that up, will you?''

"No problem."

"Isn't this exciting?" she said. "Wrestling!"

Doug subscribed to nineteen periodicals. He had hours of decent reading waiting for him at home, and instead he was going to wrestling matches. They were seated down front but out of immediate range of the falling and tossed bodies, chairs, managers. Rhonda was shrieking with excitement. Lahey was pointing out the finer points, making up names of wrestling holds as he went along in order to impress her.

"It's the double back lock, darling."

"Isn't that the Heimlich maneuver?" Doug said and then slid lower into his seat. He had slept uneasily the previous night and was close to nodding off, thinking dreamily about Antonino Rocca, the star wrestler when Doug was a boy, whom Doug watched on the off-brand Sky King seven-inch set his parents bought on time, and he didn't know then that the matches were fixed. Maybe it's better to be like Rhonda.

"What do you think?" Lahey asked as Rhonda went to the ladies room.

"It's Roller Derby without the skates."

"You could use that. But I was asking what you thought of Rhonda."

"I like her. To come here and find something to cheer about. But where does this leave Carla?" Carla was Lahey's previous woman.

"I'm still seeing her, too. You know how it goes—"

"I don't. My social life is not that intricate."

If only it were. If only I were dating Jacqueline Bisset and Julie Christie at the same time. No, one of them would be enough. Either one. They both have good diction. We wouldn't go for wrestling, we'd go for Chinese. Or I could make tuna croquettes at home. This was one

22

of his main short-order dishes for the children, loaded with protein. These successful actresses, they've had enough exotic food in their lives. The children could be there, too, at the outset, part of the appeal, a solid father, a good short-order cook. He had seen a picture of one of the actresses recently. She was at a European film festival with a good-looking guy, the kind of European guy who probably has women all the time. Were Jackie and Julie accustomed to European guys? He wondered if he could last long enough to satisfy them. Or Rhonda. How did Rhonda get into this? Like FM drift, the signals were sliding, his fantasies blurring. The last person he slept with was a dress buyer, a health food aficionada he had met through his friend Jeannie. They were together a few nights, they ate in health food restaurants, and at home she made steamed vegetable dinners, no butter, no salt. Everything was theoretically healthy about the affair and bland like the vegetables. "Recreational sex" the magazines were calling noncommittal couplings. "Interchangeable sex" was more accurate to Doug in describing these unfulfilling little affairs that don't lead anywhere. He was interrupted from his reverie by the noise in the arena from the main event pitting Mega-Killer Chandler and Bronco Billy Chandler in "The first fight to the death between blood brothers." The match ended when Mother Superior Chandler, the boys' mother, a wrestler herself, wearing a nun's habit, entered the ring and vanquished the forces of evil, knocking out both her sons.

Doug had done his research, he decided he was not going to file a column on these burlesque routines. As Doug, Lahey, and Rhonda made their way up the aisle, Doug was approached by Raymond Morri, a boxing promoter, a short, stout man in his 50s.

"Doug Gardner, just the man I wanted to see. I got myself a wrestler. You remember the Swedish Angel?"

"I do. There was even a later Swedish Angel, as I recall. Sort of Swedish Angel Two."

"He's in that mold. You gotta do a piece on this guy. He's fabulous."

They reached the lobby and Morri was still promoting.

"He's five feet five and weighs about four hundred pounds. I call him the Swedish Meatball."

"The Swedish Meatball. A fitting end to this evening."

"When can we set up an interview?"

"I'm going to pass on this. But I'll send it along if we ever get a food editor."

HE RECEIVED A NOTE IN THE MAIL FROM SUSAN; HER new company was having start-up problems with slow-paying accounts and they had missed their first two pay-rolls. Could Doug pay the bill enclosed for the children's winter jackets? She would make it up at a later date. He wrote back and told her he would pay for the jackets and she could reimburse him for her share when she had the money. Three hundred ninety-five dollars for two ski jackets. He had gone through several childhood winters in a twenty-five-dollar navy peacoat.

He took the children to buy sneakers on a Saturday morning, one pair each, and a few pairs of socks, and the bill was over a hundred dollars. Susan generally took them clothes shopping, Doug was the sneakers-and-shoes man. This dated back to the children's younger days when buying shoes was a difficult process in overcrowded shoe stores and you had to cajole them into being calm. He always had patience with them. He could lose himself in their world, in their bedtimes, bathtimes, the bubbles and ducks. He thought he might have been better at that, at being a father, than he was at anything else.

On Saturdays at eleven in the morning Karen attended

a gymnastics class for a couple of hours and Andy usually read or did homework. On this clear, cool day, after they bought the sneakers, Karen went off to her class and Andy suggested he and Doug take a football into Central Park. Although he was uninterested in athletics, occasionally Andy would make such a suggestion. They went out to the park. As they threw the football, Andy's passes were erratic and he caught awkwardly. Nearby, another father and son began to play, the boy several years younger than Andy and smaller. The boy threw swift, accurate passes and caught the ball fluidly. Andy's face was downcast, Doug reading him as saying, "I wish I could do that. I wish I could do that for you, Dad." No, not for me. This should only be for you. He wanted to gather his 15-year-old in his arms, embarrass him with kisses, hold him as he did when he was little. I don't care. I love you more than you could know. You don't have to be a ballplayer for me.

DOUG'S CLOSEST FRIENDS WERE JEANNIE MARTINS AND his lawyer, Bob Kleinman. The three had met when they had shares in a singles summer house in Amagansett. They had stayed in contact with each other through single life and married life and, after their divorces, through single life again. Bob Kleinman specialized in legal disputes between law firms and between individual lawyers. He was Doug's age, overweight; the constant adversarial nature of his work seemed to be written in his face and he tended to be sullen and suspicious. He had been married to Helena, a matrimonial lawyer and a feminist. When they were divorced, Bob created a master plan for his next wife. After a year he found her, Sarah Steinmetz, who had taught in a synagogue nursery school but believed a higher calling for a Jewish woman was to be the wife to a man like Bob, the mother of his children and the provider of his hot meals. Bob sat through the lighting of candles he had never bothered with, and the observance of Jewish holidays he had never heard of, to gain a male-dominant position in his household so complete Doug imagined one would have to go to the animal kingdom to find its equivalent.

"Let me ask you something," Doug said over lunch. "Do you ever masturbate?"

"What?" Bob became very concerned with his image and looked around the Chinese restaurant to see if anyone could hear.

"Shall I define my terms?"

"I understand the word. Why are you asking me?"

"Who am I supposed to ask, Dr. Ruth?"

"Are you talking—regularly?"

"I'm talking—ever."

"Look, I have a decent marriage."

"Bob—"

"Well, let's say we've gone a while without having sex. We've been tired. Sarah's been sick, flu, a cold—"

"I'm familiar with upper respiratory illnesses in New York."

"And I might see somebody at a dinner party. There's one incredible-looking Israeli girl we know, and you sort of fantasize under the circumstances of not having sex lately, I mean, in that circumstance."

Bob looked very uncomfortable and was adjusting his tie.

"Just don't quote me."

"At least I know I'm not the only man in America my age doing it," Doug said. "I'll tell you what inhibits me. That I'll have a coronary right in the middle and when they discover my body I'll be found caught in the act and without a date on a Saturday night."

"If I ever got found that way, Sarah would probably count what I did as cheating on her."

"Here's the jackpot question. After you split up with Helena, did you ever masturbate fantasizing about *her?*"

"You've masturbated to Susan?"

"I'm afraid so."

"So have I," he whispered.

"You have? Behind my back?"

"Only after you were divorced."

They were laughing at the absurdity.

"But did you ever do it to Helena?"

"Never," he said, still laughing. "I wouldn't want to give her the satisfaction."

ROBBY REYNOLDS CALLED DOUG FROM HOUSTON. "HOW ya doing up there in Noo Yawk? Must be real busy not to give the publisher what he's looking for. Where's wrestling, Doug?"

"It's in the paper. I see you're running wrestling standings, just as you said you would."

"Do you know what ranks among the highest in total attendance among spectator sports in your very state?"

"You're leading me to say wrestling, but it's not a spectator sport."

"Then what are all those people watching?"

"Scripts. I think we ought to straighten this out, Robby. I don't want you to keep looking for wrestling columns from me. I don't write about variety acts."

"You write so many columns. I don't understand why you can't do a piece now and again."

"I just told you why, Robby. I'm a *sports* columnist."

"I understand. Integrity. I'm for integrity. And I respect your integrity. It's a commodity on the paper."

"My integrity is a commodity?"

"It's popular with readers. So you keep your integrity, Doug, and I'll work around it. Let's do it this way. Give me one wrestling column. I'm not telling you what to write. I'm only asking you to address yourself to the subject."

"Why is this so important to you?"

"Because wrestling's become important. And we haven't heard from you about it."

"With good reason."

"We just want to hear your voice here. People want to know what you have to say about it."

"What I have to say would be negative. You're not looking for that."

"All I'd like is one wrestling column from Doug Gardner. Now is that a deal breaker? Am I being unreasonable? One column. *Anything* you want to say. How can you possibly object to that?"

"I can't," Doug said, finessed. "I guess this is why I work for you and you don't work for me."

HE SLEPT POORLY THAT NIGHT, TOO, AND DECIDED IF you have work stress and money stress and ex-wife stress you shouldn't be sleeping alone. He phoned Monica Davidson, a woman he had met recently at an ABC Sports press party who worked for a casting office. She was in her early 30s, a bouncy blonde with her hair in a ponytail. On their first evening together they had gone to a Mexican restaurant on Third Avenue she had recommended where he was among the oldest in the place and the noise level was so high the waiter shouted the dinner specials like a racetrack announcer. Monica ended the evening abruptly saying she had to be at work early in the morning, and took herself home by taxi. When he called this time she seemed pleased to hear from him, though, and invited him to join her in seeing the musical *Cats*. She was interested in a few of the cast members for television commercials. Monica claimed that in an instant she could tell who was headed for success and who was not, and he was fascinated by her youthful certainty. How much she actually knew, he questioned. On their first evening together they passed a store which had a poster of Clark Gable and Grace Kelly, a black-and-white blowup as they appeared in *Mogambo*. She knew who Clark Gable was, having seen Gone *With the Wind*.

"Who is she?" Monica asked.

"Grace Kelly."

"Oh, that's Grace Kelly. I thought so. She was before my time."

Casting executives making decisions that can influence people's careers and they can't identify Grace Kelly.

They sat in the theater and Doug put on his new glasses to read the program.

"Ever consider doing commercials?" Monica asked, studying his face.

"*Moi?* as Miss Piggy might say."

"We keep an eye out for ordinary-looking people."

"Ordinary-looking?"

"You don't look like an actor is what I mean. You're an ordinary person."

"This is getting worse as we proceed."

"I'm not saying it right. You have an interesting face and you don't look like a professional actor."

"Thank you. Let's hold it right there."

Cats began and he sensed they were having different responses to the show. Doug, brought up on the traditional American musical theater of integrated book, music, and lyrics, was restless and looking for a number like "The Rain in Spain," while Monica was loving the musical's showmanship.

"Isn't it fantastic?" she said.

"I figured it out. This really is about cats."

This time she permitted him to go back to her apartment for "a quick nightcap."

"I feel I should tell you," she said as they were finishing their drinks, "I don't go to bed with everybody. I have to love a man first."

"What is love anyway? Love is like a moment's madness."

"What?"

"That's from a song."

"Oh."

He looked around the place, a studio apartment apparently without a bed.

"Monica, where do you sleep when you sleep?"

"The chair opens up into a bed."

"God, single life is getting minimalist. Well, they're opening chairs at night, but not for me. . . ."

"What?"

"That's also from a song, in part. Thank you for the show."

"I mean it about doing a commercial."

"It's not one of my goals, but I appreciate the thought," he said.

She was cute and rather pleasant in her way. He knew the virtues of going out with younger women, their soft skin and unwrinkled faces, their flat stomachs. You could feel young yourself with such a young thing, and wasn't that the Main Idea? They were teaching that to Karen in school, how to extract the Main Idea from material she read. Surely I, a 47-year-old man, watching my weight and my hair, can grasp the Main Idea. And yet, apart from the fact that Monica and her age group had no personal reference to World War Two, Roosevelt, Stalin, Churchill, Korea, the Kennedys, or Grace Kelly, she didn't know love is like a moment's madness either. After sex with one of these young bodies he was whimsically singing "How Long Has This Been Going On?" and when he suggested that it was one of the best ways of saying "I love you" in the history of popular music, the girl didn't know what he was babbling about. You

30

are babbling with them. They don't know Ira Gershwin. They couldn't hum the verse to "Star Dust" if a Caribbean holiday on a game show depended on it, and they probably never heard of the Harry James solo from "Sing, Sing, Sing." They wouldn't know Irving Berlin wrote "Better Luck Next Time" and they couldn't hum that either. How can you be involved with women who don't even know your songs?

3

"GOOD DAY DOUG," THE MESSAGE ON HIS MONitor began. "We had an understanding. One column. America waits. Robby." He envisioned an electronic nightmare: he would turn on the television set in his bedroom one night and find a message from Reynolds leaking in on the cable, "You cannot hide from me or wrestling, Doug. We will track you down."

Obliged to file the column, he avoided the overexposed stars of wrestling, and covered a minor-league card in Trenton, New Jersey. He wrote that this was wrestling with the ribs showing. One wrestler was kayoed by a flying leap that missed him by three feet, another knocked himself out, a turn that must have looked good in the pre-match editorial session, he wrote, but did not play well in a small arena. The featured performer was "Mafia Joe Falco." He worked in a wide-striped suit with black shirt and silk tie and took advantage of the referee's wandering attention to remove from his clothing, variously, a knife, a gun, and a rope, and feigned strangling his opponent, the unfortunate "Little Filipino Mike."

Gasping, Mike was counted out, holding his throat, appealing to the crowd, Mafia Joe wildly jeered for his scurrilous behavior. For the young and naive, Doug wrote, this was theater, not a sport, and concluded the piece by saying of Falco, "His is a performance that can give the Mafia a good name."

"Nicely done," Reynolds said to him on the phone. Reynolds had been in South America and had called Doug on his return. "We're getting some outstanding reader response. Wrestling fans aren't too happy. As if you said there's no Santa Claus."

"I imagine that's next. A guy will come out with the long beard and red outfit and knock people out with his belly or gift-wrapped boxes."

"You could put that in the next column."

"There is no next column."

"There has to be now, Doug. We've got about three hundred letters. We're going to run a Wrestling Mailbag with the best of them. Then we're sure to get letters on the letters. We can keep this going a long time. You've got to do a follow-up."

"We agreed to one column."

"That was before you did such a good job. You can't let this kind of response just sit there."

"Yes, I can."

"Doug, I'm not asking you to do another column from scratch. All I'm asking is that you respond to the readers who bothered to respond to you. It's an update. A responsible journalist has to do this."

"Really now—"

"If you were a political columnist you would. You'd respond to a ground swell from your readers. This is your journalistic responsibility."

"I'll take a letter or two and I'll answer them in print."

"That's all I'm asking."

"Okay, Robby."

33

"Then a month or so later on, I think you should look in on Mafia Joe and do a column on how he's faring. Just as a follow-up to what you've already written. It's simply good, solid journalistic procedure. Nice talking to you, Doug."

HE WROTE THE COLUMN QUICKLY, TRYING TO CONVINCE himself that the speed with which he did it would neutralize the fact that his new publisher had manipulated two columns on a subject he did not wish to write about and was now expecting a third. On the day the second column appeared he received a call from Tony Rosselli, apparently recovered from the wolf girl saga.

"Doug, this is for you since you're such a wrestling fan these days."

"That is a misreading."

"I haven't talked to anybody else about it."

"I'm not interested."

When Doug left the building that evening, Tony was waiting outside in a shiny black suit.

"I realize this is nervy of me, but trust me. This is a great story."

"Sorry, Tony."

Rosselli motioned toward a car parked at the curb and a small, wiry Oriental man, barefoot, in a white belted robe came bouncing out.

"This is Kwan Doo Duk."

The man bowed.

"He is the world's tallest midget wrestler. A master of the art of Hinsai wrestling. It's very rare. So rare it's never been seen in this country."

"Probably with good reason."

Doug walked away. Suddenly, there was a loud shout *"Hayaii!"* and the man grabbed Doug around the leg.

34

He was curled up in a ball and locked around Doug's leg with his arms and legs.

"What the hell is this?"

Doug was shaking his leg, trying to get the man off, but he would not come loose.

"This is the beauty of it. There's no known answer for the Hinsai leg grip," Rosselli said, now partly addressing the crowd that was gathering.

"Call him off, Tony!"

Rosselli pried him away.

"Do you speak English?" Doug said to the man. He shook his head no. "Your first lesson in English is to learn a useful phrase. 'This-is-not-the-way-to-get-into-print.' "

"We went a little overboard here, Doug, but this is a class performer. We're going to do it with gongs, the works."

"I don't even think he's a midget. How tall is he?"

"Five five."

"Tony?"

Undaunted, Rosselli smiled broadly. "That's what makes him the world's tallest."

JEANNIE MARTINS HAD BEEN THE YOUNGEST IN THE Amagansett summer house with Doug and Bob; she was now a middle-aged woman with frizzy red hair and a slender figure for which she said she brutalized herself at exercise classes. She had divorced her stockbroker husband at the height of the women's movement, when she and Susan were in the same consciousness-raising group. Jeannie held a party in her office to celebrate the anniversary of her company. Doug stood to the side with Bob and his wife, Sarah, an unfashionable woman, chunky, with plain features, brown hair and eyes, wearing an unstylish dark dress. The three were the most

35

conventionally dressed people there. Doug was expressing his feelings to them about his recent experience with Monica and the night of *Cats*.

"Doug, you're crazy," Bob said.

"Crazy rhythm, you go your way. . . ."

"I mean it. If you tell me a woman is talking about love before she goes to bed with you, I can understand a problem. But if you tell me you don't plan to see her again because she doesn't understand the merits of Ira Gershwin—"

"These are cultural differences," Doug said. "If you're dating somebody from Paraguay—Paraguay is a factor in the relationship."

"Models, Doug!" Jeannie said, coming over to them. "Have you met anybody?"

Doug looked across the room at several glamorous women in studied poses.

"Do you have any idea of the vastness of my inexperience? I have never made love to a model or to a black woman, no Russians, Eskimos."

"There's a Hawaiian model here. I'll introduce you."

"Hawaii sounds good. The drinks are a little sweet, but I'm interested."

"What's on their minds?" Sarah Kleinman asked, referring to the models sprinkled through the room like confetti.

"Looking perfect," Jeannie said.

She located the Hawaiian model, a tall dark-haired woman in her 20s promoting her ethnicity by wearing a floral top and a sarong. Her first words privately to Doug were, "You think I can score some coke here?" and Doug, laughing at the impossibility of the matchup, said, "I don't even think you can get a Mai Tai."

When the party ended, Doug, Bob, Sarah, and Jeannie remained drinking tea and coffee.

"I wonder what those models do when their looks start to go," Sarah said.

"They get a few good years," Jeannie answered. "By then they should be married to someone successful and get taken care of."

"That is definitely a pre–women's lib idea," Doug teased.

"Frankly, I'm getting a little shaky on the subject as I get older."

"From what I see, women's lib is dead," Bob announced.

"In your case it was never alive," Jeannie countered.

"I can tell in business," Bob said. "Women are confused. The pendulum is swinging back."

"We'd be right where we were before the arguments," Doug said. "Then what did we get?"

"What we got was divorced," Jeannie answered.

WHAT WE GOT WAS DIVORCED. AT HOME AFTER THE party, he thought about that time, the 1970s, the rhetoric, the media attention women were getting, the articles, the books, and then the articles and books about the articles and books.

They were at a dinner party; Bob Kleinman, the host, had cooked and served the meal while his first wife, Helena, sat in triumph and self-contentment smoking a cigarillo, looking like Wyatt Earp. The men were in disarray. All five present had risen and bumped into each other in an effort to briskly clear the dishes and prove, There are no pigs here. It was a historic period, the Time When the Men Cleared.

Every Wednesday night Susan went to a consciousness-raising group. She had a secret world. Her expectations about going, the afterglow, seemed to Doug what it must be like to watch as your wife left for assignations.

One night she returned from the group and did not acknowledge him. She sat in the living room, thoughtful.

"How did it go?"

"It was extraordinary."

"In what way?"

"I can't even begin to describe it."

"What do you mean?"

She did not answer.

"Susan—"

Wearily she tried. "The emotions. The currents in the room."

"For instance?"

She just shrugged. It was not describable. It would be trivializing to tell him.

Susan announced she and her sisters were going to make serious changes in their personal lives, with fixed schedules outlining new, equal divisions of labor in their relationships. Doug would have to agree to a specific schedule which covered shopping for meals, cooking meals, doing dishes, bathing children, straightening the house. He was against the idea of legislating this. He spent more time on household and children than any man they knew.

"It's so trivial. I can't believe that after a year of sessions, this is what you women have come to."

"Don't say 'you women.' And it isn't trivial. It's fundamental, the way we conduct our lives. And it's nonnegotiable."

To keep peace in the marriage and out of what he regarded as his libertarian sense, he maintained the schedule. He detested it, the watchfulness required to administer it. He didn't need a schedule to tell him his role. He knew the role. He was there for the viruses and the conjunctivitis and the hacking coughs in the early hours and the dead goldfish and the hamsters, the hamster he nursed back to life after it was stepped on and

38

which then turned around and bit him. Was that Andy's hamster or Karen's? Their viruses and their hamsters had begun to merge.

Eventually Susan went back to work. She had been a sportswear buyer before the children were born and the new job was with a buying office whose accounts were out-of-town stores. They hired a part-time housekeeper and the schedule became irrelevant. Doug was involved in the household as he was before, and when Susan left this job because she wasn't "happy," Doug was responsible for the bills as he was before. When she left her next job because of "personalities," the myth of equality in their roles was over. The financial burden of the family was his as it had always been. She slept nights and he was up at 1:36, 2:49, worrying about money.

"IF THE BILLS ARE KEEPING YOU AWAKE, EARN MORE money. Who says you have to work at the *Post*? You didn't come into the world employed by the *New York Post*. John McCarthy walked away from it and does fabulously. You could do what he does."

" 'As Told To' books?"

"Books, PR for a ball club, I don't know. I didn't tell you to do this kind of work, you picked it. If you're so worried about money, make more money. Don't look at me."

"I find this extraordinary from a feminist. Make more money. Scratch the surface and what you really want is a sugar daddy."

"And wouldn't you like a sweet little wifey who waits for you at night and wiggles her tush and fetches whatever lambie pie wants?"

"Look at us. Right out on the ramparts of modern marriage and I don't think we could do five cogent minutes on the Donahue Show."

39

* * *

THEIR STYLES WERE DIFFERENT. WHEN HE WAS IN charge of the children he let them take care of their own schoolwork, bedtimes sometimes became extended. Susan felt that by being too relaxed they were not teaching them responsibility.

"I don't like always being the bad guy around here."

"Susan, this is not network TV. It doesn't matter if they run a little over."

She began to free-lance as a consultant for a fashion-merchandising service. Her hours and pay were erratic. Their arguments about money, life-style, the children were repeated so often they could phone them in, and with Susan visiting department stores in other cities and Doug on the road at times covering ball games, they *were* phoning them in. He sometimes thought their marriage was like an urban area that reaches a tip point before which there is hope, after which nothing can salvage it from blight. They drifted in the marriage, a momentum provided by details, the overseeing of school-age children, buying the clothes, the bicycles, the shoes. Doug resented the time she spent away from the household, trips, Saturdays and Sundays she was out researching retail stores, business dinners and after-work drinks she said were necessary for her work. He believed she was using work to place distance between them, she argued her hours would be acceptable if she were a man. And the relationship tipped. As she became more involved in her work, she became less involved in his work and in him, and he became less involved in her work and in her. They were carried along by random reminders of what attracted them originally, flashes of warmth, of humor, of sex, a marriage running on a minimum energy level.

He remembered their wedding, when he got up with the band and sang "I Married an Angel." And his 35th

40

birthday when he was feeling glum. Imagine feeling glum at 35. 35 is a laugher. Susan walked into a record store and pulled out every Frank Sinatra album in the rack and gave it to him on the spot for a present. What a great thing to do, Susan.

And a crisp day in October, the leaves in Central Park tinged with near-reds and near-yellows, city trees trying to be autumnal. It was late in the afternoon, the sun was low, long shadows. Susan was wearing an Irish sweater and dungarees. He was in chinos, a flannel shirt and a Shetland sweater. They were walking back toward the apartment from the playground. She had her arm across his back and around his shoulder and he had his arm around her waist, their sides lightly touching as they walked. The children—God, were they ever that little?— were trailing behind like loose wash. And he thought that anything in the world he could conceivably want was contained in that moment.

When they were first married they were like a great balloon in bright colors floating over the city. Every year a little leaked out, small amounts one would hardly notice, until, at the end, there was nothing left.

On a weekday night when the children were with him, Doug was reading in the living room, Andy doing homework in his bedroom, and Karen came and snuggled next to him on the couch.

"How's dear old Dad?"

"I'm good."

"Seeing anyone lately?"

"Nobody in particular."

"I used to think you and Mom would get married again. That was my fantasy in the beginning. Now I know you won't."

"We can't. We grew away from each other."

41

"I know. But you're both so nice."

It still hurts you. And I can't fix it. I'm so sorry.

The children looked weary to him. He didn't know if it was because of the demands of their schedules or the custody arrangement. They had been living under joint custody for over two years, going between apartments, coping with the system, the transience, the oversights, the articles of clothing and the books suddenly needed that were left in the other apartment. There wasn't a previous generation who had lived through joint custody. These children were the first. Was it trendy, like "in" food? Doug wondered. Was joint custody the pesto of divorce?

He wanted to discuss this with Susan. Their usual coffee-shop meeting place didn't feel appropriate and he suggested they get together at the Hyatt Hotel for a drink after work. In the morning he selected his best shirt, tie and jacket combination, annoyed with himself for doing it, doing it anyway, thinking he would finally be free of her when he could arrange to see her and not spend any time worrying about what he was wearing.

Over drinks he asked if she had noticed signs of weariness in the children or if they had complained about the living arrangements. Susan said she thought they had a difficult schedule, but they hadn't complained to her.

"In my darkest moments," Doug said, "I wonder if they'd have a better life just being with you."

"I say we let it all be. I don't want to give them any choices. Because if we did—" her voice faltered and she looked more vulnerable than he had seen her in a long time—"they might choose you over me. And that would break my heart."

"I wasn't looking for that. Just what's best for them."

"To have part of each of us. And we'll all muddle through."

For a moment it looked as if the grocery-store correctness between them was changing, then Susan gathered herself and became formal and businesslike and so did he. Doug went home speculating about the corrosive nature of badwill. If goodwill between people can carry a relationship through troubled times, then badwill, once established, becomes impenetrable. Neither his doubts about the children nor her vulnerability were going to soften the atmosphere between them. Once we were Mama Bear and Papa Bear. Now we're the Badwill Bears. That isn't so amusing.

A few weeks later he received in the mail an announcement that was astonishing to him. Susan was opening her own company for the creation of store promotions. She had been working for the previous company only a few months. He was certain the move would cut into her share of the expenses, that much was inevitable. She's out there expressing herself, and I'm stuck with the bill again.

DOUG WAS SUMMONED TO HOUSTON FOR A MEETING with Reynolds. He would have to put in an eight-hour day flying down and returning to accommodate Reynolds's needs. The office was immense, white throughout, the artwork consisting of color blowups of Houston Enterprises holdings. Reynolds sat behind a large white desk. He was wearing a double-breasted tan linen suit and snakeskin boots.

"Doug, boy. Good to see you here."

"Quite a space you have. I don't know why I landed at the airport. They could have gotten a plane right in here."

Reynolds buzzed his secretary on the intercom.

"Send Bill in."

A stocky crew-cutted man in his 30s appeared. His name was Bill Wall, and his face was without a trace of warmth when he was introduced to Doug, who thought he looked like an FBI agent.

"Bill is our new resident genius. Market researcher extraordinaire and vice-president in charge of operations."

"We're installing state-of-the-art research, Doug, in all aspects of the *Sports Day* operation," Wall said. "Within a year, through the proper research and marketing techniques we can revolutionize the newspaper business."

Wall made a detailed presentation of circulation projections for the newspaper and marketing strategies for sales to consumers and advertisers.

"At four hundred thousand we're sitting right behind the *Houston Chronicle* and *Newark Star Ledger* if you compare us to conventional newspapers," Wall said. "We can pass them both within a few months and move up on the list."

"And now for you, Doug," Reynolds said. "This should make you real pleased."

Wall placed a graph in front of Doug.

"You have the highest percentage of readers of any of our five columnists. And the highest percentage of 'finishing the article, once begun,' " Wall said.

"As our main all-around columnist, you can help bring us even bigger numbers," Reynolds told him.

"Each week we'll be surveying our readers on the sports and sports personalities they're following," Wall continued. "We'll send you computer printouts by geographic region, by age, by sex, telling you what our readers want to read about next. We expect you to use this as a guide in deciding the columns you write."

"Computerized journalism?" Doug said.

"It's for your guidance, Doug. You have a responsibility to your readers and to the newspaper to reach as many people as you can," Reynolds said.

"Robby, I spent over twenty years covering sports to reach the point where I can trust my instincts, write about what I'm feeling and have a pretty good idea that people will respond to it. That's my craft."

"Nobody's tampering with your craft," Reynolds responded. "Write your columns any way you want. All we're telling you is to be guided by the scientific data. You've got carte blanche."

"That's a very loose interpretation of carte blanche."

"Doug, this is not a debate. When you see the newspaper moving up the list and you see your column racking up even better readership results, you'll know this is the way to go."

"You'll be receiving the first guidelines in two weeks," Wall said.

"And use them, Doug! It's going to be a great combo, that Gardner style and integrity directed at what we know people want to read about. It's a no-lose situation. So there we are. It was great to see you."

"A pleasure," Wall said, fixing Doug with a hard look.

"Gentlemen—"

"Thanks for dropping by," Reynolds said, the way one might to a person who had merely stopped in from down the hall.

HE WOULD HAVE THOUGHT, CONSIDERING THE LENGTH of the day and with traveling between cities, that he would have fallen asleep easily that night out of fatigue. He was kept awake by speeches he never made to Reynolds about this new computerized journalism, speeches he could not afford to make. This is what Doug did for a living, there were few jobs in the field at his salary, none he knew of that were available. He couldn't walk away on principle. Susan could afford to do that, Susan, who was supposed to pay her share of child care, and one day—when would that be?—pay half the tuition, Susan was free to leave her job and start a new business.

When he was growing up the absence of money in the Gardner household was like an insufficient supply of oxygen, and they all had trouble breathing. He would sometimes awaken in the night and go into the kitchen for juice and see his father, awake, hunched and exhausted at the kitchen table, bills scattered in front of him. Doug, reflecting on the events of the day, took a deep breath in his anxiety, trapped by money like his father before him, as if it were in the genes.

4

DOUG ATTENDED A PRESS RECEPTION FOR ADVERtising personnel and the media presenting "Jocks," a new modeling agency featuring professional athletes as the models. Several women were introduced as "Jockettes." These were not the Pete Roses or Chris Evert-Lloyds of the endorsement field, this was the bench.

He brought Jeannie Martins to the party; they provided an escort service for each other, they passed along information about parties, and sometimes accompanied each other so neither would feel any more single than they really were. Scheduled for the cocktail hour, this event, at the Roosevelt Hotel, was well attended; the place throbbed with people socializing, young men and women and a fair number of middle-aged men.

"Madame Jeannie, telepathist. I can look across a room and pick out the married men."

"The ones wearing wedding rings."

"Sometimes they take them off. I can tell by their moves. They're in a big hurry and very aggressive.

47

Near them was a woman in her 30s in a working-girl's outfit, tailored suit, white blouse with a ribbon tied in front, high heels, her Reebok sneakers protruding from a canvas bag. She was sturdy and vigorous-looking with a pug-nosed, all-American face.

"Do you think this Jocks idea will go over?" Doug asked her.

"Absolutely. It's a solid marketing concept."

He wondered how one used words like "solid marketing concept" and pretended they were part of the language. But she followed up with a smile. "Cathy Vindell," she said.

"Doug Gardner."

"What brings you here, Doug?" she asked, and with a nod, Jeannie smiled knowingly, waved goodbye and dissolved into the crowd. Cathy was employed by Merrill Lynch, and Doug managed to find a common ground with her: of his nineteen subscriptions, two were for business magazines, and they went from discussing the "solid marketing concept" to market conditions to Reagan's economic policies, which carried them to dinner in a ribs restaurant. She invited him to her apartment for a drink, a one-room place on Columbus Avenue, a renovation of an old walk-up. Doug knew the neighborhood from his childhood, and he imagined an Italian shoemaker and his wife had lived there before he lost his store and apartment to gentrification and this was the result, a stock analyst with color television pouring wine for a man she met at a media event. They began to kiss, mouths open, tongues, he was intrigued how quickly they went from economics to tongues and he was fondling her naked body on her Yves Saint Laurent sheets. He was going to focus on her, take time to explore with his fingertips and tongue the light fuzz on her body and the moistness inside her. Time stops, Reynolds stops, the column stops, the tuition stops, Susan's share of the ex-

48

penses stops. This must be what it's like to be on drugs. He was concentrating on nothing but her body. He lasted longer than he usually did and then he entered her again after a while, no complexity, no particular tenderness from her or from him, just physical sex and finally he dozed off next to her. "Hey, tiger." She was poking him on the shoulder. "I've got an early meeting tomorrow. You better go." He dressed, jotted down her number from the phone and she gave him a perfunctory kiss on the forehead, much as a working girl might give to the butcher for having saved her a nice chicken. "Call me sometime," she said. Not "Call me tomorrow." "Sometime." He did call her a couple of days later. Her secretary took a message. She did not call back. After several days he called again and she spoke to him.

"Hi, how are you? Look, I'm in a relationship. If it doesn't work out, I'll get in touch with you."

In a relationship? Since him? Before him? This was his best shot. He had set aside everything else in his mind to focus on her body. He couldn't screw any better than that. Did she get laid like that all the time? When he was in his 20s the younger kids seemed to be having more sex than he ever had when he was a kid. They were a sexual revolution ahead of him. And now this. You miss one sexual revolution and you never catch up.

ONE OF THE FIRST SURVEY GUIDELINES FROM HOUSTON indicated a high percentage of people interested in reading about Pete Rose. Doug had no objection to doing a piece on Rose even though the world could live without another one. Rather than interview Rose on himself—Doug thought that might be number 4,000 on the subject—he called Rose in Cincinnati and asked how he regarded some of the new hitters in the league. Doug did a follow-up column after talking to the hitters about

Rose's comments. The columns were not technically about Rose, but Doug felt they were close enough and that he was covered in Houston for a while.

Jeannie offered Doug the phone number of a woman she had met in her exercise class. Phone numbers were not uncommon for him, Jeannie was a source, Sarah Kleinman met people at various discussion groups she attended and Sarah, too, was a source. He wondered if it was better simply to be a sex object with someone like Cathy Vindell than the matrimonial object he often was with "the hysterics." These were the never-married middle-aged morose, or the formerly married middle-aged morose he encountered on the singles circuit. Their passivity was painful, the hysterical eagerness to please, the listening so hard to the dumbest, most banal things he had to say. Throw out twenty years of women's liberation and all the back copies of *Ms*. magazine. Men are wonderful. And he used Scope, his clothes were clean, he was clean, straight, he had a job, he wasn't on drugs or booze. This was Eligible.

The woman Jeannie suggested, Vicki Moss, owned an American crafts shop in SoHo. He called for her at the store, a small, bright place with handcrafted objects. He liked the store. He thought he was going to like her, a brunette in her early 40s, a bit overweight, with luminous brown eyes and long black hair. They went to dinner at a nearby restaurant and he was off. One of those nights. You can't buy a base hit. If he tried to be witty the remark came up empty. He talked about work, far too much about work, falling into a monologue about Reynolds. Boring. An 0 for 5 night, go home and try again another time, and yet she sat there for it, her eyes wide with the wonder of him, or the eligibility of him. He asked questions about her work, how did she find the pieces she sold, were the new craftsmen markedly different from the old craftsmen? He even cringed at the quality of his questions, which he also found to be boring, and she answered succinctly, letting him do the talking, and he filled the spaces with more inane chatter about the newspaper and market research. She looked interested in what he had to say. I am a boring man tonight. How can you be interested? What I am looking for is someone who wouldn't be interested. Who would have asked to go home an hour ago. Someone I'd have to show up for with a marching band for her ever to see me again.

"I apologize for tonight," he said, as they walked to her apartment. "I've been too preoccupied with work lately."

"What do you mean?" she said, the hysteria at the corners of her eyes. The evening didn't go well, you won't call again, we won't get married within a year? What do I mean? he thought, pained for her. That's what I mean.

"I PROBABLY GET HYSTERICAL MYSELF SOMETIMES," Jeannie said to him. They had gone to see a revival of *The Seventh Seal* and were having hamburgers at the Blarney. "You're at a cocktail party, you look around the room and you think, it's over. There is not one more surviving healthy single male in the world. As of this minute the species is extinct. But the one who's crazy is that Merrill Lynch girl who went to bed with you. To just pick up a guy—"

"Not just a guy. Me."

"You could be anybody. I do it myself. Crazy stuff. I was at a bar a while back with some women from business and I went home with the bartender. Big, good-looking Irish guy. Why do men think they're so fascinating?"

"There are off nights."

"They really should just have their mothers listen to them."

"Sexism, Jeannie?"

"Right. All those consciousness-raising sessions and all that intensity. I'm forty-four. Maybe I made some progress in my career, but I'm not in a relationship and I screw a bartender whose idea of a deep discussion is to tell me how he makes a perfect Kir Royale."

"Maybe you made some progress?"

"So I have my own business. Sometimes it's hard to pinpoint the gains. I got rid of Buddy. I never should have married him. But once I married him, maybe I shouldn't have divorced him. They say it's lonely at the top. I'm here to tell you it's lonely in the middle, too."

They were quiet for a few moments, then she said, "I had lunch with Susan the other day."

"You did?"

"She asked if I'd get together with her. It felt peculiar. Basically, I got you in the settlement. She wants me to do PR for her, get her into *Women's Wear*, do what I can, and she'd pay me. I didn't want to give her an answer until I talked to you."

"I don't have any objections. Anything that can help."

"She really is Miss Driftwood, isn't she? But this new business has possibilities. She has a retainer from Filene's."

"Take the account. It's in the public interest."

"She was wearing a great outfit, all put together from odds and ends. A waiter's jacket over a lacy blouse, silk pants, and she had on a skimmer. She *has* style."

"So I recall."

On the way home he thought about Susan and her style. Sometimes I'm in a store and I can't make up my mind about a jacket or a tie and I want to turn to you and say, "Susan, what do you think?" Susan . . .

ON A FRIDAY NIGHT DOUG WAS WATCHING A KNICKS basketball game on the television set in his bedroom. Karen, who sometimes watched weekend sports programs with Doug, looked in intermittently. Andy came and sat next to Doug and asked a few questions about the game, which was unusual for him. A few nights later the Knicks were playing again and Andy watched with his father. Over the succeeding weeks Andy became a Knicks fan and started following the team's progress in the newspapers. Doug wondered if the sudden interest came from school, if he had been playing basketball there, but he had not, nor did he want to now when Doug offered to shoot baskets with him. The Knicks were playing a Saturday afternoon game and Doug arranged for tickets for the three of them. At dinner that night, Doug, the old-timer, talked about previous Knicks teams and their championship years.

"It was a wonderful time to be writing sports, the line disappeared between being a writer and being a fan. It all became one during the playoffs, the city, the crowds at the Garden, people watching at home and in bars. The last game in the playoff against L.A. in 1970, you'd never forget it. Willis Reed could barely walk and he limped on the court, made his first couple of baskets and L.A. was in shock. When the game was over and we won, people spilled out onto the streets, out of bars, out of apartments, strangers standing around on sidewalks as though they were friends, congratulating each other."

Doug caught himself. He was talking as if they were at a campfire.

"I feel like an old man of the mountain and this is our folklore. But it is, the old Knicks."

"I'm glad you got to see it," Karen commented with affection.

"I love the way you said, 'And we won.' It must have been something," Andy added.

You're something, both of you. He knew that Andy was saying, I can't play ball, Dad, but I can do this. I can be a fan for you like other kids. Doug put his arms around them and hugged them both. Andy wouldn't have been comfortable with it alone, but both at the same time, Doug was able to get the hug in.

"We're the new Knicks," Doug said.

Reynolds came to New York for a publishers' conference and passed through the *Sports Day* offices. He paused to look over Doug's shoulder at the monitor of his computer while Doug was working on a column about the Westminster Kennel Club dog show. Doug had taken his dog, Harry, to the show as a "researcher," the column a view of the all-pedigree show as a mutt like Harry might perceive it.

"It's nice, Doug," Reynolds said, "But it doesn't have anything to do with our guidelines. Two out of twenty-one columns written to our guidelines is not the ratio we're looking for."

"We have different approaches, Robby. You take a reading of pulse, then you respond. I like to—"

"—wing it. Seat of the pants. A real New York kind of guy."

"I *am* your New York columnist."

Robby closed the door of Doug's office.

"Doug, I'm telling you the future of this newspaper doesn't reside exclusively in New York. This is a national publication, and when we feed you survey results to boost our national figures, you don't do the *Sports Day* team any good by ignoring them."

"I don't know how accurate those surveys are."

"They're accurate, and it's not your job to worry about

54

the accuracy. I've got people for that. Circulation is up ten thousand. This newspaper is going through the roof. But we don't want to have recalcitrant columnists. Especially, popular ones. You've got to understand the reality, Doug."

"The reality is you're a strong-minded guy with a need to put your stamp on this newspaper."

"Only partly true. I'm also very successful. And very smart. You think I'm some dumb cowboy because I wear boots? I made businesses grow in other industries and I'm going to do it here. But I can't have such an important writer on my paper working against me. So you make up your mind. You can quit. You can turn down a chance to be even bigger than you are in your field, with even more readers, on a paper that keeps getting bigger, with ads to the public featuring you, with a ten percent pay increase. Or you can take some suggestions on subject matter for your column. Once every two weeks you follow the guidelines and write a column on a designated subject. Nobody's telling you how to write it, but I expect you to work with the surveys. Accept those terms, Doug. Give one to our numbers every once in a while. Take the raise. Or quit. Whatever you decide."

I can't quit. I can't afford to.

"What's it going to be?"

"I'll play, Robby."

"Great, Doug. Welcome aboard."

JEANNIE PLACED A STORY IN *WOMEN'S WEAR DAILY* about a circus-motif promotion Susan created for Filene's in Boston. Jeannie told Doug she learned from Susan the initial money for the new business came from a loan given by Susan's parents, Dr. and Mrs. Brook.

Susan's father was a man of medium build with a porcelain-smooth face, his nails always manicured, his hair cut by a barber who came to his office once a week. Ethel Brook was a petite woman with Susan's dark-brown eyes and hair, a heavy shopper who changed her clothes so often Doug used to think she could have had a nightclub act. Doug never called his father-in-law Charles or Dad. Mrs. Brook referred to him as "the Doctor," even to Doug, and Doug called him Doctor, and the man was comfortable with this. Doug was aware of how disappointed they were that their daughter chose a sportswriter. From their tone over the years, and the fact that they seldom read his pieces, they made it clear they considered him to be in the blue-collar section of journalism. When Karen and Andy were born and there were birthdays to be celebrated, Doug and Susan's apartment became the place where both sets of grandparents mingled across social lines. After the divorce, Doug's parents and Susan's parents never saw each other.

Doug's father, Frank Gardner, was a portly man, bald, with dark features, five feet six, with a double chin. Norma Gardner was similar to Frank in size, a round woman, a half inch taller than her husband, with a face that was moon-shaped, the outline of a face crying out for jolliness but fixed in the melancholy of financial struggle. Norma had worked for years as a cashier in a coffee shop. Frank was the owner of a small costume-jewelry company, Norma Creations, which made "items," as Frank referred to them, mounted on white cards, which sold for under ten dollars. His dream had been to sell Woolworth, if only he could have sold to Woolworth, and they would have been rich and lived in an elevator building instead of a walk-up on Amsterdam Avenue. When the Woolworth chain began to fade economically he tried without success to sell to the new suburban stores in shopping malls. He placed his line in the five-and-ten-cent stores that were still scattered throughout the country, using a novelties wholesaler, which reduced his profits. His efforts to upgrade the line always failed. He never could move to that position in business where his leading "item" was on a piece of satin in its own box, for twenty dollars. Norma Creations leased space in a plant in the South Bronx where two men physically produced the line that Frank created in rough pencil sketches. That Frank Gardner evidenced no other artistic interest, never went to a museum, and could barely draw the designs that became the "items" had always been disturbing to Doug. He believed his father had little flair for his profession and was a man permanently pinned to the wrong card.

FRANK AND NORMA GARDNER CAME TO THE APARTMENT on a Saturday to visit with Doug and their grandchildren, Frank carrying a plastic bag of flounder he had caught that morning on a fishing charter out of Sheepshead Bay. "Sweet as sugar," he declared, then cleaned the fish and expertly cut them into fillets. Doug observed his father and the pleasure he took from his fish, working at the sink with powerful, precise movements, humming. Fish moments such as these were the only times Doug saw passion in his father.

Rain was falling, and they spent the afternoon indoors. Frank and Andy were busy with gin rummy, Norma and Karen made a cake for dessert, then they all played Monopoly together. After dinner Norma drew Doug aside.

"Paint is chipping in the rooms."

"I know. A couple of years and it starts to go. The steam does it."

"So why don't you get it taken care of?"

"Because the landlord uses a painter who'll ruin the place and the estimate for a regular painter was about two thousand dollars and I wasn't ready to spend it."

"I saw on TV, children can eat it, the lead in paint."

57

"They're big children. They don't eat paint."

"They eat it and they die," she said, not quite tuned in to his station.

"That's not going to happen."

"Next weekend your father and I will come and fix the rooms. You buy the paint."

"It isn't necessary."

Two roly-polys wearing paint hats arrived the following week, to remove any evidence that could suggest their son was not making Big Money.

For the past three summers Karen and Andy had gone to a day camp with grounds in New Jersey. Andy, too old to be a camper the previous summer, had worked assisting the counselors. Doug thought they might enjoy being at a sleepaway camp, freed of their continuing home and home series for a while. The day-camp director had a partnership in a camp in the Berkshires where Karen could be a camper and Andy could have a job as a waiter. The children liked the idea, and after researching camps, favored this one. The camp fee for Karen was twenty-five hundred dollars. Susan offered to pay half when she received payment in the fall from a project she was working on for Neiman Marcus in Dallas. Taking Karen and Andy by cab to the bus-departure point near Lincoln Center, Doug was the one nearly carsick from the separation.

Visiting day was the last Saturday in July. He and Susan were not in touch with each other, and he rented a car and drove up to the camp alone. He parked in a clearing for cars and entered the camp area. In the distance was a girl with a resemblance to his daughter, brown from the sun, hair blowing freely, a towel wrapped around her neck, cruising on a bicycle. "Daddy!" Karen shouted and pedaled toward him. Her movements, the emerging sexual being that she was, startled him. She had been momentarily unrecognizable. They walked arm in arm toward the bunks, and he saw Andy sitting with his back to a tree, reading a book. His hair was unkempt and wild and he, too, for a beat, did not look familiar to Doug. Susan appeared in an antique Victorian lace dress with an antique bonnet, a ribbon down the back, moving elegantly through this background of children, rustic cabins and casually dressed parents like Claudia Cardinale in a Fellini movie. Over the next hours the generally reasoned acceptance about sharing the children with each other, the knowledge that the children needed the other parent, collapsed. She was there everywhere he turned, an intruder, and he was there everywhere she turned. By nightfall they had had enough of each other, and after they said goodbye to Karen and Andy they walked to their separate rented cars without another word.

AS HE DROVE BACK TO THE CITY HE THOUGHT ABOUT the time they decided about the divorce. They had exchanged unpleasant words over nothing, it seemed, over reading habits. On a Saturday night they were sitting with the early edition of the Sunday *New York Times* scattered on the floor. Susan was looking at a fashion supplement, which Doug would not have bothered to read. He had the sports section and the Week in Review.

"You still do that. The Week in Review is one of the first things you pick up. Nobody picks that up first."

"I also have the sports section. Do you ever bother to look at it? I am in that field, you know."

"Would you read the fashions? Do you read *Vogue*? All your magazines, and you never read it. I am in that field, you know."

"It's a little different. You don't write for *Vogue*. I write sports."

She glanced at the front page of the sports section. The lead story was about a horse race at Aqueduct.

"I'd read the sports if I were a jockey. I'm not a jockey."

"Maybe we should have an electric scoreboard and keep a tally on cutting remarks."

"Maybe we should just call it quits."

"That's a good idea."

There it was, after years. "Maybe we should just call it quits." "That's a good idea." Once they started the discussion of how they would break up, they never questioned whether they would, and they were soon talking to lawyers. "Maybe we should just call it quits." She had offered that tentatively, not, "I want a divorce." 'I'm moving out." "You're moving out." If he had said anything other than "That's a good idea," might they have stayed together? he wondered. He saw himself again sitting there with her. You don't say, "That's a good idea." You say, "It's not a good idea." You say, "No, Susan. When the kids were little we were involved with each other and we worked together. We have to work together again, on the marriage, on doing things together, on taking an interest in each other. And it starts right now. Give me the fashion section. Give me *Vogue*. Let's talk hemlines. Let's talk anything. I love you." And you get up. You get out of your chair. You cross the room. You take her in your arms. And you do that the next time and the next and it starts right there. Get up! Walk across the room. Don't just sit there. Get up!

He recalled his culpability, the times he returned her distance with his, her doubts with his, the times he had not transcended their arguments, their crises by saying, "We have to survive this. *We* are crucial." He had joint custody of the failure.

* * *

DOUG WAS GOING TO BE 48. WHEN HE WAS A CHILD HE wanted so much to be older he expanded his age. "I'm almost nine." As this birthday approached he never would have said, I'm almost 48. On his birthday the children gave him a sports encyclopedia as a gift, and they went to dinner in a Chinese restaurant where Karen and Andy arranged for Doug to be served a pineapple for dessert adorned with sparklers, several waiters singing "Happy Birthday." "If you have to be forty-eight, you're the people to be forty-eight with," he said to his children. He also received a few birthday cards, from Jeannie, his parents, his brother and sister-in-law. For people my age maybe they should have the reverse of belated birthday cards. "Sorry. I remembered."

AN IMPERIAL RUSSIAN BALLROOM WAS SUSAN'S CREA-tion for Neiman Marcus, a fashion show against a backdrop of mirrors, chandeliers, hostesses in gowns, uniformed guards, Russian wolfhounds. The event was covered by *Women's Wear Daily* through Jeannie's efforts. Doug received a check from Susan for her share of Karen's camp expenses and checks continued to arrive at intervals to be applied toward the children's tuition. Then she sent him thirty-five hundred dollars, her full share of the children's latest tuition bill, the largest check he had ever received from her. His first response was elation. Irony took over. It would envelop him at random times, while he was paying bills, while he was at work. He would have a sinking sensation in his stomach like an anxiety attack. This is my own invention, an irony attack. Is it possible you're going to become successful now, when we're not married anymore? All those years when I lay awake nights worrying about the bills, when I felt everything was on my shoulders and you weren't concerned about finances and you become concerned now. If I were going to mess up a marriage I should have been smart enough to wait for you to earn some money. But for you to make a move to be successful *now*. That has a real edge to it, Susan. It's the ultimate Fuck You.

5

THE NEW YORK CITY MARATHON PRODUCED A number of calls to Doug at the newspaper, people looking for publicity, the first Abraham Lincoln to run the race (this was an actor promoting his one-man show), a Watusi warrior in full regalia promoting "Watusi Tall Fashions," Grandma Peters, an 81-year-old marathoner representing "Grandma Peters Exercise Equipment," and Tony Rosselli for Kwan Doo Duk, "the world's tallest midget wrestler-marathoner."

Doug wrote a column related to the Marathon, ignoring the publicity seekers. He discussed the prize money in track as a means of resurrecting the reputation of a forgotten distance runner of the 1950s, Wes Santee. Santee had been America's foremost miler. The A.A.U., which presided over American track-and-field athletes, had accused him of accepting a total of fifteen hundred dollars over "allowable" expenses for seven track meets. Santee insisted at the time that he had not committed a crime, expense money was routinely accepted by competitors. Doug pointed out that in later years it became required, along with substantial prize money. Santee's position was a challenge to the power of the A.A.U., which terminated his career, barring him from track for the rest of his life. As Doug wrote, Santee was banished for crimes that ceased to be crimes and perhaps never were.

Reynolds and Wall passed through New York, Texas-tornado style, conducting a fast-paced meeting before going on to Boston where they were going to have a similar meeting. They presented the results of a new survey showing readership of articles within the newspaper. Wall pointed out that sports which tallied high on a recent "Which sport do you follow?" survey did not always perform well in "finishing the article" statistics.

"Our conclusion is," Wall said, "the articles were not well-written enough."

"So there are going to be replacements in our bureaus, unless people can improve their 'finishing the article' stats," Reynolds said.

Wall presented another set of tallies, "finishing the article" for *Sports Day* compared with the *Chicago Tribune* and *USA Today*.

"We do better than the *Chicago Trib*, which is not surprising, since we're a special-interest newspaper, but not as well as *USA Today*," Wall told them.

"Why do you think that is, fellas? Doug, surely you have an opinion here," Reynolds said.

"You're comparing apples and oranges. What *USA Today* is all about is the short piece. They do a very good job on short, compact pieces and features. If you're looking for 'finishing the article,' of course, they're going to score better. That's what they do."

"I think you're right, Doug," Reynolds said. "And that's why we're initiating a new policy. All news stories and features will be cut fifteen percent in length. All columns five percent. Only five percent, Doug, because we see the reading patterns for columns are a little different, a little more brand loyalty."

"These changes will be effective immediately," Wall said. "The computers will be programmed so that if you file copy that's over your line quota, you'll get an indication on the screen."

"It's exciting, fellas, to identify a pattern and to be able to act scientifically," Reynolds said. "We're going to pass the *Inquirer* next, guys. Keep it up!"

Reynolds and Wall left the conference room.

"Not so bad," Wilkes said. "We get the same amount of money for writing less."

"That's an opportunistic way of looking at it," Lahey said. "So long as you don't mind your copy getting cut."

"Mr. Gardner," Sally, the receptionist, called to him, "Mr. Reynolds is still here. He wants to see you."

Reynolds was standing in Doug's office.

"I wanted to mention that track column. Wes Santee? This is not a history seminar we're running here. It was very self-indulgent."

"That's what a column is, Robby. By definition it's self-indulgent or it wouldn't be a column in the first place. It would be a news story."

Reynolds looked at Doug as if he were being entertained.

"Sounds to me like while I'm trying to educate you, you're trying to educate me. Who do you think is ahead?" And he walked out of the office.

INDEPENDENCE FROM THE FATHER WAS NECESSARY FOR the growth of children. Doug knew the text. For all the hours he spent with these children he thought somehow he might receive an amnesty from generation gap. Not a chance. "Yes, we heard that before, Dad," Andy would say to him. Karen, too, sometimes said, "Yes, you told us."

Am I repeating myself more often? Is my brain disintegrating even as I speak?

Andy asked Doug about the movie *Shane*, which one of his friends had recommended. "Did you ever see it, Dad?"

"I did. It's a good movie."

"Is it in black and white?"

"That's how you place me? All my movies were in black and white?"

DOUG TOOK KAREN AND ANDY FOR A WEEKEND TO HIS brother and sister-in-law's vacation house in the Poconos. Marty Gardner was a year older than Doug, a short man with reddish hair and a cheerful face; his wife, Ellen, was a shy, pretty brunette, five feet one. When they met she had been a salesgirl in a dress shop on Seventy-second Street. Marty had a job nearby. After graduating from high school he worked in a dry-cleaning store and fashioned his dream, to have his own dry-cleaning store. He eventually bought out the owner, who retired, he started a second store, and was able to buy a little country house on a half acre of woodland in a middle-class development. Marty and Ellen had two girls, Sandy and Ricky, 17 and 16, both very physical, mountain climbers, cyclists, and when Doug visited with Karen and Andy there was considerable outdoor activity, long walks, bicycling. Marty was a social director in his house, eager for everyone to have a good time. "Okay, we'll take a nice walk, we can go boating, the kids can ride bikes, anything. I've got beautiful steaks for dinner and I rented a couple of movies for the VCR, we can make a fire, watch a movie, play Ping-Pong, whatever you want." The adults and children walked to a lake where they took out rowboats. Karen set up her easel and worked on a watercolor of the scene. On the way back Marty and Ellen's golden retriever and Harry took turns chasing each other. At the house Marty set up his gas-fired barbecue grill.

"You don't have to eat steak, we've got hamburgers, too. What do you like?" When people requested hamburgers, he said, "Any way you like it, medium, I can do medium-rare, just say the word. Are you having a good time? That's not too well done for you, is it?"

Marty. He offered anything they wanted for dessert, ice cream, apple pie, sundaes, anything anybody wanted, he would go out and get something if they didn't have it in the house, and Doug put his arm around his brother with affection. After dinner the two brothers went outside to look at the night sky.

"Isn't this great? God's country. Tomorrow we can get the papers, sit around and read, take a bike ride, have a nice lunch."

"You hit a grand slam in your life, Marty."

"I just got lucky with Ellen, that's all."

"How's business?"

"Food stains are up. Young working kids in the neighborhood, they've got a lot of clothes and they eat out a lot."

"Would you do another store?"

"For more headaches? No. So what's cooking with you?"

"Nothing spectacular."

"What are you reading, anything I should know about?"

"A good baseball piece. On black barnstorming."

"I'd like to read it. And how about women? Anybody?"

"Not at the moment."

"I wish I had somebody for you. I should be able to

67

come up with someone. All these single girls come into the place. But it's hard with a customer. You don't know how they'd take it—'How would you like to meet my brother?' "

"I appreciate the thought."

"I'll keep looking. Someone with nice clothes," he said with innocence and sincerity.

Marty admired Doug for having gone to college, for being a sports columnist. But Doug admired his brother for something Marty would not have thought significant—for the scale of his life. He had his wife, two children, and a dog in the same apartment. People brought in clothes and Marty got the clothes clean. If it all could be so simple.

DOUG SPENT SEVERAL HOURS SHOPPING FOR A GIFT FOR Karen's 13th birthday, finally selecting a sports watch and a book on the art of Georgia O'Keeffe. She was happy to have the gifts, which cost sixty-five dollars, and he gave them to her at a roller-skating party for her friends, which Susan organized. When Karen next came to his apartment she was wearing a luxurious cable-knit pink cashmere sweater, her birthday gift from Susan. It must have cost two hundred dollars.

The Christmas school vacation had to be divided between both parents, and Susan phoned to suggest they combine resources for a skiing vacation. She said the children were interested in trying it and she thought that for social reasons, skiing was a sport that should be in their lives. Susan had found a two-week package at a lodge in Sugarbush in Vermont. She would split the cost with Doug and be with Karen and Andy the first week, he would take over the second. So tentative was his commitment to the idea of skiing that if they manufactured disposable ski wear he would have bought it. In a discount sporting-goods store he found a cheap parka and pants. He took a flight to Burlington, where he was going to rent a car for the drive to Sugarbush. The terminal at Burlington was busy with people carrying boots and skis, high school or college students, he could not distinguish between the age groups, and various people who did not look as young, singles, young marrieds. A depressing thought occurred to him while he was standing on the car-rental line. Am I the oldest person in this entire airlines terminal? A few moments later an elderly couple passed with their grandchildren. All right, then. Am I the oldest person going skiing in the entire terminal? On the way out of the building he saw Lars or Sven, in his early 60s, Nordic, trim, in a beautiful ski jacket. Lars or Sven skied expertly when he wasn't making love to countless women. I have my category now. I am the oldest *beginner* in this terminal, maybe the world.

Susan returned to New York and Doug began his week, signing up the following morning for his first class. Karen and Andy helped him with the equipment. He ached just from bending to get his boots on. They guided him over to the class and said they would meet him at lunchtime. A week of skiing and they already belonged on a different part of the mountain. After two hours of hobbling sideways and falling in the snow, Doug discovered a sport he loathed more than jogging. The instructor, a strapping lad named Mark, was very enthusiastic, and by the afternoon session he had Doug falling off the rope tow.

By the second day he was now doing snowplow turns at a downhill speed not much faster than the rate at which icicles form. The children glided by to offer encouragement, and in order to turn and say hello to them he fell, for about the thirtieth time in two days. The afternoon of the third day he was so tired he had developed his own snowplow wobble. I am a 48-year-old man on a ski slope in Vermont, my nose is running, my feet are cold. I am doing this to compete in some way with my ex-wife, who is not even here and who is probably in a heated room wearing a normal person's clothes. I am doing this for my children, for their social advancement, and they are already so socially advanced they breeze by me to say hi. The one person I am not doing this for is me. At which point he hit ice, skidded rapidly and out of control, fell, landing on his rear, and as he slid downhill, his el cheapo pants split and were filling up with snow. He saw skiers at the bottom of the hill and beyond them a lodge. He imagined himself going right down the hill on his rear, past the skiers, crashing through the lodge and coming out the other end, bumping into Lars or Sven, who would look at him with disdain for being so déclassé. He came to a stop and attempted to regain his dignity and his upright position. He felt foolish at this age to be so comically inexpert at anything. Tots on skis were gliding past him. Susan, I give you Sugarbush, Aspen. I give you the beginner's slopes, the intermediate slopes, the advanced-intermediate slopes. I retire from skiing.

FOR SAKS IN WHITE PLAINS SUSAN ORGANIZED A FASHion show against a background of one hundred sports cars. For Neiman Marcus in Houston she produced Highland games with pipers, folk dancers, and athletic competitions to feature woolens from Scotland. Her share of the tuition payments were now paid promptly and in full. During the Washington's Birthday school recess she took the children to St. Thomas. They had never gone to the Caribbean when they were a family—they took less expensive vacations then. One summer they went to the Jersey shore for two weeks. Another to Fire Island. Lake George. Tanglewood. Not elegant but good times. Susan and I talked so much in those years. So many details about the kids. And the birthday parties. Karen's 6th birthday when the teenage magician lost his rabbit and it ran terrified through the house making all over the place, and the children howling with laughter. It was better than any magic trick and Susan and I laughed ourselves to sleep that night. The playgrounds. The hours in the playgrounds switching off between the swings and the sandbox, sitting on the benches talking about the children, about schools, about what they needed and what kind of parents we should be and who they were going to become. And the physical labor required to get them through a weekend happy. When they're young, you're so intense. Then the physical labor stops, the playgrounds stop. They get too old for playgrounds and you never set foot in one again. But we were good at it, at the playgrounds and the vacations and the parties. I forget that sometimes. We were a really good team for a while.

OCCASIONALLY THE OLD HOUSEMATES FROM SINGLE DAYS would meet for lunch during the week. Jeannie, Doug, and Bob were at the Oyster Bar and Jeannie announced she and Susan came to a mutual parting on her press representation. When Susan opened a promotion out of town she was looking for local publicity Jeannie was unable to provide, and Susan was hiring a larger public-relations firm. Bob was fascinated by the cost-efficient nature of the business Susan created. She developed the ideas and produced the events but the department stores paid the entire costs of the promotions.

"If she keeps coming up with accounts, she can pass us all by," he said.

An article appeared in *Women's Wear Daily* featuring Susan, "Rising Star of Store Merchandising," with several pictures, Susan in her New York apartment, Susan at her Highland games, Susan at a horse-show event she staged in Denver. Doug noticed the living room of their marriage had been completely redecorated. That she managed to pay for redecorating and for her share of the children's expenses, the tuition, the skiing, the Caribbean, was evidence to him that she had already passed him by.

He did not know how he could hold the children's interest within his budget against treats such as winter vacations in the Caribbean.

Taking him by surprise, Andy said, "Knicks-Atlanta Saturday night. Dominique Wilkins. Can you get us all tickets?"

"You really want to go?"

"I do."

"Karen?"

"Great."

When they left Madison Square Garden, Karen took her father's hand and Andy let his hand rest on Doug's shoulder.

He smiled and said, "You're my MVPs."

SPORTS DAY MOVED AHEAD OF THE PHILADELPHIA INquirer in circulation, and compared with conventional daily newspapers, at 510,000, was now among the top fifteen in America. A celebration dinner of spareribs and champagne was held in Houston for a hundred staff members from the home office and the bureaus. Reynolds had recently installed a new managing editor and a news editor, men in their 30s who had worked for *USA Today*. He introduced them and they stood to applause. The addition of editors from that newspaper appeared to be consistent with Reynolds's thinking. He was copying the successful *USA Today* format and layout, *Sports Day* looking more like an all-sports version of *USA Today*. A six-minute film was shown called "*Sports Day* Is Coming at You," which would be used by the advertising department to sell space, and the presentation ended with a professional singing group performing, "Have a Nice Sports Day," from the new radio advertising campaign. Doug did not applaud at the conclusion. He was still absorbing the idea that he worked for a newspaper that had its own song.

JOHN MCCARTHY, DOUG'S FORMER COLLEAGUE AT THE *New York Post*, asked Doug to meet him at Brooks Brothers. It was Susan who had originally encouraged Doug to shop at Brooks, and McCarthy followed Doug's example. Now, in keeping with his position as a prominent sports-journalism packager, McCarthy had his suits custom-made there. McCarthy's wife, a nurse, worked in Westchester, so McCarthy sometimes asked Doug to help him at Brooks with a second opinion on alterations. In his 50s, with thinning brown hair, McCarthy had a light complexion that turned ruddy when he was drinking. He also had a beer belly which Brooks's custom tailoring could do little to conceal. Doug observed the latest fitting and confirmed that the tailors were doing their best. They adjourned for a dinner of hamburgers and beer at the Blarney.

"So how are you getting along with Hopalong Cassidy?" McCarthy asked.

"He's not a cowboy, he wants you to know. Even as he rides over everything we were brought up on."

"Is he giving you a hard time?"

"I think I amuse him. He seems to be making a cause out of me."

"Well, you're getting good money, good exposure, pretty good license to write what you want. Where is it better?"

"I feel like I'm in some terrible newspaper-sci-fi movie, 'Hecht and MacArthur Meet Computer Man.' "

"You could try free-lancing."

"It's too unstable a life for me, John. Not with my bills."

"Look at it this way. You've got something I don't have: You write pretty much what you want. I have to take what's out there."

"He's like a dark wizard. Whatever I may think, he keeps building circulation."

"Do you want to try 'As Told To' books? I can help. I can't write them all."

"That's nice of you, John."

"You're the custodian of my secret information. You knew me when I was a good writer."

"That's supposed to inspire me to join you?"

"I just turned down a book you can have. Pat Cawley, America's new tennis phenom."

"He's a racket-throwing, foulmouthed brat."

"That's the title, *Brat!* The money's pretty good. There's got to be a fantasy you could fulfill with the money."

I've got a fantasy. I'm back on the *New York Post*. We're together as a family again. We're at Tanglewood. Susan and I are lying on a blanket. The children are playing tag nearby before the concert begins. Susan and I are watching them, our fingertips touching, smiling at our good fortune. The concert is about to begin and the children come and lie near us, fitting themselves back into a pattern with us. We are arranged as if a painter has placed us there, the four of us again.

"Doug, where are you?"

"I'm sorry, John. I'm going to pass. Now if it were Hulk Hogan," he said unseriously.

"I'm already doing Hulk Hogan."

74

SEVERAL WEEKS LATER SUSAN CALLED DOUG AT HOME in the evening.

"I have some important news. Doug, I'm getting married."

I have some important news. Those were the words she used when she first told him she was pregnant with Andy. She sat across from him on the floor that time, took his hands in hers and said, "I have some important news." Was it intentional? Or was it a phrase she was accustomed to using at crucial times? He heard himself saying the right things. "Congratulations. I hope you'll be very happy." The words had nothing to do with him. What he wanted was to yell, *how?* How did you do it? I'm not even out of the starting gate and you're getting married. And what happens with the children, how do we live, how does this work? "I wish you the best," he said.

He imagined himself on a track with Susan, running along as she drew next to him, then passed him, pulling farther and farther away, receding from view, their history together disappearing until he could no longer see her with his middle-age eyes.

6

AN ENTITY EXISTED IN HIS LIFE THAT TOOK PRE-
cedence over an ex-wife announcing her remar-
riage. The column. The work. Three times a week the
column had to appear. A columnist cannot dwell on the
fact that he doesn't have someone other than a platonic
friend to see a movie with, while his ex-wife has her
situation so under control she is already replacing him,
that this person he carried along financially waits until
he is off the premises before she earns the money which,
if she had earned it then, might have reduced the tension
that contributed to the end of the marriage. The screen
of the monitor was waiting. He felt its impatience. Fill
up my spaces, man. I'm only here for words, and where
are they? Millions of dollars of technological research to
create me and you sit there thinking about your ex-wife.
You're going to have sexual fantasies about her, I bet,
you pervert. Come on, write something. All the writers
around and I end up with you. I could be working for
John "As Told To" McCarthy. James Michener. He'd
have chapters by now. Finally! Players' injuries on arti-

ficial turf. Don't ask me what I think of it. I'm only interested in quantity.

ON HEARING NEWS OF THE MARRIAGE FROM DOUG, BOB Kleinman said he wanted to analyze the information. Apparently to emphasize the seriousness with which he viewed this, he asked Doug to visit him at his law office.

"I don't trust a woman in this situation. Her payment of the bills, the new man. You may be looking at a move on her part to alter the arrangement with the children, based on a change of circumstances."

"I can think of many ways of getting depressed on my own. I don't need help."

"This is what you have lawyers for, to point out what could happen."

"She's not going to alter the arrangement. I know Susan."

"You know Susan. I've seen brother and sister fighting over objects, furniture, jewelry when a parent died, relatives screaming and pulling hair over who was promised the pearls."

"All we have here is her intention to get married."

"She's establishing a stable financial situation with a husband, while you, a bachelor, are screwing all over the place."

"Could we define our terms?"

"Her lawyer could claim this. You're very vulnerable on custody right now. You might want to consider moving for sole custody yourself. Then we'd settle for the status quo, which keeps her from getting them."

"Are you looking for a little extra work? Do you have some children's orthodontics to pay for?"

Bob's pessimism troubled Doug sufficiently for him to ask Susan if they could get together and she offered breakfast at the coffee shop. Doug started to look for one of his better shirts that morning and then said the hell with it. He took the first shirt on top in the drawer. She didn't care how he looked, she wouldn't be impressed one way or the other. She was getting married.

Susan was radiant, a person who had managed to find a marriage in the singles world of New York, the middle-aged singles world, which made this more of a win.

"I should ask the musical question—who?"

"His name is Jerry Broeden. We met about a year ago and it got serious about six months ago. And we decided to get married."

"What is his field?"

"Apparel. He manufactures denim."

Denim. Laughable. Once again the doctor's daughter doesn't marry a professional. A sports columnist possibly outranked a denim man on the social ladder. And then he figured it out. Denim. Did he have any idea how much denim was worn?

"He must do pretty well."

"You can't believe how much denim is out there."

"Right."

"He's very nice, Doug, very playful with the children."

"Where do you plan to live?"

"We're buying a co-op on Central Park West."

"Are you?"

"There are families in the building. The kids should like it."

"It's a big step to take children into your life. He must love you."

"Yes, I think he does."

Doug appraised her over their drinks, a desirable, successful woman. When you marry young, you marry potential. I married the potential and this Jerry Broeden comes along and claims the results. He gets the career woman with her picture in *Women's Wear Daily* and her aura of success.

He doesn't get the early childhood illnesses either, the fevers in the night as the children thrash around and you cannot absorb their pain for them, the chicken pox and worrying how badly scarred they will be. He gets none of that. He doesn't even get the bills to handle all by himself. He gets to sleep with a star and to sleep nights.

"Susan, how are we going to work this with the children?"

"The way we have. They'll have two weeks with you and two weeks with us. Do you have any other thoughts?"

No, just that I could kiss you for that. I knew you wouldn't try to take the kids for yourself, and I never would have done it to you. You know that about me, don't you?

"That sounds fine."

They finished, walked outside and as they were about to part he did kiss her spontaneously on the cheek in thanks. He quickly rushed off before either of them would have to react to this.

IN THE FOLLOWING DAYS HE NEVER SAW SO MUCH DENIM. Everywhere he looked he noticed it, on the street, in his closets. His assumption was that Jerry Broeden manufactured all the denim he was seeing. Jeannie told him that Broedenco was one of the largest manufacturers of denim in the United States. Broeden bought himself a family with his denim money. Doug had worn out the images of Susan with men, now he thought about the theft of his place, this man padding around the house while the children were there.

AT THE CHILDREN'S REQUEST, DOUG SERVED HIS TUNA croquettes, a dish handed down from his parents' kitchen, the artlessness of the meal amusing him. On the table it looked a step above what they might have eaten on a lucky night in *The Grapes of Wrath*. He wondered what other single parents served their children. If he were the kind of man who owned a show dog, would his children be eating tuna croquettes?

"So Mom's getting married," he said, unable to make it sound casual.

The children looked at each other as if they had been waiting for this.

"Yes, that's true," Andy said.

"What is he like?"

"He's all right," Karen offered. "He kids around a lot."

"In what way?"

"He's kind of mischievous," Andy said.

"I don't understand."

"Fooling around kinds of things," Karen said.

He saw how easy it would be for him to be subversive, to be sarcastic about "Denim Jerry." That could fit nicely. And how did "Denim Jerry" fool around today? An ongoing game he could play with them and it could start right here, they had given him the opportunity. And nothing would be gained. The best for their well-being, he conceded, would be for them to like their stepfather and be comfortable with him and happy living with the sonofabitch.

"And I hear you're moving. Have you seen the new apartment?"

They nodded yes.

"Is it nice?"

Andy said, "Yes, it's nice," with such reserve Doug interpreted it to mean the new apartment was huge.

* * *

HE HAD BEEN ATTEMPTING TO WORK WITH THE SURVEY guidelines on subject matter. One area he was supposed to write about and had been ignoring was personal fitness, which he simply didn't consider a sport. Reynolds sent him little reminders on the computer, "Are you fit today, Doug?" "Fitness keeps you and your boss happy." And after a couple of weeks a change in tone, "Let's shape up on the fitness front." And finally, "Where is a fitness column?" To quiet the screen, he wrote a column about jogging, surely jogging falls under personal fitness, Robby. He called jogging the castor oil of physical activity, so bad it had to be good for you. He included his own jogging experience, watching the world's tushes pass him by as he plodded along. How it was best when he ran with the dog while listening on a personal stereo to National Public Radio. With the dog and the news program he managed to place as many layers as possible between himself and the act of jogging. Reynolds responded, "The jogging column barely covers you on personal fitness, but I'll let it pass," sending this on the computer, obviously savoring the notion of being an omnipotent high-tech Wizard of Oz.

ON A SATURDAY EVENING WHEN THE CHILDREN WERE at Susan's, Andy called and asked if he could stop by for a schoolbook he had left at the apartment. When he arrived for the book, he was with a girl. She was chubby, with a sweet face.

"This is Lesa. Dad, Lesa."

"I'm very pleased to meet you, Mr. Gardner. I've read many of your columns."

"Required reading," Andy said, smiling.

"I'd like to be a writer some day. And I like sports. I'm on field hockey," she said.

"Dad was an athlete once," Andy said.

"Really?"

"I played some baseball. High school and college. A long time ago. It was in black and white."

DOUG WORKED, WROTE INFREQUENT COLUMNS TO THE surveys, marginally close to his quota, read books and periodicals at night. When he was in elementary school he and his classmates would go to Rockefeller Center on Saturdays for school projects and wander in and out of the tourist bureaus of Latin American countries asking, "Got any information?" and they would be given tourist information. He had information but no woman to share it with. A new feeling at night began to overshadow the anxiety attacks and the irony attacks, and it was loneliness. The kind you might have if you go into Macy's to buy a lamp for your bedroom and you see a young couple in their 30s buying a sofa together, holding hands, and you find yourself watching them like an old person on a park bench looking at the young ones. This was a Frank Sinatra "Wee Small Hours of the Morning" loneliness, arrangement by Nelson Riddle.

Doug was ready for phone numbers from any source. He went out with a pastry chef, courtesy of his brother, an airline stewardess from John McCarthy, a librarian from the Kleinmans, a divorced housewife from Bob's secretary's cousin. A new veterinarian, unmarried, came into the office where he took Harry for his appointments and Doug went out with her, meaning *Harry* had fixed him up.

Some of these women he saw for a drink or dinner and not again, some he slept with and did not see again. He was dating wildly in a mad attempt to do what? What am I doing, trying to meet someone fantastic I can elope with before Susan gets to the finish line? Or just trying to meet someone interesting, whatever that means. A couple of women he saw once perhaps he should have seen a second time, one or two he saw a second time perhaps he shouldn't have seen again. His need to have someone in his life was turning in on itself, he was creating social chaos, losing his judgment, and he didn't know what he was looking for any longer. He went to a Columbus Avenue restaurant called Pasta!!! A West Side newspaper had written that Wednesday night was "networking" night at the restaurant, young professionals came for "an exchange of resources," and since he was desperate, he attempted to "network." He watched as people not anywhere near his age exchanged business cards and interest in each other.

"What do you do?" a fairly good-looking blonde in her 30s asked him over the din.

"I write a sports column."

"I'm looking for a job in advertising. I'm a copywriter."

"Do you use a word processor?" he said lamely, trying to get *something* started.

"I don't use anything. I'm unemployed." And she moved on. He looked at the networking throng, buzzing bees, and the awful part was that several of the women, happy to alight elsewhere, looked attractive to him. Listen out there. I have something a lot of these young guys might not have. I have experience. I have some wit, some intelligence. I love dogs. Eavesdropping, he decided that for all the exchange of business cards and contacts, "networking" in a public place was another word for pickups, and he wasn't picking up and it wasn't his network.

HE CALLED A SERVICE THAT ADVERTISED VIDEO DATING. Perhaps he could find a terrific woman so committed to her meaningful work that she hadn't the time or the inclination to meet men in the ordinary rituals. For one hundred dollars you received three phone numbers obtained after viewing videos of women talking about themselves. You, in turn, submitted a video of yourself which they could judge. Doug sat in a room with the video camera on for his interview with Mrs. Patterson, in her 40s, stylishly dressed, who, in the preinterview, exhibited a condescending manner which suggested to Doug that she was saying, "You're needy. *I'm* married."

"What are you looking for in a mate?" she asked with the camera running.

"I never articulated it so baldly. Someone who can adjust to a man having teenage children. Who can accept sports and knows the Tampa Bay Buccaneers are not from an Errol Flynn movie. Who knows who Errol Flynn *was*." He paused, beginning to feel ridiculous. "Someone who is as personally degraded by this as I am. Who sympathizes with the need to meet a kindred spirit that would lead you to make a video so someone can gape at you in this electronic meathook."

"Sir? Our customers are not negative about our service and we're not promoting negativism here."

"*That's* the woman I'm looking for, the one who's negative about your service!"

"We're going to return your money. We reserve the right to do so."

"No, I want all this in. This is my presentation."

"The interview is concluded. Cut."

"That was possibly a great dating video," Doug said. "It might have gotten into a museum. *Video vérité.*"

"HOW IS IT DONE?" HE SAID TO JEANNIE AT DINNER. "I don't know how you connect with anybody."

"I don't know what you do, either. Some women start to go out with younger men. I've got to wonder about the men who go out with women too much older than they are. After you do that, then what? Already I see myself dressing younger than what's appropriate. I was Audrey Hepburn. I'm turning into Blanche DuBois.''

''You look wonderful, Jeannie.''

''What do you know? You look at me like I'm a sister.''

''Younger sister.''

''I appreciate that.''

''What's the forum? Sports columnist. Has half a dog, half of two children, good seats for sports events, subscribes to nineteen periodicals.''

''Nineteen? Really?''

''Actually, I sound terrific.''

''We both are. It's the system that's no good. The thing is, marriage doesn't work. But not being married doesn't work either.''

THE DAY. SUSAN AND BROEDEN WERE GETTING MARRIED in Paris. The children flew over with them as did members of the immediate families. This was Susan's custodial time and by extension the dog's time with her, and Susan asked Doug if he would take the dog. If not, she would arrange to place him in a kennel. Doug kept Harry with him and on the wedding day took him jogging in Central Park. He was back at the apartment by 11 A.M. He had another thirty hours or so before the children were to be returned to Manhattan by a cousin of Broeden's while the newlyweds honeymooned in Europe.

''What are you doing today?'' Bob said to him on the phone.

''I've got some articles to read.''

''What you need is a steam bath, a massage, a movie, then dinner.''

''What is this about?''

''We start with the steam bath and the massage.''

him. He could feel Bob's belly pressing against his, and the whiskers on his cheek. He had never held a man so close—his father when he was little, not anyone as an adult. Doug and Bob stood on the sidewalk hugging, in a zone of intimacy neither was familiar with, and they did not want to let go, they held each other a long time, holding onto the moment, not caring who might see.

A FEW WEEKS LATER DOUG MET JERRY BROEDEN, Susan's new husband, for the first time. On a Sunday night Doug was returning from the supermarket, and as he was about to enter the building the children arrived with the dog for their two weeks. Broeden had driven them there, and he came out of the car to introduce himself. Doug had expected a movie star. Broeden was a slim, unexceptional-looking man of five feet eleven, light brown hair, brown eyes, dressed seriously in Ralph Lauren, the tweed sports jacket, the Shetland sweater, the twill slacks, the Ralph Lauren loafers Doug knew to be out of his price range. And Broeden was young. This may have been the Main Idea here. He appeared to be several years younger than Doug, possibly younger than Susan. He looked 40, nearly.

"I'm Jerry Broeden."

"Doug Gardner."

"I guess we'll be seeing each other now and then." He called out to Karen and Andy, "So long, guys."

They waved, carefully watching the interchange between Broeden and their father. Aware of their concern, Doug played it elegantly and gave Broeden a warm smile and a handshake.

"Good to meet you," Doug said.

"Same here." And Broeden returned to his car.

Doug didn't have a car and had never owned a car. I could have a car, I suppose, but I don't really need one.

Since Doug didn't own a car and didn't care at all about cars, he didn't know exactly which model of Mercedes Broeden owned. It was black and large, as large a Mercedes as Doug had ever seen. The kind of Mercedes he imagined would have been used by Hermann Goering.

7

SUSAN AND BROEDEN APPEARED SO FREQUENTLY IN *Women's Wear Daily*, Doug wondered if their marriage was being represented by a press agent. Jeannie mailed him clippings, Susan Brook creating a Mexico Week for Saks, Broedenco commissioning designers to create a highfashion look in denim, Jerry Broeden and Susan Brook at the opening of Sparta, the new hit nightclub in SoHo.

"Maybe I shouldn't be letting you know about these things," Jeannie said to him.

"No, I'd like to read about these whiz kids. I'm not sure why, exactly."

He changed his mind when Jeannie sent him yet another clipping, Susan gorgeous in a sumptuous gown with Broeden in a tuxedo at a fashion-industry fete, and he decided he knew enough about their stardom. Susan continued to use the name Brook in business but was now Mrs. Broeden in her personal life. Doug phoned the apartment for the children and a Spanish-accented female voice said, "Mrs. Broeden out. Children back soon."

This was Carmen, the Broedens' live-in housekeeper from Venezuela. Andy said he spoke Spanish to her and this was going to help him with Spanish for school. Doug was preoccupied with the live-in aspect.

"How big an apartment is that?"

"Twelve rooms," Andy said.

Apparently even Harry had his own room, a separate laundry room in the apartment, and the dog slept there at night.

"He's so cute," Karen said. "He just gets up at some point at night and walks all the way to the other end of the house and goes to sleep." Doug attempted to visualize the size of an apartment where you would say, "All the way to the other end of the house."

"Flash Broeden" he was now referred to in the media. Susan and Broeden expanded from *Women's Wear* and now were mentioned in column items in the *New York Post* and the *Daily News*. Broeden opened several retail stores, calling them "Flash," stores projecting exactly that. Doug had to pass one every day on the way to the subway, Broeden's investment invading Doug's landscape. Flash on Broadway was on a site that had been a supermarket, the place now a tribal gathering place for young people, largely teenagers and slightly older, shopping for the brightly colored clothing, punk styles and costume jewelry that characterized the Flash look. People shopped as rows of television sets played rock videos, the sound augmented by disco-quality sound systems. A Flash opened on Forty-second Street, another in Greenwich Village, and Broeden was quoted as saying he planned to take the concept nationwide.

WHEN DOUG WAS FIRST PRESCRIBED GLASSES HE COULD still read a newspaper in the morning without them, although holding the pages at a distance. Now he was be-

91

ginning to inch the newspaper away *with* his reading glasses. He was disinclined to see the charmless young Dr. Jeffrey Weiss for a follow-up examination and he asked John McCarthy for a recommendation, Weiss having been suggested by Bob Kleinman. McCarthy gave him the number of Dr. Max Rothstein, a man who immediately inspired confidence in Doug. He spoke with a slight European accent and was possibly 70 years old. Now this was a doctor. A bald little man in a lab coat, Dr. Rothstein moved around the office with rapid steps, making adjustments in the testing equipment. The consultation took place in a brightly lit room, Doug's confidence beginning to ebb when he saw Dr. Rothstein squinting over his notes.

"So. You use your eyes much?" he asked Doug.

"Yes."

"Your eyes are slightly weaker. You need a more emphatic prescription."

"It's only been a few months."

"This is normal. And it must be said, once you wear glasses, the condition is irreversible."

"Oh."

"You don't expect your eyes to get stronger. When you reach our age—"

Our age? You see us as the same age? I've come for an eye examination to Mr. Magoo!

Doug took the prescription, had the lenses changed, and despite his waning confidence in the squinting Dr. Rothstein, who called him "Mr. Garner" as Doug was leaving, he noted the improvement when he now read. But "irreversible." That's not a word you want to hear at this point in your life. What else is "irreversible"?

KAREN AND ANDY ARRIVED AT DOUG'S ON A SUNDAY night with fresh luggage tags on their suitcases.

"You were in Montreal?"

"Jerry and Mom wanted to go for the weekend," Karen said.

"Was this for business?"

"No," Andy said. "For a restaurant. They wanted to try it."

"You flew to Montreal to try a restaurant?"

On their next school vacation, they were going to Antigua the first week; Doug had to work during the second.

"We'll have sort of a vacation in New York," he said. "Go to the theater, restaurants, movies, a ball game."

They went on to have a pleasant week in the city as sightseers, but there was the oddity of their appearance. He was pale and they had three-thousand-dollar suntans.

A "GREEN DAY" WAS ANNOUNCED IN THE NEWSPAPERS, a march and speeches in Central Park to protest nuclear proliferation. He asked the children to go with him. They were already planning to march with school friends but invited him to join the group. He tagged along behind a dozen teenagers with three other parents. At the end of the speeches people in the crowd joined hands to sing "Give Peace a Chance." He maneuvered to get next to Karen and Andy and take their hands, feeling possessive about their idealism, which began before Broeden. This is a new way of measuring time: "Before Broeden."

After the demonstration he brought them to the Blarney for hamburgers. A college football game was playing on a large-screen television facing the bar.

"We just got one of those," Karen said, referring to the set. "A Mitsubishi. It's fantastic for sports events."

"I'm sure it is."

"Jerry says if you're going to watch sports, you might

as well see it big as life," Karen continued. "And it really is great. You should get one, Dad."

Jerry says?

"It's kind of grainy" Andy added. "It might be too big for some programs."

"Where in the apartment is it?" Doug asked, thinking of the sheer size of those units.

"The entertainment room," Karen said.

The entertainment room. Of course. If Harry has his own room, why shouldn't the Mitsubishi?

"What else is happening these days?"

"Mom and Jerry have been going out to the Hamptons," Karen said. "They're looking at land."

"Not to farm," Andy commented.

"I imagine not."

"I hear it's pretty bleak in the off season," Andy offered.

"I'm sure it's lovely."

A few weeks later the Broedens decided to buy an existing house in Westhampton on the ocean with a pool situated in the deck.

Isn't this something? My children are richer than I am.

BROEDEN'S NAME CONTINUALLY ENTERED KAREN'S conversations, general information she learned from him such as how the light in the Hamptons was different from other areas in the North because of the particular relationship of the land to the surrounding water. "Boron" got to Doug. He wasn't sure he would have dealt with graphite or wood-Plexiglas any better. The children arrived on a Sunday night and Karen had a $250 Boron Prince tennis racket with her. Broeden bought one for each child. Karen was taking tennis lessons every Wednesday night at an indoor court where Broeden had a regular game with friends, and he arranged for the pro to give a group lesson to Susan, Karen, and Andy, as well, if he chose to go.

"I know it's our time with you," Karen said. "But would you mind Wednesdays when we're with you if I go to the lesson? You really have to keep up the rhythm."

"It *is* your time with me, Karen. He has half of the year to turn you into Martina."

"But if you don't play regularly Jerry says each week you miss you only get back to where you were when you stopped."

"Andy, are you playing?"

"He got me a racket. I take the lessons now and then. I'd have to say I'm not going anywhere in the sports world with my tennis game."

"Please, Dad. I love it so much. And if I stay with it, I can teach you."

"All right. Keep your Wednesdays. But you come back here."

"Thank you." And she gave him a big kiss on the cheek.

Broeden had managed to buy into Doug's time with Karen, and he was succeeding in including the children in his interest, Karen, anyway, going over to the game of the new man. This is like Sal Maglie jumping to the Mexican League. And he gets to see them now in the times before bed, Karen in a nightgown, Andy in his pajamas. Does he kiss them? Do they kiss him? He saw them kissing him, laughing with him. Where is it you're told how to handle this? Is there a Dr. Spock for this, when your wife marries a man and he's where you once were, and your daughter can't give up her precious Wednesday nights with him because she's playing tennis with her 250-goddamn-dollar racket?

* * *

95

ANDY, A HIGH SCHOOL SENIOR, WAS MAKING HIS APPLIcations to colleges. The infant with soft brown eyes who sat immobilized by his snowsuit, strapped into his stroller as they went to see Patty Cake, the baby chimpanzee in the zoo, had more phone calls coming into the house than Doug, and from girls who had evidently replaced Lesa, calling to ask, "Is Andy there?" Andy was circumspect about these activities. Doug insisted he tell him where he was going and when he would be coming home. Andy's late nights were restricted to weekends, and Doug tried to stay awake for the click of the door without drifting off and was not always successful. When they were with him, Karen and Andy often watched *Saturday Night Live* after he had fallen asleep. Once Doug had sat in living rooms necking with girls while their parents were supposed to be sleeping. He wondered then if the adults were lying awake inside, listening for the unclipping of their daughter's bra, ready to come storming in on him. He had the answer. Those parents, those old farts, were the same age as he was now, and they were sleeping.

"MR. GARDNER, MR. REYNOLDS WOULD LIKE TO SEE you in his office for a meeting at one tomorrow," Reynolds's secretary said cheerfully, as if Reynolds wasn't suggesting he drop everything and get on a plane.

"Doug, boy, our shining light. Look at this." And he showed Doug a glossy four-page folder with Doug's picture, the copy extolling his virtues with excerpts from his columns, the folder ending with "Doug Gardner, one of the people who brightens *Sports Day*, the fastest-growing special-interest newspaper in America. Reserve your advertising now or you'll get caught off base."

"I suppose it's flattering to be promoted like that."

"You sell papers, Doug. You also sell advertising. So it makes me uncomfortable to have such a key guy in our starting lineup dragging his feet so much. Let's talk personal fitness.''

''I did a jogging column.''

''A while ago. And an antijogging column is not a jogging column. Let me give you the reason I'm so eager about this. We've got a new survey that shows we're not doing as well as I'd like with women readers.''

''Isn't a sports newspaper going to have, primarily, a male audience?''

''True. But some women enjoy sports and we should have more of them reading us. The way to hook them in is with articles they're interested in, like personal fitness.''

''What does that mean, Robby, diets?''

''It means *you*. I want to run you on the subject, with the authority of your position.''

''Then as an authority I say we should stay a true sports paper.''

''I'll put it to you bluntly, Doug. You're being disloyal.''

''I'm trying to be honest.''

''Look, give me another piece on personal fitness and I'll give you a five percent pay hike. You can think of it as a point in money for every point out of your column.''

''That's insidious, Robby. What if I say no?''

''Why would you say no? Who says no to a raise?''

''Obviously it wouldn't be the raise I'd be saying no to.''

''Lyndon Baines Johnson, when he was President of the United States, said, 'I don't trust a man until I've got his pecker in my pocket.' Extraordinary, such rough language from a President. But I can understand it. You're running a big operation, you don't want people who are against you. You want people to be loyal and you don't get that loyalty unless you have the pecker.''

''I don't agree with that kind of thinking, Robby.''

"I don't care if you agree or not. Your vote doesn't count here. I've got the oilfields and the buildings *and* the paper you work for. So come up with something on personal fitness that you can live with and I can merchandise, and you can grumble all the way to the bank."

"Robby, how crude are we going to get on this? My pecker is not for sale."

"Give me the column, Doug. I need it to promote women readers. So figure out a way to keep us both happy and cut the New York shit!"

With John McCarthy confirming that it wasn't better anywhere else, with Andy going to college soon and a higher tuition to pay, he didn't see any alternatives. Resign and be scraping around for money while Broeden captivated his children with Borons and Mitsubishis? He was not in a position for gestures. He could solve this, however, if he could come up with the right piece.

"Okay. Would this satisfy you? Jane Fonda. Who's more personal fitness than Jane Fonda? I'll get a Jane Fonda workout video, I'll work out with it and write a column about it."

"Great! Entertaining. Promotable. And it doesn't cost you your integrity."

Reynolds rose with a broad grin and put his arm around Doug, leading him to the door, concluding in a few minutes this meeting for which he had Doug come from New York to Houston.

"Easy money," Reynolds said.

Doug ran the video on his television set. Jane Fonda worked him out into exhaustion. He wrote for his column that in the beginning, while doing the exercises, much of what transpired with Jane was in the area of sexual fantasy, but after a while he realized not only was he not in good enough shape for a woman like that, he didn't want to be in shape for a woman so driven for bodily perfection, and he watched the end of the tape eating a half pint of butter pecan ice cream.

DOUG AND HIS PARENTS WERE AT THE APARTMENT OF Doug's brother and sister-in-law for dinner. The Jane Fonda column had appeared that day and Doug's brother complimented him on the piece.

"My contribution to personal fitness," Doug said. "Hopefully, my last."

"What do you mean?"

"Our publisher. He has the editorial judgment of a television programmer."

"Who?" Frank Gardner said, coming into the kitchen where they were talking.

"It's nothing. Just work problems," Doug said.

"You should leave work at work is my advice," Frank said.

"Good advice," Doug replied. "I wonder if Robby Reynolds does that. I wonder how *he* sleeps."

"You get along with this man?" Frank asked.

"We engage in a dialogue."

"You could lose your job?"

"I think I'd have to push it before I'd actually *lose* my job."

"You're getting fired?" his mother said, joining the conversation by way of her own anxiety.

"No, as a matter of fact I just got a little raise. He hands out raises like gold stars. Nicely done, see the cashier."

Frank was looking into the rear courtyard from the kitchen window, a faraway expression on his face.

"You stand up for yourself," Frank said, and he turned and clutched Doug's shirtsleeve.

"I will, Dad."

"They think they can buy and sell you, those people. But they have no right!"

His father became aware of the grip he had on his son's shirt and, embarrassed, patted Doug's arm.

They. Doug's experience with Reynolds apparently summoned for Frank a lifetime of injustices *they* had committed.

DOUG WAS RESEARCHING A COLUMN ON WOMEN'S TENNIS and set up an interview in the *Sports Day* conference room with two promising teenage players on the women's circuit. The arrangements were made with their lawyer-business adviser, who was with them for the interview, a woman in her 30s, Nancy Bauer. The tennis players were from California, both blondes, one tall and thin, the other short and stocky. A doubles team, they were aggressive on the court and in the interview. They talked fast, finishing each other's sentences, two ambitious whirlwinds. The lawyer sat quietly, composed, a slight smile on her face. The only time she contributed was when the girls were rattling on about cheating by players in junior tournaments and she steered them away from this, saying, "That's a side issue. We don't want to go on record about other people's cheating." She had such composure and presence, Doug was drawn to looking at her during the interview. She was a willowy brunette with long hair that fell loosely around her shoulders, hazel eyes, high cheekbones and a large, full nose. Doug thought that with a slight variation of her nose she would have been very pretty. In his perception the nose tipped the balance and she was "attractive," but considering that he kept looking at her, he amended that to "very attractive" by the conclusion of the interview.

He asked if they could have "a drink" that night. She agreed, they met at the Algonquin, the time passed effortlessly, and Nancy said she had to leave. She only had time for "a drink" and that was all he had offered. A few days later he noticed *The 400 Blows* was playing at the Bleecker Street Cinema; he hadn't seen it in years. He called and invited her to see it with him, and when she said yes he made sure to mention they would go somewhere afterward, lest she say they only agreed to "the movie." At John's Pizzeria on Bleecker Street they discussed Truffaut's body of work.

"We sound like two film students," she said. "Not that movie talk doesn't have its place. But I've been with you for three hours and I don't know anything about you."

"Have I been boring?"

"Remote. And yes, boring."

A woman who is not hysterical about connecting? Who won't sit still for me when I'm boring?

"How boring have I been?"

"On a scale of ten, if ten is comatose—seven."

"That's very boring."

"Yes."

"Someone who tells me I'm boring when I'm boring! This is like the scene from *Spellbound*! Aha, that's the secret moment that unlocks everything! I love you. I know that's not serious, but in the context of not being serious, I love you."

She had a hearty laugh and he laughed along in the contagion of it, wondering, hearing his little laugh, if this was another function of age and his laugh was becoming constrained, that the laugh of him was receding along with his hair.

The conversation became more personal, she told him that after Barnard and Columbia Law she worked for a Washington law firm doing labor-relations work and was now with a large New York firm.

"I'm thirty-five. I probably shouldn't have said that, but it's on my mind."

"I'm forty-eight. I never said that to a woman before. Of course, I've never been forty-eight before."

"What else? I've never been married. I was engaged twice, once in college, once in law school. Both would have been disastrous marriages of people too young. But when you're young you can get your first marriages out of the way much easier. You get older and your standards go up and your possibilities go down."

"I'm afraid I know what you mean."

"I work a lot. Carter, Lynde has about two hundred lawyers. The firm does a pretty fair job on pro bono work, and in the good deed area I do a little more than I should on my own. But I started out more idealistically than I'm becoming, so it helps me to convince myself I'm still slightly pure anyway."

She lived on West Eleventh Street in Greenwich Village in a three-room walk-up. In the bedroom was a home-office area, an antique rolltop desk with a computer on a stand nearby. The small living room had a fireplace, a reading chair next to a green-shade floor lamp, books in floor-to-ceiling bookcases, the room having the overall feeling of a den. Nancy served tea, and when she stood he rose and took her in his arms and kissed her. He slid his hands along her hips, drawing her close to him, and she pulled away.

"I can't."

"Why?"

"I want it to mean something, at least a little."

"It will mean a great deal to me," he said with mock seriousness.

"No, it won't. Not after one evening together."

"This is the second."

"That one drink doesn't count."

"Maybe it wouldn't have if we had the drink standing. We had it sitting."

"You sound like a lawyer. Another time, Doug, please. I don't want to rush this, because in the context of not being serious, I love you, too."

The next time he saw her, Nancy served wine, cheese, and crackers, fresh flowers were in a vase on a coffee table. He was chastened by seeing the flowers. Going out with women had become such a businesslike procedure for him he had begun to forego softening acts, such as bringing flowers himself. The care she had taken, the chilled wine, the cheese, the flowers made him want to go back outside, buy a rose, a Whitman's Sampler. Does anybody give Whitman's Samplers anymore?

They decided to go out for a hamburger and he suggested the Blarney. "It really is just a joint."

"I've been to Lutèce."

They sat in Doug's booth and talked for a couple of hours.

"We have to check periodically for boring," he said.

"I think we're doing fine."

"Listen, would you like to be my girl? I've been looking for a girl. Old-fashioned type of girl, the kind you used to have. Do you know that kind of relationship?"

"I think so. Does that mean we try to be friends? I wouldn't mind that."

He stopped the cab a few times on the way to her apartment to run into late-night drugstores, finally locating Whitman's Samplers.

"This may be two years old, but it's the thought behind it."

At her apartment they sipped wine, then he led her into the bedroom. She kissed his eyes when they were making love. He couldn't remember in his recent experience a gesture of such tenderness. What he had been involved in, evidently, with "recreational sex" was an extended series of athletic performances.

"There you are," she said after they had lain quietly. "This is me. I wish I had bigger breasts and a smaller nose."

"Please—"

"The breasts I would never do anything about, although some women have. The nose was fixable. I was in high school and one year all the girls were spending their summer vacations getting nose jobs, the same precious little nose. I was too serious for that, or I thought I was too homely, and wouldn't it have been doubly terrible if I had the nose done and it still didn't help? So I never went for the nose. I used to say to myself it would mar my personal honesty. I'm not so sure if I wouldn't have been better off with less honesty and less nose."

He placed his hand gently on her face.

"I hope my nose and my breasts are out of the way, as it were. It stands as a definition of a friend, if I could say that to you."

"You've opened it up. We've got my bulging middle, my thinning hair, how well hung I am—shall I go on?"

"I say you're perfect."

"And I say you are, too."

ON A RAINY SUNDAY NIGHT DOUG WAS AT HOME BY HIM-self. Nancy was in Washington on business and this was the children's time with the Broedens. He was reading while listening to a sports call-in program on the radio. He liked to listen to those shows occasionally. This kept him in touch with public taste, and he also enjoyed matching himself against the fans, people who called in and tried to stump listeners and the host with such as

Dominic DiMaggio's lifetime batting average, and what was the name of the third ballplaying DiMaggio. Like Name the Fourth Marx Brother. Doug didn't know what Dom hit, the other DiMaggio was Vince, also he knew Zeppo Marx. One would have to search for Dom DiMaggio's batting average, which was not readily available in sports digests and world almanacs. Why did this person care? What was the passion for statistics in sports? He thought that it could be a search for order. In a chaotic universe, if you could quantify circumstances, you were not hurtling meaninglessly through the void. It was worth a column perhaps.

Andy called with concern in his voice.

"Dad, Karen's got a temperature. A hundred and three. Carmen's out on Long Island and Mom and Jerry are stuck in Boston."

"I'll be right over."

He couldn't get a cab in the rain and he ran to the building on Central Park West and Sixty-sixth Street. Andy brought him into Karen's bedroom, the dog following Doug as if he were trying to figure out, What are *you* doing *here?* Doug kissed Karen on the forehead, feeling for her temperature with his lips.

"Not so good, huh, angel?"

"I feel very achy."

"It's okay. Anything else, any other symptoms?" he said, looking for rashes, pressing her glands.

"No."

"Don't worry. The doctor is in."

Susan phoned and he spoke to her on a cordless phone.

"Seems to be just a fever. Probably the flu," he said to Susan. "Has she taken anything yet?" he asked Andy.

"Not yet."

"I'm going to give her some Tylenol. Do you have any?"

"Yes," Susan said. "Doug, the storm's going to have us here all night. We can't get out."

"I'll give her a little ginger ale to sip. And I'll stay here tonight."

"I'll call back in an hour or so."

He took Karen's temperature, a shade over 103.

"I've seen hundred and threes before. Don't worry," he said to Karen.

"You can go back home, Dad. We just didn't know whether to call you," she said.

"You did the right thing. I'll be here tonight."

He administered the Tylenol, gave her ginger ale, and sat with her and read to her from *The Once and Future King*, which was on her bedstand, staying with her until she had nearly fallen asleep. She was no warmer to his lips.

"You're going to be fine. Sleep, angel. I'll be right here."

Susan called again and he assured her that Karen was not in danger and was resting. She asked how he would sleep suggesting he use the guest room where they had a convertible couch with clean linen. A guest room in a city apartment?

"Can I serve you something, a drink or something?" Andy asked in the awkwardness of the situation. He was the host and his father really didn't belong there.

"I'll take something if I wish. Thanks."

Harry came by, squeezing between Doug's legs.

"We've overloaded his circuits tonight," Doug said.

Andy said goodnight to his father, Doug kissed him on the top of his head, and Andy withdrew to his room. Doug did not follow him in. Somehow, being with them on a night when he was not supposed to be underscored his nonexclusivity. There were men who got to be with their children every night.

106

He sat on the floor in the hallway outside their rooms and waited for Karen to fall asleep. He checked her, she seemed slightly cooler to him, and sleeping soundly now. Harry was following him, his part-time dog.

"You've got it good here, boy," he said. "There's no way I could get you an apartment like this."

He hadn't taken notice of the apartment when he first entered. He walked through the rooms as a tourist. The living room was probably twenty-five by fifty, nearly as large as his apartment. Adjacent was a separate dining room. The children's rooms, the maid's room, Harry's room, and the kitchen were on one side of the living room-dining area. The den, guest room, entertainment room, two offices, one for Broeden, one for Susan, and the master bedroom were in the other wing. Because of Broeden's "Flash" he imagined the decor would have been gaudier than it was. The furniture was modern without ostentation, the colors muted, and he saw Susan's eye in this. There was custom cabinetry in most of the rooms. At New York City prices the work must have cost as much as some people's homes. And he noted the gadgets, the cordless phone, the large-screen television, the housewide stereo system. The maid had a nineteen-inch television set. Only the dog was without television, and Doug surmised if Harry knew how to ask for it, he could have had one, too.

In Broeden's office over his desk was an exquisite watercolor that Doug recognized as Karen's work, a landscape of a marsh, one of the best paintings she had ever done. Doug was distressed. This painting was in Broeden's office and Doug had never even gotten to look at it. On the wall of the den he came upon a montage of framed photographs, Broeden, Susan, Karen, and Andy together on weekends, on vacations, smiling, mugging for the camera, an intense, ongoing life involving his children, and another man was in his place. The sight filled him with such extreme sadness, he was suddenly nauseous. This is not something I should have seen. Find the missing face in these pictures.

8

M EETING THE CHILDREN WAS DUE, SINCE DOUG
had been seeing Nancy for weeks. He decided
it should be conducted over ever-reliable Chinese food.
They went to Chinatown and he sat nervously while
Nancy and the youngsters ran the dinner. Nancy, nervous
herself, asked questions, trying to get to know them
quickly, as if this might be the one chance she was going
to get, and these old pros slowed the pace, asking questions about her. At one point, Andy, noting his father's
tenseness, said, "It's all right, Dad. We're relating."

Also due was the answer to How did I get to be here—
single? They were at Doug's apartment, lying quietly in
the dark, and Nancy introduced the subject.

"I was in Washington. My first job. He was a partner
in the firm with the house in Georgetown I never got to
see, the hostess wife, the two children I never met. It
lasted for three years and I was very much in love with
him, and one day, it was always one day, he was going
to leave his wife. I saw a little humor book once and it
said, 'Waiting for him to leave his wife is the same as

waiting for Godot.' I finally got out of Washington and came to New York and eventually I fell in love again. I was thirty-one. He was forty-four and had never been married. A sculptor, he had a teaching position at Princeton. Commissions, shows, fairly heady stuff. He had a gorgeous loft in SoHo, everything in it he constructed himself, a man of skills, an intellect and flawless, if I had been about nineteen. We made wedding plans now and then, which were like some prospective project he'd get to one day. Three years into the relationship, I was a year into therapy and still waiting for Godot. When I finally came to see he was never going to get married, or at least not to me, we were losing it, and in my fervent way I had invested several years in relationships that ended with warm wishes for my best well-being in the future, with whoever was next. Therapy's given me some sense of my own passivity in the relationships, having been so 'butch,' if you will, professionally that I wanted to just collapse traditionally into the man's arms, to give you the shorthand on it. But I'd fallen in love a couple of times to people who didn't marry me, and not getting married is all right in this day and age, except the relationships didn't last. And now I'm thirty-five.''

"I'm jealous of them both.''

"I should be jealous. You were married.''

"We lived through the height of the anger in the women's movement, and we were casualties, which is also shorthand. I didn't do enough to keep us together. I've thought that with an entirely different set of outside circumstances the marriage might have lasted, but that's probably not true. Because Susan ultimately married a much more high-powered and financially successful man than I was or will ever be.''

"We don't know—

"We know. I'm not thirty-five and we know. As far as

110

the time since the divorce I've been in a few ball games. Not many went into the late innings.''

"What inning would you say we're in?''

"I'm not sure, but I know we're past the first.''

TONY ROSSELLI SURFACED SPEAKING ON THE PHONE IN an excited voice. "Doug, you've got to meet me at the bowling alley at Forty-first and Eighth some morning this week. When can you do it, tomorrow, the next day?''

"Let me guess. The world's tallest midget championship bowler.''

"This is big, Doug. Colossal.''

"I'll meet you before I go to work, eight A.M. Thursday.''

"This is so big I can barely speak.''

Doug entered the bowling alley. Rosselli was wearing a shiny green suit, pacing. On the floor in front of him were two shoe boxes with holes punched in them.

"In the history of sports,'' Rosselli said, making his presentation, "there have only been a couple of kinds of racing for betting. Horse racing. Dog racing. Both of them require big outdoor settings, big investments of capital. I introduce you to a new concept. You ready?''

"I'm breathless.''

Rosselli removed the cover of each box, reached down and produced the participants.

"Turtle racing!''

He walked to the top of an alley and placed two turtles on the surface. They did not move, their heads and extremities pulled within their shells.

"You have to give them a minute to adjust,'' Rosselli explained, setting food out in front of them.

"Obviously stage fright.''

"Picture this. The turtle-racing track is set up in the casinos of hotels where there's gambling. Or in a ballroom, say. You line up eight turtles. They race for the food."

"Race? Do we have the same definition of the word?"

"The beauty part is the race isn't over in a minute. It can take maybe five minutes, even ten agonizing minutes."

"I can see where it might be agonizing."

A turtle's head slowly appeared.

"After I get it established, I'd set up turtle tracks all over. People will get to know their favorites. It can go nationwide, international."

"You're thinking of TV, I suppose. A tie-in with *Wild Kingdom*?"

"TV. Offtrack betting."

A turtle began to crawl a couple of inches to the left.

"I don't understand it. They were going fast in my apartment."

"Maybe they're not ready to turn pro."

Another period of waiting passed. The second turtle's head appeared, the turtle did not move.

"Tony, you might be able to tie in with funeral parlors because at this pace people will be expiring."

Rosselli looked at his turtles dejectedly. Doug patted him on the back.

"I thought I had it," Rosselli said.

"Some day you're going to come up with something, Tony."

Doug headed for the exit and Rosselli, for Doug's benefit and his own, yelled, "You blew it, you dumbells! You coulda been stars!"

A WEEKEND APPROACHED WHEN THE CHILDREN WERE scheduled to be with Doug. On the phone Andy told him he was going to a late movie Friday with a friend and would be sleeping there. Karen said she didn't know if she would be around at all for the weekend.

"Where do you plan to be, honey? It's your time with me."

"Jerry has to be in Quebec on business and he said he'd take me."

"Why doesn't he arrange it for when it's their custodial time?"

"He's opening a Flash store there and it's this weekend. Quebec, Dad. I hear it's really unique."

"So—"

"Well, if I come to you, I'd miss it. We can make up the time. It's not a big deal."

"Jerry seems to be making it a big deal or you wouldn't be so eager to go."

"There's going to be a big party and I'd get to see the city. Please!"

"I'll see you Sunday night."

"Thanks, Dad. Love you."

That he went out the very next day to buy the Mitsubishi forty-five-inch projection screen was transparent, his attempt to compete with Flash, but he did it anyway. He needed the handyman to help him find a place for it in the apartment. The set would have overwhelmed the living room and seemed more appropriate in the bedroom, if a forty-five-inch screen could be appropriate in an apartment this size. When Andy entered the apartment he was amused to see it looming in the bedroom.

"So you got one, huh, Dad? Well, it's large."

"It *is* good for sports," Doug said, trying to be low-keyed. "Daddy, terrific!" Karen said when she arrived on Sunday night.

"Yes, we have Mitsubishis here, too," he said.

It may not have been textbook fatherhood, but he asked only a question or two about Quebec and then cut off the

113

discussion, since Quebec apparently was "absolutely wonderful."

ANDY WAS ACCEPTED BY THE UNIVERSITY OF PENNSYLvania and Wesleyan University. He chose Wesleyan. Broeden happened to be a graduate of the Wharton School at the University of Pennsylvania. Doug had tried to be neutral, "in the best interests of the child," but he was overjoyed at Andy's choice of Wesleyan over Penn. He didn't want his son going to Broeden's alma mater.

WHEN THE CHILDREN WERE WITH HIM, DOUG NEVER had a woman sleep in the apartment, thinking it prudent to keep his sexual activities private. Neither Doug nor Nancy was comfortable with the idea of adolescents on the premises, even sleeping ones, while they were in the bedroom together, so she did not stay over during his custodial periods. In all other respects the growing relationship was undisguised. Nancy and Doug cooked meals for the children, they all went to a Knicks game together, and to dinners in neighborhood restaurants. Doug spent a Saturday interviewing high school coaches for a column and returned to the apartment expecting to find the children there. At about 6 P.M. they came into the house with Nancy. They had gone to the Museum of Modern Art and a movie, an arrangement he hadn't known anything about. Nancy had called in the morning, she spoke with Andy, asked what they were doing, and invited them to spend the afternoon with her. The three of them were glowing when they came into the house, pleased with themselves for doing this. On another Saturday, when Doug had to work, Nancy asked the children to join her for a revival of *You Can't Take It With You*. Doug sensed the ease with which the children were dealing with Nancy, their acceptance of her was a way of telling him "This is a good person for you. Don't lose her."

One of Nancy's clients was playing in a tennis tournament in New Orleans and Nancy asked if Doug would like to spend the weekend there. They flew to New Orleans on a Friday evening and went to the match the next day. The girl lost, but that she played at all was significant. She had injured her knee in a fall during a match the previous year, her career as well as her ability to walk properly had been in question. Nancy was of the opinion athletes were entitled to earn whatever money they could, their careers were so unstable, and Doug generally agreed with this, having written several columns on the subject. They talked about it at dinner and he said, "You're like a boyhood fantasy come true. A girl who'll sleep with you and appreciates sports."

"A boyhood fantasy. I'm sorry I'm coming into the picture so late."

"It's never too late for that fantasy."

They stayed at a hotel in the French Quarter and immersed themselves in New Orleans food, Dixieland jazz, sex. On Sunday they paused to listen to a last set of Dixieland in a bar before leaving for the airport.

"Wonderful food, sex, and a woman who understands your profession. Not a bad travel package," he joked.

"I think you're supposed to say 'wonderful' about the woman."

"Thank you for the weekend." And then, preoccupied, he became absorbed with the music. "You know," he said after a while, "I haven't listened to live Dixieland since I was a kid. We'd go to Central Plaza, a huge place, and you'd drink beer like a Big Guy. And later you'd try for heavy sex with your date who was supposed to appreciate what a Big Guy you were for drinking the beer and taking her there. I rubbed up against so many girls in apartment-house hallways after Dixieland jazz. None of it lasted. Where are those girls now?'' He kissed the tips of her fingers. "This was a lovely gift, Nancy."

"A hot time in New Orleans?"

"The chance to do a rewrite."

ANDY INVITED NANCY TO HIS HIGH SCHOOL GRADUATION, which was to be held at the Beacon Theater.

"It's very kind of him," she said to Doug. "But I don't know if it's my place."

"He invited you. It's his graduation."

"Who else will be going?"

"My parents. My brother and sister-in-law. Karen, Susan, her husband, her parents."

"Ouch."

"I'm an outsider myself with some of those people."

Before the doors opened for the ceremony, Andy's guests waited on the sidewalk, divided by divorce. Nancy was coming from a breakfast meeting downtown.

"So who is this person you're bringing?" Doug's mother asked.

"She's the mystery guest. A lawyer I've been seeing. Nancy Bauer."

"This is serious?"

"Leave him alone, Mom," Marty said.

"Leave him alone? He *is* alone."

"We saw a program on TV," Frank said. "About single parents."

"The man," Norma explained, "if he doesn't have a wife, he can develop his *feminine* side."

"These are very saucy programs you're watching," Doug said.

"That one," Norma said, referring to Susan, "she got married. She didn't wait around."

Nancy arrived and was introduced to both families,

116

Doug's parents' faces tense—is she the one who'll save our unfortunate son from his feminine side?

Doug whispered to Nancy, "This is much too modern for me, you and Susan at the same time."

"Think of us as just a couple of ladies you've slept with."

Susan's parents greeted Doug with warmth, the brooding disapproval of him had passed. He was old news. Doug had not seen his former in-laws in over three years, and in this period the Brooks had crossed a threshold into advancing age. Dr. Brook had been 67, he was now 70, and beginning to look less hearty. Susan's mother, despite the typical Brook finery, also looked considerably older to him.

The Bradley chorus sang a Bruce Springsteen medley. At Doug's high school graduation, in the fashion of the day, the chorus sang "You'll Never Walk Alone." June 1952. Over thirty years ago. Nearly as long as this woman I'm with has been alive. Give me strength. I could use a little "You'll Never Walk Alone" myself right now.

As part of the ceremony three seniors delivered speeches about their views of the future. One was Andy Gardner, who spoke on the environment, an idealistic speech, but with documentation as he named prominent corporations that had been found to be polluters. The main commencement speaker was a former Bradley student and currently a domestic aide in the Reagan administration who delivered an inspirational message about American life and the vigorous job market that awaited these young people one day. Doug thought he might have been back in the Eisenhower years.

After the ceremony, while they waited for Andy, Broeden worked the crowd, passing along congratulations, asking other parents, "Who is your graduate?" so he could tell them his was Andy, "one of the speakers." They went to Pasta!!! for lunch, and under arrangements made earlier in the week through Susan, Doug would share the expenses of the lunch with Broeden, Doug paying, Broeden sending him a check later on. As they were entering the restaurant Broeden said to Doug, "I'd like to pay for champagne for the lunch. It's been such a great event."

"Champagne is fine, but you don't get to pay for it."

"My pleasure. I want to do it."

"We're splitting this. You don't get to feel any more important than anybody else around here."

"All right. It was just a warmhearted offer. But let's get a good champagne, okay?"

"That was Flash Broeden," Doug said to Nancy.

"Yes, the flash is apparent."

The mood in the restaurant was festive, other graduates were present with their families, youngsters were busy table-hopping. Andy and Karen told stories about school, laughing. Doug joined in the high-spiritedness and then began to reflect on the tangled path leading to this particular grouping, to be celebrating his son's high school graduation with his ex-wife, her husband, his ex-in-laws, his current girlfriend, his brother and sister-in-law and his parents, who didn't talk to the other side. He looked at Susan and at Andy, remembering.

"I'M SO SCARED. WHAT IF THE BABY DIES? WHAT IF WE both die?"

"Nobody's dying. Just do the breathing. Come on, honey, a little while longer."

"If I die and the baby lives, you'll get married again soon, won't you, so the little baby will have a mother? Say you'll do that."

"Susan, shh. You're going to live. The baby's going to live. We're all in this for the long haul."

* * *

"IT'S AN ABSOLUTE, CLEAR-CUT DA-DA. HE'S BRILliant, Doug. Yes, that's your Da-Da. And I'm your Ma-Ma."

"WHO AM I NAMED AFTER?"

"Nobody in particular. We picked the name Andrew because we liked it. Right, Doug?"

"Right. It's a great name."

"I like my name."

"You got good gifts today. Five years old. What a big boy you are."

"OKAY, DAD, IS THIS YOUR CARD? THE FOUR OF CLUBS?"

"It is. How did you know that?"

"The Great Andy knows the secret. Should I do it again?"

"Show Mom. Susan, you have to see this!"

"WE LOVE YOU EQUALLY AND THAT'S WHY WE'RE DOING it this way. We love you too much for both of us not to stay in your lives."

"A BOY, DOUG. A SWEET LITTLE BOY. OUR BEAUTIFUL baby."

BROEDEN WAS GRANDLY ORDERING ANOTHER BOTTLE OF Dom Perignon for the table. Doug left to go to the men's room, not wanting the sonofabitch to see him with tears in his eyes.

* * *

"I WOULD NOT CALL THAT MY FAVORITE EXPERIENCE," Doug overheard Andy saying to Karen as they unpacked their belongings on a Sunday night.

"What?" Doug asked.

"We went to Westhampton by plane," Andy said. "With Jerry flying."

"Give that to me again slowly."

"He has a pilot's license and he used to fly," Karen said. "But he stopped for a while when he didn't have a plane. Now he has one. He keeps it in New Jersey."

"Harry came too. He didn't understand the lure of flying. He threw up."

"Harry threw up. And Mom was there?"

"She was a little nervous, too, at first," Karen said. "You get used to it and it's really fantastic. You see everybody stuck in traffic below."

"Yes, we ordinary mortals," Doug said.

This playboy is taking my kids up in a plane with him flying, and I used to worry when we went on the Staten Island ferry if there were enough life preservers!

Doug didn't want to call with the children nearby and he waited until the next day, phoning Susan at work from his office.

"I understand Jerry took my children to Westhampton and back in a light plane."

"He's an accomplished pilot."

"Is he? You married Smiling Jack, did you? This is dangerous business, Susan."

"Based on my stomach, I don't imagine we'll be traveling much that way."

"Not much. Not ever. I don't want them in any light planes with any weekend pilot."

"It's safer than we think."

"It may be safer than *you* think. Susan, what's going

120

on? Did you leave your intelligence in the glove compartment of the Mercedes when you married this guy?''

''We don't need that, Doug.''

''Don't do this again, please. Little planes crash all the time. Rich people die all the time in their darling little planes. Even if the children go up on your two weeks, I don't want to bury them on mine.''

A few days later, Karen called the Broeden apartment looking for a book she needed for school and Broeden said he would drop it off. Doug went down to wait for him.

''I want to talk to you.''

''Sure,'' Broeden said and came out of the car.

''I told Susan and I'm telling you. My kids are grounded.''

''Do you think I'd take chances with them?''

''I don't know what you'd do for your life-style.''

''You may not be able to understand this, but I don't take orders from you.''

''You do about the kids. If they ever set foot in a light plane with you flying—''

''What?''

''Don't try it.'' Doug took the schoolbook out of Broeden's hand and for emphasis he gave a little kick to the tire of Broeden's car.

''What the hell do you think you're doing? Don't you kick my car. I want an apology.''

''I'll dictate one in the office.''

Doug turned to leave and Broeden grabbed him by the shoulder.

''I mean it,'' Broeden said. He had not let go of Doug's shoulder. Doug pushed away Broeden's arm. Broeden shoved him. Doug shoved him back. They began shoving each other with increasing intensity. Broeden was slightly taller than Doug, younger, his movements swifter. Hockey players. That was the best comparison Doug had for this, the kind of dumb brawl hockey players had. Using a hockey move, Doug grabbed Broeden's jacket and pulled it over his head and shoved him again. Broeden got free of the jacket and tried to twist Doug's arm. In pulling away, Doug's feet became entangled with Broeden's and he fell, Broeden falling with him.

"Would you like your new wife to see you like this?" Doug asked as they were sprawled on the ground.

"You don't look so wonderful yourself," Broeden answered and they picked themselves up.

"It's a good thing we don't do this for a living," Doug said, walking back to the house.

Doug doubted the skirmish would qualify for "Greatest Fights of the Century." He returned to the apartment and the children, embarrassed. Like a bimbo, I've just been battling your mother's husband in the street. He tried to whistle his way through the rest of the evening, trying to ignore the pain in his left shoulder, his bad shoulder, from overextending his arm in the shoving, and the bruised hip from the fall to the pavement.

A middle-aged body did not like to be pummeled and flopped to the ground. It liked to keep steady hours without violent surprises. And it did not respond quickly to warm baths. Doug conceded he shouldn't have kicked the tire. But Broeden made the first physical intrusion. What kind of hothead was he? Doug toyed with a *Rocky* fantasy. He would get Moe Askin, a boxing trainer he knew, to give him instruction. He would work out, run up the steps of the Forty-second Street Library, punch pastramis, and if Broeden ever shoved him again, he would get decked by Kid Pastrami.

HE HEARD NOTHING ABOUT ANY FURTHER PLANE TRIPS. The children returned to camp for the summer, Andy working as a junior counselor. Doug and Nancy rented

122

a car for visiting day. Susan and Jerry were on the grounds when they arrived, Susan in a white dress, Broeden in a white suit, white shirt, white shoes and a Panama hat. Claudia Cardinale had been joined by Marcello Mastroianni. Doug and Nancy hugged the children. The two couples stiffly acknowledged each other. Andy was nearly Doug's height now, dark and good-looking. Several of the girl campers giggled their way past him. Karen was growing taller and more womanly. Did any of the boys here try to take her to the boathouse at night? the father speculated. They all visited Karen's bunk and went to the arts-and-crafts shed where she was working on an oil landscape of the campgrounds. While the others were content with general words of approval for a lovely painting, Marcello said, "Nice light. Good greens. Reminiscent of the Hudson Valley School." Andy brought them to his bunk where he worked with the youngest children in the camp, 8-year-olds. When the children saw Andy, three of them gathered around to meet his family. Doug noticed that when Andy talked to the children, he dropped to one knee to be on their level. He had done that with Andy, who was followed by these children as if he were the Pied Piper. You're going to be a good Daddy one day.

Karen took them to see a new ball machine installed on the tennis courts, and Broeden raced off to make a change, appearing for tennis with a T-shirt that said "Flash." He tested the ball machine and declared it "acceptable," and played with Karen for so long he was asked by other parents to leave the court so they could have some playing time with their children. "I want to see it all, do it all," Broeden said as they toured the grounds. He kept up his high energy throughout the day, and while they were watching Karen in a girls' volleyball game, Broeden cheering loudly, Nancy walked over to him. They exchanged a few words away from the others.

123

She came back toward Doug, a grim expression on her face.

"What just happened?"

"I thought I'd say something to him. I told him, 'Why don't you ease up a little?' He knew exactly what I meant, but he looked at me with a look I recognized very well from business, a look that says, 'We hire and fire lawyers around here,' and he said to me, 'I'm not paying for your advice.' "

Doug had eagerly looked forward to seeing the children, but he could not wait for this day to end.

49 YEARS OLD. HE HADN'T THOUGHT ABOUT HOW HE was going to deal with his birthday; the best idea he had was to ignore it. The children hadn't mentioned celebrating and this was all right with him, the only relevance he could find for 49 was that it was one year from 50. He came to Nancy's apartment. They were planning to go out for a casual dinner and he walked into a surprise party which she had organized. Karen and Andy were there, the Kleinmans, Jeannie, Marty and Ellen, Doug's parents. Nancy and the children had worked together on a gift for Doug; the children had secretly removed from a file box in Doug's apartment clippings of his pieces dating back to his earliest news stories. Nancy made copies and had the collection bound in a leather volume. If he had been asked, he would have declined a celebration. He was grateful to Nancy, though, for doing all that, for being more celebratory than he would have been. But 49? 49 going on 50.

"NATIONAL OUTLOOK. THOSE ARE THE KEY WORDS THIS month, Doug. When you sit there thinking about what you're going to write, ask yourself, am I being too provincial?''

"Probably. I'm Kid Pastrami.''

"How's that?''

"Robby, what's my quota this time?''

"Don't be so sensitive. No quota. Just think national outlook. Will it play to all our readers out there?''

"Doug?'' Bill Wall came on the line.

"Yes, Bill.''

"If you have any doubts about a column not being national enough, we've got a new way of pretesting your columns *before* they appear. We can't do this with all columns because of timing. But since you usually have a few in reserve, we can pretest some of them, then you can go back and actually tailor the pieces for maximum demographic impact.''

"A little from the sides, a little from the waist.''

"What?''

"Sorry, I was being too New York again.''

KAREN AND ANDY WERE AT THE BROEDENS, AND WHEN Doug called to speak to them, he learned from Andy that Karen was away for the day. She and Broeden had gone to Westhampton in his plane. In what was apparently a concession to Doug, Broeden had hired a professional pilot. Doug called back later. Karen was home, she was fine. But later on he imagined the children in the plane, and while Broeden was congratulating himself about being above the common citizenry, the plane would crash and they would die. Or Broeden would take them on a fancy vacation to the Caribbean, scuba diving, and the apparatus would fail, or skiing, and the chair lift would break. The worst images were those where Broeden lived and the children died, where they were in a situation they never would have been in but for Broeden, but for his money and life-style, and Susan's, Susan was part of it, although it was mainly Broeden and his wealth that led them to the death of rich children.

By morning he managed to purge himself of these thoughts, accepting that accidents could happen unconnected to money, they could happen any time, anywhere, they could happen when the children were not with Broeden, but with him. He wasn't sure of his own motives any longer. Was he looking to ground them out of concern for their safety or because of that excited look in Karen's eyes as she described flying above traffic, the obvious delight she was taking in the deliciousness of her new life with Smiling Jack? He called Teterboro Airport. He had to know how much the plane cost that Broeden owned. One hundred and fifty thousand dollars. I put up with Houston and surveys and little messages on the computer to make enough money to meet my expenses and stay competitive with His Flashness and I have as much chance of matching him as Rosselli's turtles have of getting on *Wide World of Sports*. I run out to get a bigscreen television, and he's got the television and the apartment and the car and the house and a goddamn *plane*.

9

THE MESSAGE ON DOUG'S SCREEN WAS, "GOOD. Let's have some more like this." He had written a column for "national outlook," the attention given to sports figures from important media cities at the expense of others less well placed.

"The diabolical part of his operation is that he can send the messages to you. You can't send a message to him," he told John McCarthy while they were having lunch together.

"I've got a suggestion. You grab a couple hundred a week extra money, Hopalong gets you down, you go out and buy some new clothes or whatever makes you happy. TV is the answer."

"TV?"

"Sports Cable Network. They need a guy for a Saturday show. I've got so much on my desk I can't think about it. You read some scores, do a little commentary. Piece of cake. I'll recommend you."

"Do I get to sing?"

"You really should think about it. Or you can tell Hopalong to shove it and write *The Donna Blayton Story*. Her life in swimming and drugs.''

"Esther Williams, where are you? I can't risk freelancing. I couldn't live with Flash Broeden picking up a share of my tab.''

DURING THE SUMMER NANCY HAD BEEN WORKING ON two pro bono projects in her office, helping an artists' cooperative buy a loft building and securing space for a child-care program on the Lower East Side. On a July Saturday, walking through a street fair on Third Avenue, he and Nancy passed a booth for Bronx Educational Services, which ran a literacy-training program for adults. Doug talked to their director, responded to what they were doing and as a means of raising funds and publicizing the group, arranged a media event for their next street-fair booth. He contacted the New York Yankees, and Dave Winfield, Ricky Henderson and Don Mattingly appeared at the booth, the press seizing upon this photo opportunity. On a variation of the idea, he secured a commitment from the Mets' pitching staff to pose for pictures in behalf of Literacy Volunteers. Doug may have thought of these ideas on his own, but he had Nancy as an example. His giving help to these organizations was a result, he believed, of having this person in his life.

The last two weeks in August they had rented a house together in the Berkshires for their vacations. They went to concerts at Tanglewood, ate at country inns. One morning they were walking along a road holding hands and Nancy rested her head on Doug's shoulder.

"Oh, that's it,'' he said. "Where has that been? I seem to have misplaced it.''

"What?''

"That feeling. To be with a woman and be happy.''

They were beginning to deal with parental restlessness. Nancy's parents wanted to meet Doug, and she suggested they all go to a ball game.

"My parents like baseball and it will put you in the most favorable light," she teased.

They went to Yankee Stadium for a Saturday-afternoon game. Nancy's father, Joe Bauer, was a trim man of five feet seven with graying hair and the prominent family nose. He was wearing a sports shirt, sports jacket, twill slacks and a vintage Yankee baseball hat. Her mother, Ruth, was a slender brunette, wearing sensible clothing, a cotton turtlcncck, slacks, a golf jacket and sturdy walking shoes. They had come to play. Both of them knew the game; Joe, in particular, was pleased about seats in the press section. He talked to Doug about his memories of ball games, the dynasties in Yankee Stadium, and games at the Polo Grounds, the Giants with Mel Ott and his kickout batting motion, slow-footed Ernie Lombardi hitting the left-field wall and only reaching first base. Following the game they went to Nancy's apartment for dinner. Nancy's parents were both high school history teachers in Rockville Center. They had gone to a ball game, and that was fun, and now it was the conversation segment. With Doug, a sportswriter, present, they had a topic for dinner and they pursued it—"Sports in America."

After they left, Doug said, "They're a very doughty pair. You get the feeling they should be from Scotland."

He stayed overnight at Nancy's apartment in the glow of his passing marks with the teachers. He was thinking of them as one of those sweet, energetic older couples who go to lecture series in New York. Then he did his arithmetic. Mel Ott. Ernie Lombardi. Those were not names out of a period of sports history Doug had read about. He saw those ballplayers, too. Joe Bauer had married Nancy's mother when he was 20. He's 58. I'm 49. I've got them as a sweet, older couple—and the man who

129

is the father of the woman I'm sleeping with is practically my contemporary!

BOB KLEINMAN CONCLUDED THE MILLION-DOLLAR DEAL he had been working on, a settlement between two large law firms. The weekend following the settlement he and Sarah went to East Hampton and bought a house with a swimming pool.

"If you don't make it by fifty, you haven't made it," he said to Doug at lunch. "I made it. Barely."

"We have to celebrate your birthday."

"I told Sarah and I'm telling you, no celebration. I don't have to commemorate the fact that I'm getting closer to the grave."

"Are you going to make it through this meal? Because if you're not, I'd like to settle the check now."

"Your fathers are fifty. You're not fifty," Bob said despondently.

"You look better than you did a year ago." Bob had been working out at a health club. "Maybe it's the exercise."

"I don't look better. Your eyes are failing you."

"They are failing me." Doug squinted at the menu in the Italian restaurant and took out his reading glasses. "I'll be needing large-print menus soon. And then large-print food."

"Maybe I'll pull a Jack Benny," Bob said. "I'll only admit to being thirty-nine. That's one way to handle fifty. With fancy bookkeeping."

SINCE DOUG WAS NOT GOING TO HAVE THE HOUSE WITH the pool by the time *he* was 50, he decided that the little extras looked attractive, the better stereo for jogging, the snappy Ralph Lauren loafers that Broeden wore, which

130

he could buy with the money John McCarthy said was available from the sportscasting job. He asked McCarthy to make a phone call in his behalf to Sports Cable Network, and Doug followed up with a call to Frank Cotton, the general manager. Cotton explained they were looking for a local correspondent for the regional portion of their Saturday-afternoon sports wrap-up show. The sportscaster would read ball scores, be involved with the editing of tape highlights of the day's events, and give a sixty-second commentary each week. Doug was asked to prepare a sample presentation, which would include a simulated reading of ball scores, a commentary, and an "expression" he could use for peak moments such as Mel Allen's "Going, going, gone!"

ON HIS WAY TO THE AUDITION HE THOUGHT OF *STARTIME* from the early days of television and the desperate looks on the faces of the *Startime* kids with their frozen smiles as they attempted to sing, tap, or accordion their way to stardom. He saw himself as a middle-aged edition of an ambitious tot vaudevillian. He smiled at the receptionist, physically sensing the lines of his false smile against the inside of his cheeks. And now here's *Startime*'s own Doug Gardner to sing "I Want to Be in Pictures."

Doug was led into the studio, where he was greeted by the producer-director, Seth Peters, a slim man wearing sweat clothes and sneakers who looked to Doug to be in his teens.

"Mr. Gardner, get yourself made up and we'll be ready for you right away. Did you bring your presentation and your expression?"

"This is it, starstruck."

"No, I mean—"

"I have it."

Doug entered the makeup room where a woman in her

50s with carrot-colored hair, wearing a caftan, necklaces, and bracelets nearly to the elbow, introduced herself in a low, husky voice as Vera.

"I'm going to make you look very beautiful," she said in a European accent.

"I thought I came in very beautiful."

"Just extra touch here and there. You are actor?"

"Sportswriter."

"I have made up writers. I worked NBC, ABC, CBS. I did everybody. Henry Kissinger. Neil Diamond. I make them all very beautiful. Who are you?"

"Doug Gardner."

"I never heard of you. You will be very beautiful, though."

As she worked with the makeup, taking more time than Doug would have liked, he said, "There is a philosophic question here. How much a journalist should allow himself to be made up?"

"Everybody gets made up. The Pope, I bet."

She was patting and tapping and he was becoming very uncomfortable.

"I think that's enough," he told her. "Very beautiful." "Not finished. I have to put more color here. Your complexion is too sallow. And the bags under your eyes, the camera, it finds you out. You sleep good at night?"

"Could we define our terms? What is good?"

"You sleep alone? I don't come on to you. I have lover. But you also look a little green."

"Green and sallow? Replaces 'Young and Foolish'?"

In the studio, Doug was seated at a desk on the set. Frank Cotton, a blond man in his 30s, five feet eleven, in a blue suit, introduced himself. Doug was fitted with a clip-on microphone by a production man.

"For my first number I'd like to sing 'Granada,' " he said to allay his nervousness.

"Let's begin, Mr. Gardner," Peters called out.

Doug did a sample commentary, artificial playing surfaces versus natural surfaces, his opinion that synthetics look better on color television but have shortened players' careers, and that in baseball it wasn't the same game any longer when ball clubs could build their teams specifically for a fast artificial surface. He made a last-minute substitution, deciding to drop the broad *Startime* smile, which wasn't playing well inside his head, for a more modest version, choosing to read the lines with what he hoped was appropriate energy, but with the decorum of a journalist.

"Very good, Mr. Gardner. Nice credibility," Peters said. "Okay, we'll do the simulated portion now. Just pretend you're reading over taped highlights and give us your expression."

"The fast-stepping Cardinals got six leg hits off Ron Darling today at Shea, but it wasn't enough. Darryl Strawberry was on the premises—and let's pick up the action in the bottom of the sixth. One man on, the pitch from Tudor, a long drive—pencil it in, pencil it in . . . write it in the record book! Two-one, Mets. Darling the win. Tudor the loss. Over at Yankee Stadium, virtually a one-play ball game and here's the play. Winfield up, bottom of the ninth, one-nothing, Twins. Two on, two out. A long drive to left, pencil it in, pencil it in . . . erase it! Caught at the wall. Blyleven the win. Righetti the loss. This is Doug Gardner for Sports Cable Network."

"Excellent," the general manager announced. " 'Pencil it in, pencil it in, write it in the record book!' And if the ball is caught, the pass is dropped, 'erase it!' "

"You've got a real good expression," Peters said.

"Writing, record books," the general manager continued. "It implies history being made," he said solemnly. "Very prestigious."

Doug was given a copy of the audition tape by the

engineer, and he and Nancy watched it that night on her video recorder.

"I'm fat. I've been found out. Green, sallow, fat, and nearly fifty."

"You look great."

"The camera doesn't lie. Cary Grant we don't have here. Howard Cosell we don't have here."

"You seem very relaxed. You absolutely look like all those people who do this kind of thing."

"This is so strange to watch yourself on TV. But terrific," he said, laughing.

Doug was hired by Sports Cable Network. He would be on the air every Saturday at 7 P.M. for five minutes, in the studio to review tape at 5 P.M., one hundred fifty dollars a week. He didn't consider this real journalism, and he kept a lighthearted approach to the enterprise. "Narcissism unbound," he said to Nancy. On the air he was casual, conversational. He had no illusions about or interest in anchoring Monday Night Football one day. The sixty-second commentary would give him a chance to talk about sports items that might be insufficient for a column. He was going to enjoy being on the air. And the children would get to see him on television—take that, Flash.

Of his first appearance Andy said, "You were really great, very professional." Karen was teenage-excited. "I couldn't believe it. My Dad! On television! Wait until I tell my friends."

Tell Broeden, too.

Karen missed his next week's show. In this time between the end of camp and the beginning of the new school year, while Andy was getting ready to leave for college, Karen slipped off with Broeden and Susan to "do a little London," she said, language she would never have used before Broeden.

* * *

"Hey, Doug, I hear you're doing some TV up there."

"A local segment. Yes, Robby."

"I don't know how I feel about that."

"You should appreciate the publicity. I'm introduced as 'Doug Gardner, columnist for *Sports Day.*'"

"Now let me understand this. You use *our* offices and your work time for me to build up your credentials, and while I am paying you more money than you can get anywhere else you sell your services to another company?"

"I'm on the air for five minutes, Robby. I do a sixty-second commentary."

"The lawyers are looking into this, Doug. We have an agreement for you to provide exclusive services to us."

"For print. My lawyer already looked into it."

"I don't know if I want you doing this."

"Why would you care if I'm on television for a few minutes in New York? Is this about power, too, Robby?"

"Of course it is. The issue is, who owns you? Do you own you or do I own you? Oh, go ahead. But you should have asked me first."

Doug arrived at Nancy's that night, still tense from Reynolds's phone call. She asked about his mood and he recounted the conversation with Reynolds.

"He certainly is controlling. On the other hand, you get a column that's read across the country."

"Are you trying to make nice?" he said, touching her hair affectionately.

"I'm trying to be realistic. I go through it every day. I'm constantly weighing A against B. How much am I giving up of myself to do the work I want?"

"He probably does think he owns me."

"He doesn't though. And if this goes beyond the limit of what you're willing to do, you can make a decision then."

"Obviously you don't think I'm at that point."

"I think you're getting more than you're giving up. You have a forum," she said.

"I also have someone who's smart and supportive."

"But what are you giving up for that, your freedom?"

"I've had the freedom. It's a little bit overrated."

DOUG RETURNED TO THE OFFICE ONE DAY AFTER HAVING lunch with Nancy and he passed Pat Lahey sitting in an undershirt, sweating, a bottle of Scotch in front of him on his desk. When Lahey saw Doug, he raised his glass and started to recite "Casey at the Bat."

"What's going on?" Doug asked.

"I did the first profile ever written in New York on Jackie Robinson. For the old *Trib*. I knew them all. Campanella. DiMaggio. He used to call me Paddy. 'How are you, Paddy?' Joe D. Joltin' Joe. The Yankee Clipper. What else, Doug? You remember what else they called him?"

"DiMadge."

"Right. DiMadge. There are people today, your readers, and the biggest thing they know about him is that he was in that Paul Simon song."

"What is it, Pat?"

"I was fired."

"Damn it!"

Doug was deeply upset about Pat, and about what Pat represented, an old-time newspaperman; the resource was not replaceable.

"Reynolds called me. That was personal of him. He could have sent it on the computer. He said they're putting in writers-at-large, a half dozen of these four-paragraph whiz kids. Wilkes is going to be one of them. They'll be rotating, coming through New York. And along with the wire-service copy, Reynolds says they can handle everything through Houston. All they need here is an office manager. Replaced by an office manager. He says he wants to do this now, so I can still get myself situated, rather than a couple of years down the line. Who does he think he's kidding? If I stay to sixty-two, he has to pay me retirement benefits. And where am I going to get a job on a sports desk at fifty-eight? Feller. I loved those Friday-night games when the Indians would open a series at the Stadium and Feller started. Or a Dodger-Giant series on a weekend. O'Malley and Stoneham. They raped the city.''

"What are you going to do, Pat?"

"I've got plans. Cousin of mine, he has a big mail-order house. He's been after me to go with him. Run his sports section. Ever see those novelty items? NFL piggy banks, football jerseys, that kind of thing?''

"You're a newspaperman, Pat."

"One is until he's not. You know, if you drink a fifth of booze fast, your heart can stop.''

"But we're not going to do that, are we, boys and girls?''

Doug took him back to Lahey's apartment. He canceled dinner with Nancy and stayed with Lahey until his daughter came from Long Island to retrieve him. The next morning the office manager arrived at *Sports Day* —Brad Smith, in his 20s, from Houston, with a degree, he told Doug, in "Office Technologies.''

Doug met Lahey for lunch that week. Doug had gone to the archives of the public library, tracked down an old copy of the *Herald Tribune* and found the profile about Jackie Robinson Lahey had mentioned. Doug had it photocopied, then laminated as a plaque.

"It's lovely, Doug. Too bad they can't laminate me.''

Lahey had been drinking before Doug arrived and his speech was slurred.

"Pat, I read it a few times. It's beautifully written."

"All these kids. They're going to start talking to each other. Short pieces by people brought up on short pieces, written for an audience just like them. Ted Williams, not giving in, hitting right through the shift, remember? The Kid. The Splendid Splinter."

"The Thumper."

"The Thumper! That was a good one. I forgot that one. Beware, Doug. New people are coming up behind you and they never even saw the Thumper or DiMadge."

10

ANDY WAS ABOUT TO LEAVE FOR COLLEGE. ON HIS last night in New York he asked Doug if they could merely bring in a pizza, and he spent most of the evening on the phone saying goodbye to people. Karen, back from London, was in her room working with charcoal in a sketchbook. She no longer painted in Doug's apartment, and once when he asked her about this she explained, "It's something about the light here. It's not optimum." She had said this offhandedly, oblivious to the possibility that she might be hurting him, that the best he had was a side street, which was not Central Park West overlooking the expanse of the park. She was making an artist's simple statement of fact: in the other apartment the light was better.

Doug helped Andy tie some of his belongings into a carton, remembering when he had left for college. He had walked out of his parents' apartment into the subway. His parents had a party back then when he was accepted at NYU on a baseball scholarship out of Haaren High School. They served cold cuts and bottles of rye at an event largely for adults: Frank and Norma Gardner got a son into college! They may have been second-generation Americans, but by social class they still considered themselves immigrants. When the children, specifically when Doug moved into American corporate life, they would finally get their citizenship papers. They would visit him at his home in the suburbs, their son the executive. "NYU. The business school," his mother said proudly, her face jolly for the moment. "He's my guy," his father added, patting Doug on the back. Frank and Norma were being congratulated on all sides by their friends, and Doug was weak with sadness for his parents, for their need to live through him.

For three years at NYU he meandered, unfocused, through vapid business courses. One day he complained to the editor of the school newspaper about what he considered inadequate coverage of the baseball team and was asked to rectify it himself. He started to write for the newspaper, taking journalism courses in his senior year. The college writing helped him to an Army job with the post newspaper at Fort Dix, and when he returned to the city he was determined to be a newspaperman. He knew there would be less anxiety about his job-seeking if he informed his parents about his plans after he had a job.

"A reporter? For sports?" his father responded when Doug said he had been hired by the *Yonkers Herald Statesman*.

They were ashen. They stared at him, disbelieving.

"You went to college for business," his mother said.

"I don't want business."

"If you're not a doctor, then all there is—is business," she said.

"How much is the pay?" his father asked.

"Fifty-five dollars to start."

More disbelief. Four years of college and the Army only to work for fifty-five dollars a week.

"That's the pay scale. It improves."

"How can it not?" his father said.

"I was a business-administration major. There isn't a business I could administer, even if I wanted to. And they wouldn't want me. My parting with corporate America is mutual."

"I never heard of such a thing," his mother said.

"I'm going to have to rent a room in Westchester."

"Why don't you become a ballet dancer, a wedding photographer with your college diploma?" she told him.

"I'm sorry if I've disappointed you," he answered softly.

He watched his parents staring at him, trying to decipher this. How did this happen to them? Who was a reporter? They were looking at him as if he were a ship slipping beneath the horizon, carrying away their dreams and leaving them with themselves.

ANDY SAID HE WAS READY FOR SLEEP AND DOUG CAME into the room to say goodnight to him.

"So—this is it. I can't believe you're the boy I used to carry on my shoulders every day."

"When was that, Dad?"

"You must have been two, three. Every morning I'd carry you straddled on my shoulders and we'd walk to the newsstand for the morning paper. Then you just got too big."

"I guess I don't remember."

"Do you remember the bread in the jar and fishing for killies?"

"Sort of."

"We were at the bay on Fire Island. And I had this trick Grandpa showed me. You take a jar, put bread in it, drop the jar in the water with a string, leave it there for a few minutes and pull it up and you have a jarful of

141

killies. You used to get so excited, you thought it was great.''

"I remember once we went to the Bronx Zoo, Karen wasn't with us, I don't know how old I was. It was a cold day and we must have gotten there very early because we didn't see any people around and the animals kept coming right over to us.''

"I remember that day.''

"We didn't see anybody else there for a long time. Just the two of us. It was like we owned the place.''

"What you don't remember because you didn't know is the day you first walked to school by yourself. And I followed you.''

"What do you mean?''

"Mom and I were nervous. We'd been over the route with you, but you were always with one of us. And the first day you went by yourself, I walked a block or so in back of you, just so we were sure you were all right.''

"You're not planning to follow me to college, are you?'' Andy joked.

"You're on your own now.''

They were quiet for a few moments with the seriousness of that thought.

"Once I was in a hallway outside the Knicks' locker room,'' Doug said. "Red Holzman was the coach. This was when Walt Frazier was his playmaker, and Holzman said to him, 'You're my main man.' You're going to need me less and less, but for whatever it is, for whatever you need, I want you to know, I'll always be there, to be your main man.''

KAREN'S GYMNASTICS GROUP WAS SCHEDULED TO GIVE an exhibition. Nancy was at a baby shower for a woman in her office, and Doug went to the gym by himself carrying a bouquet of roses. The head of the gymnastics

142

school, Elsa Vladic, a compact woman in her 40s, conducted the proceedings briskly, head up, chin erect. Doug felt out of shape just watching her stand.

Broeden was seated in the front row with Susan and he was wildly enthusiastic, applauding and calling out, "Way to go! Fantastic!" as Karen performed. She did a dazzling turn on the parallel bars and Broeden was on his feet yelling "Bravo!" Doug was also in the front row farther along the line, applauding, but he wasn't sure Karen saw him. I watched her on the monkey bars. I pushed her on a swing when she was little. I put up a chinning bar in the apartment and brought home a trampoline. I told her how wonderful she was when she really wasn't yet and needed the encouragement. I was there all those hours, you loudmouth.

When the performance was over, Broeden moved through the gym congratulating Elsa Vladic, Karen, the other children, their parents. He had elected himself mayor of this event.

Doug made his way to Karen and gave her the bouquet.

"You were wonderful."

"Thank you, Dad."

Then she had to leave. This was Susan's custodial time, and Susan and her husband were taking his daughter to lunch.

"Wasn't she terrific?" Broeden said to Doug.

"Yes, terrific."

As he led Susan and Karen out of the gym, Broeden was still beaming.

You've even stolen the smile I should be smiling.

At the University of Minnesota the results of a study were announced concerning parents' responses to children leaving for college. As reported in *USA Today*, fathers were hit particularly hard by separation, especially those who had spent considerable time with their children. I could have told them that.

Doug felt his situation with Karen was now especially precarious. Without Andy shuttling back and forth with her, an ally in custody, would she just as soon forgo the arrangement and live in one place? He doubted she would choose the apartment where the light was not "optimum." And yet she was not sullen in his presence. She announced one night she wanted to start a Chinese food festival with him, they would try every new Chinese restaurant in New York at least once. "It's a lifetime project," she told him. "Someone said they have the same chefs, who rotate. Wait until they find out it's the same customers." He volunteered to distribute literature for Bronx Educational Services at a street fair. Karen asked to go with him, working alongside her father for several hours on a Saturday. And she still liked his being on television. He could not say his daughter had *rejected* him. With the small but obvious signs—tennis, trips, references to Broeden, liberties she took with the custody arrangement—he would have had to characterize her as *partial* to being around Broeden. Partial. After the years, the commitment to her, to have her come up partial to another person—he may not have been *rejected*, still—*partial* was a terrible word.

Doug was talking on the phone with Susan about their joint disposition of checks for Andy's college expenses, a typically flat conversation for them. When the business was concluded, Doug said, "I miss him so much." Something in his voice, or in the fact that Andy had been their little boy, suddenly, dramatically altered the mood.

"I miss him, too," Susan said. "Very much."

144

"Separation is healthy, but it's awful."

"I know. You've been such a good Daddy."

"Daddy. That's archaic usage with them."

"Right. I haven't been Mommy for a long time."

"It's late for this, Susan, but I have to say I owe a lot to the women's movement."

"Can we inform the media on this?"

"It's just that I realize I was a good father, but it did make me a better one."

"If only I were still in a consciousness-raising group—"

"You could have done a good ten minutes on that."

"Doug, there's a gymnastics competition coming up in Philadelphia in a couple of weeks. Karen wants to see it. It's on our weekend, but why don't you take her?"

"I'd love to. But how come, Susan?"

"Because a girl still needs her Daddy."

"WE ARE GOING TO FILL YOUR LIFE WITH SO MUCH JOY and intellectual stimulation, you will not believe it," Nancy announced one childless evening to Doug.

"When does this begin?" he asked and jokingly checked the time.

"A week or two. If we're uncomfortable with it, or if it seems silly or forced, we'll stop, but if it works, we'll have fun with it."

Nancy commenced a series of Friday-night events at Doug's apartment. She invited several people from her office, he asked Jeannie, Bob and Sarah, John McCarthy and his wife. Two of the single women who worked with Nancy brought men, at other times they came by themselves. Buffet dinners were served and each evening was devoted to a subject for discussion—politics, events in the news, sports. People were told the subject beforehand and they were to read what they could about it in advance of the gathering. On some weeks, instead of the

145

discussion groups, they had musical events: they rented a piano and had a sing, another time they read scenes and sang songs from *Guys and Dolls*. When they began, Doug thought the idea was ridiculous and he felt foolish participating. But the evenings developed their own momentum. People weary of repetitive dinner parties and the sameness of their social lives responded to the gatherings. Doug understood that for Nancy there were two projects here—the events were one and he was the other. She had managed to widen his social circle and bring activity into his quiet rooms, showing him there was life after the empty nest.

"You're fabulous," he said to her after one of these nights. "You're creating a little community."

"We are."

"No, it's your doing."

"It's us, don't you understand that?"

"I was just trying to give you a compliment."

"I never would have thought of these evenings if not for us, all the magazines you read, the musicals you love—that came from you and *then* I had the idea."

"I'm sorry."

"You should be. I'm very upset with you."

"I only meant it's something I never would have done."

"Well, it's not just you. There's another unit here and it's called *us*."

DOUG WAS JOGGING AROUND THE RESERVOIR ON A SATurday morning thinking about ideas for columns, about bills, about future tuition payments, about Reynolds, who had sent him a computer note the previous day, "How about another column on personal fitness, Doug? You're getting slack around the middle on this," and near the mile mark he felt a pain in the back of his leg, a seizing sensation. He limped back to the apartment. The leg continued to hurt over the next two weeks. He had read that for some serious joggers their passion for running resembled addiction. When these joggers could not run for a while they experienced the same kind of depression that accompanied drug withdrawal. But not me, not a slow, non-Marathon type like me. And yet he was becoming moody about not exercising, and he observed a gradual weight gain.

"I was running to relieve my stress, thinking about what makes me stressful when it happened. It's like a self-inflicted wound," he said to Bob Kleinman at lunch.

"People die jogging. Actual death. All you got was a pain in your leg. You're several limbs and life functions ahead."

The pain persisted and he went to see the orthopedist who had treated his shoulder, a man in his 60s with a practice that included several professional athletes.

"It's a muscle tear, Mr. Gardner. No running or long walks or any strenuous flexing of the ankle for about six weeks. You'll be back to normal."

"I don't understand it. I was fully warmed up."

"That's what happens."

"I never had this before. Is this from my inexorably advancing age?"

"Do you want me to tell you the truth?"

"You just have."

"As we get older, the muscle fibers aren't as elastic any longer."

He was to wear a small foam pad in the heel of his shoe to relieve the strain of his injured left leg. Wearing the pad and compensating for the muscle tear, unconsciously he changed his gait. After a week he had a pain in his theoretically sound *right* leg. Andy came into New York for a weekend and asked Doug if he wanted to spend some time with him. Doug was unable to walk

147

more than two blocks without discomfort. They took a cab to the East Side and saw a movie. Doug went to the studio for his television segment, Andy came to watch him, then linked up with friends, while Doug returned to the apartment to soak in a warm bath. First middle-age eyes. Now middle-age legs.

Doug and Nancy were at Marty and Ellen's apartment for dinner, Doug was helping Marty serve drinks, and Marty inquired about his leg.

"It's healing slowly, Marty."

"My back gets me now. Goes in and out. Ellen says it started around my birthday. On account of my fiftieth."

"Please don't say that. You're my model of mental health."

"Me? I was Looney Tunes. The closer I got to fifty, the loonier. It's like I didn't have enough, my life wasn't enough. I was making deals, negotiating for leases, I was going to buy businesses, go into donuts, nut shops. I was the nut shop."

"Marty, if fifty got *you* . . ."

"I've had some wild ideas. Ellen straightens me out. And the thoughts. Do you ever see yourself at your own funeral?"

"Is that next?"

"Incidentally, thank you. At mine you said some very nice things about me."

Doug was too suggestible to let this pass. He emerged from the subway on his way to work Monday morning and saw himself lying on the street, a simple, basic heart attack brought on by the very act of worrying about his death. The funeral is well attended. Pat Lahey is there. He steps to the lectern "I knew Doug Gardner and I just want to say—he was a newspaperman." John McCarthy nods, concurring, as do the other mourners. Wait a minute! That's it? That's my entire eulogy? "He was a

148

newspaperman.'' I find it a little terse guys. His dog, Harry, has come. He speaks. Harry speaks! Harry, if you could have done this when I was alive, we would have been in clover. Harry says, ''He was a fine owner. He never forgot to walk me.''

KAREN ARRIVED ON A SUNDAY EVENING AND WAS TELL-ing him about events of the past two weeks. ''The big news, I'm so excited, is that Jerry told me I can design a line of clothing for teenage girls and he'll manufacture it and put it in the Flash stores. He says since I'm artis-tically inclined, I can do it. Can you imagine? He'd have his staff make up samples and we'd see how they turned out. He said there could be a whole sportswear line called 'Karen.' And I'm going to start right away. I'm supposed to go around to different stores and see what they're sell-ing and look at what kids are wearing and read the mag-azines and this isn't just playing at it. If the line worked out I'd get paid just the way a regular designer who worked for him would. In the meantime I'm going to be sort of a consultant on some new clothing they're doing and I'll be going into an office after school. He said he'd give me my own little office to do sketches and read the magazines so it would be professional. Nobody I know does anything like that. None of my friends. I mean, they're all consumers. But to be the person who thinks it up. *Karen!* Isn't that the neatest?''

''Yes. I would think it can be very exciting for you.''

She spoke to Broeden from Doug's apartment several times during the next evenings, thrilled about her project. She talked about it at dinner with Doug; she was filling sketchbooks with ideas. Doug could not decide if Broe-den was being the greatest guy ever, which Karen evi-dently thought he was, to give her this opportunity, or if he was finding another way of luring her away from him.

149

After two weeks, Karen returned to the Broedens, eager to get there.

"I'm really unclear about my feelings," Doug said to Nancy over dinner at her apartment. "It's possibly a wonderful chance for a kid. On the other hand, up to now she's been a serious young artist. He's going to put her in the fashion field. It's like he's commercializing her. Is that patronizing of me?"

"I can't say."

"I'm not suggesting she's going to be a major artist, but before she can even think about it, she's being deflected into commerce."

"I suppose if she becomes a brilliant fashion designer, everybody could live with that," Nancy said with a sharp edge to her voice.

"What is it?"

"What is it? You have children problems. And I say to myself, in a few weeks I'm going to be thirty-six. If I keep going like this I'll never have an Andy or a Karen of my own. I know I signed up for this. I was going to have the career and that seemed right when I was younger, but the biological clock is ticking and I've got this pattern of drifting with men. We've been together for six months. And then it will be another six months. It's not the same six months as when you're twenty-three. I want to be married and I want to have a baby. And seeing you with your children, it's not just a baby in the abstract I'd want, but a baby with you. Is this too much for me to say?"

"No."

"I'm terrified of drifting with you and then breaking up and having to start over again, and eventually it will all be too late. I love you, Doug, and I want to have your baby."

"I'm very touched—"

"You just said the wrong thing. In my head you say,

150

'I love you and I want to have a baby with *you*.' But you have to think about it. We can't just go on and on.''

HIS LEG HEALED SUFFICIENTLY FOR HIM TO JOG AGAIN and he wrote a column on middle-age legs and the unhappy recognition that he needed that form of exercise, however monotonous—the column his contribution to Reynolds's personal fitness quota. He and Nancy celebrated her 36th birthday at the Four Seasons. They told stories about their families, and about their worst and best birthdays, laughed, and stayed clear of the issue Nancy had raised. In the next weeks Nancy did not bring up marriage or children again, and yet Doug felt the issue, having been introduced, was now part of the relationship.

BOB ASKED DOUG TO MEET HIM FOR LUNCH IN A JAPA- nese restaurant on East Sixteenth Street, far from their usual meeting places. Doug was escorted to a small private dining room secluded by screens. Bob stopped speaking every time the waitress, whose command of English was extremely uncertain, came into the room, and he waited apprehensively until the screen door was closed before resuming.

"Why are we here, Bob? This is the kind of place where you'd pass state secrets.''

"Close. You have to promise me you won't tell this to anyone. Not Nancy, not Jeannie, not a soul. You promise?

"I promise."

"Not anyone."

"I promise I won't tell anyone.''

"I'm having an affair.''

"What?''

151

"It's one of the most exhilarating and simultaneously depressing things that's ever happened to me."

"Of course, depressing."

"It's been going on for five months."

"Five months?"

"At first it was just a flirtation, then a one-night stand, then it developed."

"Does Sarah know anything about it?"

"It's against her religion to know anything about it."

"Bob, who is she, what does she do?"

"Connie Davis. She's a psychotherapist."

"Is she aware that you're married and you have two kids?"

"Of course."

"Isn't this against the rules? Don't they take a kind of Hippocratic oath?"

"I don't imagine they should sleep with their patients, but she's a vital, normal single woman living in the twentieth century. Almost the twenty-first," he added.

"What are you going to do? You have a family."

"I don't need that tone of moral superiority from a buddy."

"What would you like, humor? I can give you humor. How Oscar Levant said affairs were all right, but it's the two dinners that kill you."

"I've eaten the two dinners."

"I didn't mean to be morally superior, if that's how it sounded. I'm just so surprised. You plotted this marriage."

"That's the depressing part. If we break up, Sarah would get sole custody. I can't do what you did. I'm not that kind of father. And there's the country house and all those plans for us to spend more time together."

"So why, Bob?"

"I can't say for certain. You always have outside temptations when you're married. It's like the way we're supposed to come in contact with viruses all the time, but that sometimes we're more susceptible than others and we catch something. My marriage got stale and I caught an affair.''

"Taking the American Medical Association position on love.''

"With Connie, at its best it's been extraordinary. The sex, Doug! I have never experienced such sexual pleasure. Miraculous. Animalism. We're like beautiful animals.''

Rotund Bob with his little tubby belly talking about his sexual pleasure, Doug could almost laugh but for the man's sincerity, and for his own experience. It was good with Nancy. Was it miraculous? Had Bob found some level of male sexuality he had never reached?

"I don't know what's going to happen, Doug. I love my kids. I still love Sarah in a way. I love Connie. It's such a mess.''

Suddenly Bob began to cry, his entire body heaving. Doug put his arm around him.

"Okay, now, easy—''

"I don't want to lose my family. I don't want to lose Connie. Tell me what I should do.''

"How can I? You and Sarah. If *your* marriage isn't working—you had it all figured out.''

"I did.''

"Then what do I know? I'm going to be fifty. I'm supposed to know something. I don't know anything about anything.''

CLAIMING WORK AS AN EXCUSE, HE SPENT A WEEK without seeing Nancy. Over the weekend he wandered through the city, gravitating toward playgrounds, watching children playing, hoping a new truth about marriage and family might reveal itself to him. From the bottom

153

of a closet in his apartment he brought out a cardboard box containing his custodial portion of the family pictures taken during the marriage, Karen and Andy when they were younger, and he shuffled the memories like cards. Beneath the photographs were old picture books nobody had wanted, the children had outgrown them, and out of sentimentality he had claimed them when he and Susan were dividing possessions at the time of the divorce: *Boris and Amos; Goodnight, Moon; In the Night Kitchen*. He thumbed through the worn volumes and realized he practically knew the words by heart.

After nearly two weeks he called Nancy and went to her apartment one evening. When he entered, she held herself away from him, joking, appraising him as if to reacquaint herself with his features. As she served wine, the tension was palpable.

"Nancy, if we start to think about marriage, it's not only marriage we're thinking about with us."

She shook her head as if this was coming on too quickly, she didn't want this. "I have the feeling this is not the right time for such heavy material. You look tired. I'm tired."

"We have to deal with this."

"Do we? Wouldn't you rather make love? I make you happy, soldier," she tried to quip, but he proceeded.

"I don't have a very good record as a husband. I don't know too many people who do."

"I move for a postponement. See me in a few months on this."

"No, you were right. We can't just drift."

"To think I brought this on. I am so incompetent."

"It has to be faced. You're talking about marriage *and* children, and I have to ask myself if I want that."

"Why did I let our future get enmeshed in parenthood?"

"It is, though."

154

"I didn't have to present it quite that way. God, if I conducted my professional life like this, I'd be out of business."

"But you were talking about children. Wasn't that the idea?"

"Yes," she said quietly.

"So I have to decide. Sometimes you read about these men in their fifties and sixties who have older children, starting all over with new wives and babies. But I don't know what their first marriages were like. I don't know what kind of fathers they were back then, how many hours they put in, how early they got home, did they buy the children's shoes, take them to doctors, all those things, or did they just come in for the main course while the wives did the rest? I was there. I spent the time. And because I was there, I know what's required to do it. And as much as I'd like to say otherwise, I don't think I can love a child, not that way again, not with all that intensity, and all those hours. And then to go through separating from your children all over—I don't think I can deal with it. And I don't have the energy anymore," he said in a troubled voice.

"I am so stupid. To give you an ultimatum. I can't believe I handled it this way. Doug, don't you know you'd make a wonderful father all over again because you are, because you were?"

"Nancy, I just can't do it again."

"You would have a wife and child who love you, possibly children loving you. Because you're terrific. And I am terrific. I am the best thing that could ever happen to you. And we would make it work!"

"There are no guarantees. It's not always what you had in mind."

"I was so happy to see you and you came here to say goodbye."

Her arms were crisscrossed and she held her sides in pain.

"Nancy—"

"No, go home. Go away. I am so stupid. But you're a fool."

11

H E WAS HOME ALONE READING, ON THE RADIO THE plaintive "I Get Along Without You Very Well" was playing, and, finally, it was not Susan he thought of when he heard the song. Without Nancy the texture of his life changed more dramatically than he would have imagined. The Friday-night events were over. The contact with her, speaking to each other during the day, having her there at night, the closeness, the stability—vanished. Whoever said, "A bum decision is better than no decision at all" wasn't approaching 50 having ended a relationship. He was unable to call anyone and go through the laborious process of beginnings. Sarah Kleinman and Jeannie gave him phone numbers. He didn't use them.

After three weeks of reading his periodicals at night he accepted a suggestion of Jeannie's. She told him the West Side Y had a singles club; she had been there a few times with women friends, and he might find someone without going through the rituals of a date. He attended a lecture to be followed by a square dance, the lecture by a professor of sociology at Hunter College on the theme "What Is Marriage?" Twenty unmarried people squirmed in their seats eyeing the "possibles" in the room as the professor, a married woman in her 40s, was selling commitment to an audience eager to get past the lecture and circulate.

Wine was served in paper cups. The younger women in the room and the younger men went to each other like iron filings to magnets. A potbellied man in his 40s chatted with Doug and lost interest in camaraderie when Doug was not a candidate for life insurance. A nearly obese woman in her 30s in a sacklike dress was talking to a man in his 40s, a half head shorter than the woman. The man was wearing a blue tweed jacket with lime-green slacks. She looked over at Doug a few times, smiled, and in politeness he smiled back. The folding chairs were moved away and the social director, an energetic little woman of about 60, called out, "Grab your partners!" She played a square-dance number on the phonograph. Doug, the heavyset woman, the potbellied man, and the man in the green slacks were watching the others dance. "Come, meet. You're not here to meet?" the social director said, pulling the outsiders into the circle. Doug danced, holding hands with the heavyset woman. After a few spirited turns around the floor, perspiring heavily on her face and under her arms, she took his hand and led him to the side, where she poured herself a cup of wine.

"I never saw you here before."

"My first time."

"I'm Donna."

"Doug."

"Doug, let me ask you a personal question. Suppose you went to a dance and a woman saw you across the room and she liked you. She saw you were different. She was in personnel and was a good judge of people. And she said to you that the other men were losers but she liked you and she wanted to take you home and screw. Screw like you haven't screwed in your life. Screw until every drop of you was drained from you and you were so limp you thought you could never screw again, until she aroused you with her tongue all around your penis. What would you say to that?''

"I'd say you've got a way with words.''

"Is this your fantasy of all time, to walk into a place, looking, and have someone just take you home and screw you limp? And I talk dirty, too, better than those phone-in things. I talk so dirty, you can come from my talking. So what about it, Doug? You can be coming inside me minutes from now.''

"Frankly—''

"I ask just once. It's your last chance.''

"It's a fantasy, all right, but it's not mine.''

She scowled at him and walked away.

"So, you're having a good time here?'' the social director said as he was heading for the door.

"This is a very peppy group.''

As KAREN RECOUNTED IT, THE KAREN LINE OF CLOTHing was still in a preliminary stage. For all her research, none of her drawings had yet to be converted into samples. The private office she was promised turned out to be a desk within the bookkeeping department. Doug could have told his daughter Broeden was being inconsistent, hedging on his offer, but she was still very enthusiastic, and the price of scoring points against Broeden was too high.

SPORTS DAY PASSED THE SAN FRANCISCO CHRONICLE IN circulation and at 560,000 was thirteenth of all newspapers in the country, second to the *Wall Street Journal* in the special-interest category. A celebration lunch for staff members was held in Houston and Doug was one of the honorees, Reynolds awarding lighthearted gifts, in Doug's case a jogging outfit with the words "Middle-Age Legs" on the back.

"That was very responsible of you, Doug, boy," Reynolds said after the lunch. "Doing that column without my prodding you."

"I'm a team player, Robby," he said, in a droll tone.

"But you're still on TV, I understand."

"You don't want anybody to be excessively a team player."

"Five hundred and sixty thousand. Am I entitled to say, 'I told you so'?"

"I suppose."

"You know we're picking up women readers. Not quite enough. How about going to one of those expensive health spas and writing about it?"

"Robby—"

"I just think it would be fun reading you in that situation."

"It's not sports."

"But to read it *would* be entertainment. Isn't there a thin line between the two? Doug Gardner Goes to a Spa. Just a suggestion, Doug. Make that a recommendation."

A PIECE IN *THE NEW YORK TIMES* ON LOCAL SPORTS-casters mentioned Doug in passing, citing "his intelligent weekly commentaries." Following the *Times* article, Frank Cotton, the general manager, offered him another two minutes on the air and an additional fifty dollars a week.

"Is there something you'd like to do?" Cotton asked. "Interviews? More commentary?"

"Well, there are people who don't even know who the Splendid Splinter was."

"Who?"

"Ted Williams."

"Oh, of course."

"If I can get the footage, I'd do a couple of minutes each week on some of the great athletes of the past."

"Doug Gardner's Memory Lane. You've got it."

I've reached the point where I'm old enough to have a Memory Lane.

With the additional time on the air he considered himself a minor cable television personality, at seven minutes a week, very minor. People would sometimes look at him on the street, having trouble placing the face. No, I'm not David Brinkley. Sometimes he stared at women first, a game from adolescence when he would look at girls on sidewalks, testing if they would lock glances with the stud that he was. He started to do this again in the barren period after Nancy, a crazy thing, staring, testing his attractiveness, his recognition factor. Some women exchanged the glance, most looked away first. Some of the younger women, while processing his stare, had a look of annoyance. What are you looking at me for? One pretty young woman appeared to be worried and he took her expression to mean, Why is that old guy ogling? Is he going to expose himself? And he terminated this behavior.

NANCY'S PRETEXT FOR CALLING DOUG WAS THAT SHE never returned the news clippings she used for the collection of his articles. She didn't want to put them in the mail, she said, and the early part of the conversation was about the clippings.

"Nancy, how are you doing?"

"Busy. Single-busy-lawyer-woman. There could be a magazine about me."

"Maybe we could have a drink sometime."

"And I could give you the clippings."

"That would be good."

"Meet me halfway?" he said.

"For the drink, you mean? I'll meet you in the lobby of the Plaza at seven-thirty tomorrow."

They approached each other with uncertainty and paused, measuring whether to kiss, embrace, shake hands, and they managed a small kiss. At the table, Nancy turned over the clippings, Doug thanked her for the clippings. They had done clippings. She asked about Karen and Andy, he asked about her work, she asked about his. They went around again, on her work, his work.

"Do you know how boring this is?" he said, and for the first time they both smiled.

"A man who'll tell me I'm boring when I'm boring."

"Nancy, it hasn't been great lately."

"Not for me, either."

"At first I thought, This is better for her in the long run. Let's hope for her sake she'll meet someone. But the idea you might actually *be* with somebody—"

"There's a statute of limitations on that kind of concern. In the world we live in it's about a week," she said.

"I miss you."

"I miss *you*."

"So if we're not happy away from each other, why are we doing this to ourselves?"

"Because it's better in the long run?"

"We have to see each other again."

"I'd do that—possibly."

"Then it's settled."

"Easy, Doug. A little more has to be discussed, such

162

as what's going to happen. Do we go back to where we were?"

"Of course. We'd be together again."

"And?"

"And we'd be happy."

She waited. He did not volunteer anything else.

"There wasn't a marriage proposal in here that I missed, was there?" she said puckishly.

"There wasn't," he answered softly.

"Doug, I want to be married and have a child. If I didn't know that about myself, or I was past the point, it would be different."

"Doing all that just seems beyond me," he said in sadness. "I wish you could understand that. I've had my children."

"I know. You've been very clear. I've been very clear. Two wonderfully clear, direct people."

"Maybe if we had a moratorium on *talking* about the relationship."

"I'm sure that would be fine, for a while."

"All right. I won't bring it up if you won't," he joked.

"How long do you think that would last? We'd always get back to the same place. We just did. A few minutes and we were right back on *the* issue again."

"Come on, kiddo. We'll live together. That's not a bad commitment to make."

"It is enticing. If I accept it your way, it's better than an affair with a married man. I get Thanksgiving."

"Well?"

"Answer me honestly," she said. "Has anything changed?"

"We know how much we miss each other."

"But has anything changed? Really?"

"No," he was obliged to say.

"Doug, it can't work. I'd bring up marriage and chil-

163

dren. Over and over. I know I would. We'd end up not liking each other very much.''

They were both silent, dispirited.

"This is for the best," she said without conviction. "This way we'll always have something good we can remember.''

Neither could say anything more. She rose, kissed him on the cheek, looked at him for a long time, a last look, and left.

DISCONSOLATE, HE FORCED HIMSELF TO USE THE PHONE numbers he had been given, a fashion coordinator from Jeannie, a nursery school teacher from Sarah. His lack of enthusiasm affected the evenings. First dates. What are your interests? He saw each woman once and not again.

"I don't think I can handle blind dates any longer," he said to Jeannie after a movie. "I'm too old for blind dates. I'm too old to date.''

"Call it something else, but you've got to keep going. I tell that to myself as I keep turning up lemons.''

He went to the Kleinmans for dinner, finding it disquieting to be in their company with his knowledge of Bob's activities. Being with them had an unpleasantness for Doug as though *he* was betraying Sarah, and he avoided further dinners with them.

REYNOLDS SENT A MESSAGE ON THE COMPUTER, "TAKE a whirlpool, try the mudpack. I'm buying." He sent Reynolds back a handwritten note: "Dear Robby. Sportswriters can't go to spas. It's a contradiction in terms.'' He then set out to do a column which had been eluding him. Billy O'Shea was the first professional football player from John Jay College, the New York City police

164

academy. He played for a year as offensive guard with the Birmingham Stallions of the USFL. A knee injury on artificial turf ended his career, and Doug wrote two columns about him, one during the time of his tryout with the Stallions, another when he had to leave football. He had seen O'Shea in the Blarney a few times and O'Shea kept referring to a good story, if he ever got around to telling it. Doug called O'Shea periodically and finally O'Shea said he was ready to talk. He asked Doug to come to his garden apartment in Bayside, Queens. O'Shea was a person who seemed to have been constructed out of a kit: in his early 30s, he was five feet eleven, weighed about two hundred seventy-five pounds, his neck, shoulders, arms and torso were so muscular they did not appear as if they could be moving parts.

"Billy, how have you been?"

"Married," he said proudly, leading Doug into his living room furnished with matching leather pieces. "Honey!" he called out and a red-haired, freckle-faced woman in her 20s came into the room. "This is Megan. Doug Gardner."

"I've heard a lot about you," she said.

"First of all, Doug, this is on the record."

Doug nodded and removed a tape recorder from his briefcase and placed it on a glass table between them.

"The superstars, they usually get the ink, but you wrote about me, which is why I'm coming to you with this. You can't have a good marriage without honesty and you can't have honesty unless you're honest."

In a painfully rendered, careful narrative, O'Shea admitted he had been a heavy user and a dealer of anabolic steroids while playing professional football. The drugs, synthetically producing the male hormone testosterone, were favored by body builders, weight lifters, and, evidently, football players for the additional strength the user felt he obtained. They were theoretically to be used only by prescription.

"The black market was so accepted in pro football, you couldn't even call it a black market anymore. It was like handing a guy a drink." He looked over at Megan, who nodded her head to encourage him. "The bad part is—I had been a cop. And I found a good source and ended up dealing."

When he was injured and stopped playing football, he withdrew from using or selling steroids. O'Shea was currently running a bodyguard service with several other former police officers. He had been clean, but ethically he did not feel "really clean," he said, unless he made this confession. Apart from coverage in *Sports Illustrated*, little had been written about illegal steroid use in professional football, and Doug told the O'Sheas he would definitely do a column about this. The column appeared, the material was picked up widely by other newspapers, and O'Shea had the opportunity in interviews to restate his contrition. In gratitude the O'Sheas sent Doug a gift basket of fruit, nuts, and chocolate, huge, expensive, and charming in its naiveté.

"HI, DOUG. HOW'S OUR NEW YORK GUY?"

"Hello, Robby. How's our Houston guy?"

"I'd like to talk to you a little about that O'Shea column. I can understand why you did it, I like that the other papers quoted us, but personally I didn't appreciate it much."

"Oh—"

"Too down. Too dark. We did a survey. I'll let Bill Wall fill you in. Here he is."

"Doug, people don't want to read about drugs anymore. Sixty-nine percent of our readers, when asked if they wanted to learn more about athletes and drug use, said no."

"They're oversaturated with drug stories," Reynolds said. "At some point, it's more of the same. And they don't want to see their heroes that way."

"If it's a legitimate story you have to run it."

"No argument. You had the O'Shea thing. You did right. But you don't have to go out of your way to look for such dark stories."

"Eighty-four percent of our readers said they'd like to read more about the positive side of America," Wall said.

"That was the positive side," Doug replied. "A man confronting his guilt."

"You probably feel good about yourself for writing that column," Reynolds said. "But it was a downer. Optimism, Doug."

"I should interview Lee Iacocca on his fitness habits. That would cover just about everything."

"If you were serious, you'd have something. Look for uplifting stories about our heroes. They're out there in this great land of ours," Reynolds said in a facetious tone. "So find them, Doug. It's your price of admission for feeling good about yourself."

THE CURRENT PERIOD IN THE OFFICE HAD BEEN TYPICAL in the number of unsolicited inquiries from people looking for publicity in his column. The lists reminded him of "The Twelve Days of Christmas," five public-relations people selling clients, four manufacturers promoting products, three athletes promoting themselves, two wrestling promoters, and Rosselli in a shiny brown suit.

Doug was working on a column about trends in salary negotiations for athletes. He interviewed Steve Macklin, a successful lawyer who represented several prominent ballplayers. Macklin was outspoken, stating that athletes gave good value to the public, and that they deserved as much money as they could get. A tall, hulking man, Macklin had the physical characteristics of a thug, a description kinder than what he had been called by some of his adversaries among ball-club owners. "If athletes are so rich," he said to Doug, "how come they don't own ball clubs?"

Doug sat at the Blarney going over notes from the Macklin interview. He noticed Tony Rosselli attempting to line himself up in Doug's field of vision. The last time they had seen each other was when Rosselli tried to convince Doug to do a column on his latest idea, nonpedigree dog racing. The owners would be ordinary citizens with their ordinary dogs. Since this was supposed to be for Everyman and Everydog, Doug agreed to go to a schoolyard in East Harlem where Rosselli was staging a demonstration for him. A track was drawn in chalk for a trial race. Two dozen dog owners held their mongrels on leashes. A teenage boy on a bicycle carrying a salami rode past the dogs, Rosselli yelled, "Go," the dogs were released, and they went berserk, about a dozen chasing the salami, others peeing, a few humping other dogs, none keeping the general outline of a track in their little minds, and Doug was obliged to say to Rosselli, "I don't think populist dog racing is a sport yet."

"You got a minute, Doug?"

"What now, Tony, cat racing?"

"This is elegant. Think about the Olympic Games, Doug. Who competes for us? College athletes, former college athletes. But what happens to the kids who never make it to college? Their grades aren't good enough or they get in trouble when they're young. The hard-luck story. The outstanding athlete who doesn't get into the system."

168

Apprehensively he looked at Doug to see if he was following.

"Go on—"

"We run an Olympics for everybody who's not in the system! The Street Olympics. We do it in public places like the running track where a certain party who shall go nameless was snookered by a certain wolf party. Track and field doesn't cost that much to run. And we can do it all across the country." He removed a piece of paper and read from notes. "We find the people who have slipped through the boards of the system and put them on a new path." He addressed Doug again. "We give a chance to kids who lost their chance. Even if they don't go all the way to the real Olympics they still might be good enough to compete in regular track meets. We get them into track organizations." Reading from his notes again: "We give them a second chance for glory." He looked up. "I have a new girlfriend, smart, a travel agent. She wrote that part. So there it is, Doug, the Street Olympics."

Doug took a moment to consider the idea. Rosselli's eyes darted nervously. Doug couldn't think of anything wrong with it. Rosselli had finally done it. This had value, it was moral.

"It's lovely," Doug said.

"It is?"

"It would be a very interesting event."

"Yes?"

"And if it comes off, you get yourself credibility in the sports field."

"Listen—"

"I'm not saying you shouldn't. Tony, I'm going to do it. You've got yourself a column."

"You mean it?"

"Absolutely. Your name, everything."

"You're not putting me on?"

"No, Tony. I'm going to write about it."

"I made your column! Jesus, I gotta go. I gotta call my girl."

Rosselli did not know what to do with his hands. He put them to his face, he shook hands with Doug in thanks, and put them to his face again. "It's gonna be in the paper!" Then he added, "I knew it was good," and he rushed off.

Doug completed the Steve Macklin column on athletes' salaries and started working on the Street Olympics piece. He formally interviewed Rosselli and also called track officials and coaches in various parts of the country for their reactions to the idea. The column was in rough draft form when Reynolds came to the New York bureau, passing through while he and his wife were en route to Europe. Reynolds came into Doug's office and scanned the monitor, which showed fragments of the Rosselli column.

"What are you writing here?"

"You'll be very happy. Uplifting. Optimistic. A column for these Iacocca years."

"Street Olympics? For street kids?" Reynolds said, reading the material. "Our readers don't want to know about street kids. Where is this in our demographics?"

"This has to be written about."

"Street kids mug people. They mug each other. Our readers aren't interested in muggers and people on crack."

"Where are you getting that? Robby, this is a first-rate idea for a sports event."

"How can you think street kids are what I mean when I say 'uplifting'? This is your New York point of view messing you up. I'm talking your Vietnam vet who runs the Marathon on crutches. Your suburban housewife who swims Lake Michigan. I'm not talking street kids. Don't spend any more time on this. It's not for our paper."

"This is my column."

"Well, I'm killing this piece. Don't submit it," and he walked out of Doug's office.

DOUG DID NOT DELIBERATE VERY LONG. HE HAD A COUple of beers at the Blarney, returned to the office after hours, wrote the column, and sent it to Houston. He was at his desk on Monday afternoon, the day the column was in the paper, when Reynolds entered his office, no Texas smile.

"I thought you were in Europe, Robby."

"We only went for the weekend."

"I'd like to do that sometime. The Concorde?"

"The column ran, Doug."

"Yes, I filed it."

"I told you not to run that column. Brad!" The office manager came to the doorway. "Get a garbage bag. Do you have one?"

"In the coffee room."

"Bring it in here." Reynolds turned back to Doug. "Anything you've got that belongs to you, dump in the garbage bag and take with you. We've got four columns in reserve. That will be sufficient. You're fired. I want you off the premises in three minutes or I'll bring in the building security to haul you off."

"And throw me out on the sidewalk like in a Western?"

"You're a real New York wise guy."

"And you're a real Houston wise guy."

"I hope you're independently wealthy, Doug. Because you're not going to get a job like this anywhere at this kind of money."

"Come on, Robby, you know this isn't about money. It's about peckers."

171

12

50. HE WAS CLOSER TO 50 THAN HE WAS TO 49. Five months away. His only income was from the television work, and that was not enough to sustain him. At a time in his life when he should have been successful, apart from a few minutes a week as a performer, he had nothing.

50! 50 was General MacArthur, admirals, the school principal. 50-year-old women were Tallulah Bankhead, Eleanor Roosevelt, opera divas. Phil Niekro, the old knuckleballer who looked ancient, wasn't even 50. 50 was Abby Meltzner, the delicatessen waiter his parents knew, who retired with the shakes. "Put down the glass, Abby," his boss had said. "You have to go home." "I'll go home," Abby replied. "But I can't put down the glass." 50 was closer to 60, which was a senior citizen. 50 was being who you are, no longer thinking about what you might become.

"You have seven months to live," Bob Kleinman announced mournfully in his law office.

"What you mean is I have seven months before the

money I have in the bank is gone. That is not the same as seven months to live.''

"You think being without money for men of our age and background isn't death?''

"Bob, do you ever see yourself at your own funeral?''

"I've been to my own funeral so many times it's like watching *I Love Lucy* reruns.''

"My dog spoke at mine. Brief, but touching.''

"What did you die of?''

"Worrying about dying.''

"I died last time of sex. Connie says I've created a crisis in my personal life because I'm fifty, because I'll never be a young man again.''

"That's where she doesn't know you. You were never a young man. You were forty when you were twenty-five. You can't be getting much older.''

"I am. This affair is going to do me in. But I need it. I realized I had never spent a Sunday with Connie. Then I had a brainstorm. I was going to Washington on a Monday-morning shuttle. I told Sarah I wanted to go down early to avoid the Monday crush and I also had work to prepare. I flew down on Sunday, called Sarah from the hotel in Washington and said there was trouble with the phones. If we got disconnected she should call me back. I disconnect us. She calls me back. Sarah is calling me back in Washington! We finish the conversation, I fly back to New York, spend Sunday afternoon and night with Connie while Sarah *knows* I'm in Washington. The next day I fly to where I'm supposed to be!''

"I'd say it's a lot of work to add to your frequent flyer mileage.''

ANDY CAME INTO NEW YORK AND STAYED AT DOUG'S apartment. Karen was with him for the first time in two weeks, and he told them what had taken place at *Sports Day*.

"It was a matter of principle," Andy said. "You did the right thing."

"And you still have the television show," Karen said.

"Yes, I still have the television show."

They had gathered around in support, but he felt tainted. Whatever his justifications with Reynolds, he was saying to his children that he had been fired. Big Daddy is not supposed to be fired. Stepdaddy never has to worry about that. He owns the ball.

Susan called him, having heard the news from Karen and Andy.

"I hope they don't take away from this the idea that mutiny is the best policy," he said. "It might not always be."

"What they see is that you stood up for yourself. Doug, what are your plans?"

"Nothing definite."

"I just want you to know you don't have to rush into anything because of your share. If need be, I'll take care of the bills on the kids for a while."

"I don't want you and Jerry—"

"We're not talking about Jerry. This is between us. You covered for me, I'll do it for you. I have plenty of money."

"Thank you for your offer, Susan."

Doug met with John McCarthy for lunch at the Carnegie Delicatessen.

"This is the constant," Doug said, savoring the sandwich. "When the pastrami here goes, we're all finished."

"I see you've been replaced by disco music and sit-ups."

174

Unable to communicate with Doug by computer, Reynolds found a new way of sending a message to him and it said, "We can live without you, Doug, boy." The space where Doug's column had appeared was given over to "Personal Fitness," a new column by Bonny Sunshine, a Californian with a hit workout video.

"Reynolds's love note to me."

"I don't know if there are any jobs around. An out-of-town paper, maybe."

"I can't go out of town. Karen's here. Andy's here sometimes."

"Could be your best shot now is TV."

"I don't take that seriously, John."

"The time is right for a good sports game show. If we come up with an idea, we can package it. You can be the host."

"A regular Bob Barker. Remember John Drebinger, used to write for the *Times* when we were kids?"

"Sure."

"That dramatic prose. You grew up on it, what sportswriting was supposed to be. There's a book out with a lot of those old *Times* pieces."

"I saw it."

"I was reading Drebinger when Bevens lost the no-hitter."

"Yanks-Dodgers, 1947."

"Henrich was in right. 'Desperately he tried to clutch the ball as it caromed off the boards in order to get it home as quickly as possible, but that sloping wall is a tricky barrier and as the ball bounced to the ground more precious moments were lost.' It's so florid and wonderful, it's almost Victorian. You start out wanting to be John Drebinger and you end up Bob Barker."

* * *

Doug received a call from Steve Macklin, the sports lawyer he had done the column about. Macklin had a proposal to make and asked if Doug would visit him at his office. Macklin was guarded about the idea and Doug presumed he wanted him to ghostwrite or co-author a book. He did not want to move into an area of writing that John McCarthy, the king of the field, regarded as distributing product. Doug entered Macklin's space in the Seagram Building, the reception area decorated with luxurious Italian modern furniture, a Picasso painting behind the receptionist, the space saying, "Whatever you thought when you walked in here, you'd better raise your offer." Doug was escorted into Macklin's corner office, a Chagall and a Degas on the wall.

"Thank you for coming, Doug."

"I feel I should be in formal wear in this place."

"Appearances. Unfortunately, it counts. So what happened at *Sports Day*?"

"Artistic differences. No, I don't think you'd want to say artistic with that operation."

"You were too good for the room there. Doug, I know Reynolds was spending money so I imagine you were making more than you'd get on a conventional paper. But I propose to you, and I've been reading you for years, that at this point in your career you've taken being a sports columnist as far as you can go. Where do you go next? You don't want to work for less money and you don't want to interview smart alecks like me for the rest of your life. Should I continue?"

"Does that mean I concede you're a smart aleck or that I'm interested in what you have to say?"

"Both can be true. The stuff you wrote, outstanding, but you did it. It's time for a change. One of the functions we've begun to perform here is to bring together corporations looking for sports tie-ins with sports events they can tie into."

"Like the Volvo Masters."

"Exactly. There are many corporations that would like to get into the tie-in business, for the PR, the customer relations, the dealer relations. The problem is to create the events for them."

"Be a marriage broker."

"Right. We can't handle the demand the way we're structured now. I've got a lawyer here to negotiate fees and contracts, but I need someone who's creative enough to think of ideas, who can talk to the corporate people, oversee publicity, someone who understands the sports world. First I thought of hiring a former athlete. But an athlete from one sport might not give the appearance of overall knowledge."

"Appearances."

"That's what *you* have, Doug. Overall savvy. And you have visibility from the TV show. I'm being blunt. That's a plus. Also you're a clever man. I bet you could come up with an idea for a tie-in right while we're sitting here."

"Steve, is this a test?"

"Yes."

"All right. Tennis. Most of the attention is given over to the top players on the circuit. The big tournaments already have tie-ins. But you could run a junior tournament. The Stars of Tomorrow. Do it in the Meadowlands and get one of those aggressive New Jersey banks or corporations and you'd have yourself a tie-in."

"You're hired."

"Am I now?"

"Seventy-five thousand a year. That's good pay and it's a final offer. I'm a legendary negotiator."

"Do I get to think about it?"

"Sure. While you do, let me tell you that once a tie-in is set up and continues, we get our fee year after year. So in bonuses—"

"I'd make plenty of money."

* * *

HAD HE TAKEN SPORTSWRITING AS FAR AS HE COULD GO? He had been doing it a long time. The job he just held paid more than he could earn elsewhere. He was now going to take a pay cut if he worked for a newspaper. Seventy-five thousand plus bonuses for a man out of work and about to be 50—

"It's better than a pie in your face," Bob Kleinman said when he discussed it with him.

"There is the moral consideration," Doug said.

"Moral consideration?"

"Are tie-ins an overcommercialization of the sports world?"

"What is this, a talk show on PBS? You're out of work and somebody's offering you more money than you've ever earned before."

"There is a question here."

"The question is, Can I get you more money and what about employee benefits? I'll negotiate with Macklin and get back to you."

Doug was concerned about the morality, though, and needed to discuss it with someone. He felt isolated. John McCarthy was not the person, he merchandised people's lives for profit. Jeannie, perhaps, but her field, publicity, thrived on exaggeration. With Bob Kleinman, issues of this kind sailed over his head like passing birds. Nancy. She had integrity, she understood balancing A against B. She would be able to help. He hesitated about contacting her and after several days of indecision about the job, he called her at home.

"Hello?"

"It's Doug. How have you been?"

"What is it, Doug?"

"Are you all right?"

"Why are you calling?"

"Well, I'm not at *Sports Day* anymore. I reached the limit."

"Really? I noticed there was no column. I assumed you were on vacation."

"Nancy, I've been offered a job by Steve Macklin."

"Doing what?"

"Creating sports tie-ins. Bob is negotiating the money, but there's a moral question."

"I see. And you call me?"

"You're my person on morality."

"Is that what I am?"

"I trust you."

"You trust me." She sighed. "What do you want to know?"

"I'm concerned about the morality of tie-ins."

"And you want my opinion?"

"Please."

"They're a fact of life. I have clients who play in sponsored tournaments all the time. If it's a legitimate sports event, it's fine. If it's a false event, we can do without it."

"That was my sense. I just have to watch it carefully."

"Doug, you can't call me up and make me think about you."

"There was no one I could ask."

"Please don't do this again. This call is very painful for me. I can't be out of your life and in it."

CALLING HER WAS NOT WONDERFUL FOR HIM, EITHER—to know he was still connected to her and that he couldn't be. But it was finished. He would not do that again.

The next day Bob Kleinman reported the results of his discussion with Macklin.

"I always considered myself tough. This guy is some-

179

thing. I got you a few things. The salary stays. Bonuses will be paid as the business dictates.''

"I could have told you that.''

"Hospitalization comes out of his company plan.''

"Bob—''

"You have to pin these things down. One serious debilitating problem and you can get wiped out, a slip in the bathtub, a heart attack—''

"I'm thinking of a new career and you have me under oxygen.''

"I did get you something. And from him it's a major victory. Five suits at Brooks Brothers.''

"What?''

"I told him you couldn't go out there in last year's suits, that an image was required, and we made it part of the deal.''

"What is this, hit the sign and win a suit? This is so embarrassing and ridiculous.'' Doug burst into laughter.

"It's the perks of the business world. And I figured you should look nice.''

DOUG WAS GIVEN A CARPETED OFFICE WITH EXPENSIVE oak furniture, a secretary, a lawyer in Macklin's office assigned to take care of the legal details of the tie-ins, an Edward Hopper watercolor on loan from Macklin's art collection, a name for his activity marked by a brass sign on his door, "Corporate Sports Promotions.'' And he started to work on his first project, the junior tennis tournament. Andy was in the city for a weekend and he visited Doug's new office with Karen. They were impressed by the surroundings. He took them to dinner at Arcadia, an East Side restaurant, for a fancier meal than they would normally have had together.

"The work has similarities to what I did before,'' he said to them. "Thinking of an idea is like thinking of a column. And you have to keep up with what's going on in sports. Except I go into that nice office every day." He did not add, although it was apparent in the new suit and the elegance of the meal, that another difference was the money.

Doug contacted tennis officials about promising junior players, secured open dates from the Byrne Arena in the Meadowlands, noticed the president of Jersey National Bank was appearing in a television advertising campaign, and approached him with the tie-in idea. After two meetings, an agreement was reached. Doug turned the details over to the lawyer, and he had his first tie-in. Macklin was a good cheerleader; he brought out champagne and toasted Doug in the office. Doug wanted to do better than champagne. He arranged for Andy to clear the time, and when Karen was scheduled to be with him, he booked a trip to the Caribbean for a weekend. They went to the Dorado Beach Hotel in Puerto Rico, he sipped piña coladas while watching his children play tennis, they all swam together. This was the most extravagant gesture Andy and Karen had ever seen from their father. A Broeden kind of move, isn't it?

"I HAVE SUCH EXCITING NEWS, DAD," KAREN TOLD HIM when she arrived at his apartment for the next two-week period. "I'm going on a safari."

"A safari?"

"Kenya. Washington's Birthday break. Jerry always wanted to do it and this year it works out best with his schedule."

"Andy, too?" he asked.

"He can't. He's not off then. Mom, Jerry, and I."

"It's supposed to be spectacular."

"Jerry says we should go now before it's all gone and gets asphalted over."

181

Doug had thought the situation had become stabilized, Karen hadn't talked much about Broeden of late, nothing about the clothes designing—he presumed that was dormant—but suddenly she was back with Broeden-induced excitement. Does he sit there with a strategy map and pins? Puerto Rico for the weekend. We can top that. Try matching a safari.

DOUG HAD THE IDEA TO EXPAND THE STARS OF TOMOR-row tennis event. His secretary, Laura Viona, an efficient woman in her 40s, was able to track down the names of key bank officials in other cities, and with the first tie-in as an example, by phone, and with a few trips to other cities, Doug was forming a new junior tennis circuit for tie-ins. There was not a question in his mind that he could do this work, he was doing it. After a few weeks of good results for Doug in the job, Macklin invited him to a dinner party at his home, a large apartment on Fifth Avenue in the Eighties. Among the art pieces were another Picasso, a Miro, a Johns, a Rosenquist.

"Beautiful," he said to Macklin. "I'm trying to think what I collect. I had marbles once."

"Keep going like this and you'll be collecting money."

People were guided from the cocktail area to the dining area by Macklin's wife, Jane. A slender woman in her 50s, her hair streaked with gray, she was a silvery shadow to Macklin's hulking presence. She circled him gracefully seeing to the needs of their guests. Among the people present were lawyers, Wall Street executives and a poised, striking woman in her 40s, next to whom Doug was seated at dinner. A slim five feet seven, with pale blue eyes, she wore a black silk dress, pearls, her straight blond hair in a pageboy, not a hair out of place. Her name was Ann Townsend. They talked about their connections to the Macklins. Ann did charity work with Jane Macklin.

"Are you married?" she asked.

"Divorced."

"Good. If you meet an attractive man, mature, who's never been married, you have to wonder about his general desirability."

She said "mature." I've heard that as a code word for Golden Agers. "Garden apartments for the mature."

"I've had my obligatory marriage," he said.

"I've been married twice."

"Then by these standards you're twice as healthy as I am."

Ann told him she was a fund-raiser for United Way. She had a grown son who lived in Switzerland where he worked in banking with his father, her first husband. She asked about his work and when he described Corporate Sports Promotions she said assuredly, "It will be very successful. Corporate executives are enthralled by sports." Ann was as culturally informed as anyone he had ever met, she had been to virtually every play, gallery, museum show in New York.

"You could do listings for magazines," he said.

"Why live here otherwise?" And he had the sense she could afford to live anywhere. She told him her family had newspapers in New England. "Old money," she said. "Something I like about the Macklins is that they take new money and make it look like old money."

"I'm not up to that part yet where you make the distinctions. Tell me, are you extremely rich?"

She laughed and said, "Yes."

"That's great."

"It is, actually. Tell *me*, are you a fortune hunter?"

"I'm not up to that part, either."

The general dinner discussion centered on the Middle East. One of the lawyers represented oil interests there, and, based on his reading of periodicals, Doug was able to offer a few passably intelligent comments. At the conclusion of the evening, he and Ann exchanged business cards. She called him a few days later and invited him to a New York Philharmonic concert, old money seats. They went for a late dinner to Arcadia and took a cab to her apartment on Fifth Avenue and Sixty-fourth Street. With its antiques, her living room looked to him like a model room in the Metropolitan Museum of Art. Ann dismissed her employees, a husband and wife team in their 60s, chef and housekeeper. Two people in help to take care of her needs. I've been a bit understaffed myself. She served wine, he came close to her on the plush sofa, kissed her, and she responded. They went into the bedroom and he thought—designer sheets and perfumed soap. The bedroom was decorated in sensual fabrics and shades of pink. On an end table was a copy of *House Beautiful* with that very bedroom on the cover. They made love in a room that was "an embodiment of romance in the 1980s." The romantic decor aside, she was crisp and efficient in bed. She left the bed quickly to take a bath, asking him if he wouldn't mind leaving, since she had to be up early in the morning.

They began seeing each other about two nights a week, concerts, the opera, catered dinner parties at the homes of her friends. In the second week of the relationship he bought a tuxedo. By the fourth week he had amortized it against the cost of renting. Ann preferred that he spend the night with her only on weekends and this was always at her apartment. Once, out of curiosity, she came to his place and they made love there. Afterward she said it was "very Bohemian." My middle-class apartment? Doug was well informed, they could speak on issues and relate on that level, but she belonged to a level of New York society he had never been near. She did not drop names, she *knew* people he had only read about. In

184

sports, it wouldn't have been the ballplayers she knew, but the owners. Her moral purpose was the surprise to him. What she had chosen to do with her time was not shopping, which would have been his clichéd thought about the wealthy, but work for a charitable organization full time, raising money.

"You're really a good person," he said to her one night.

"Some of us are," she teased.

Ann held a black-tie dinner at her apartment, sixteen guests, not a Blarney crowd. Ann was at one end of the table, Doug at the other, placed tactically next to the chairman of Trandex, a rapidly expanding computer-manufacturing company. A former college baseball player for Williams, he was interested in Doug's latest idea for a corporate tie-in, a World Series of Softball, a nation-wide competition for the best American amateur teams. They made a deal on the spot. The ease with which business could be conducted in these circles was startling to him. From what he could overhear, his was not the only deal being transacted at the dinner. Now *this* is networking.

After he made the arrangement with the Trandex man he shook his head slightly in wonderment and Ann saw this and smiled knowingly. Behind her was a floor-to-ceiling mirror, and he could see his reflection as he sat in his privately owned tuxedo, rich people in formal wear to his left and right. He imagined someone might come running into the room in umpire's clothes, Harpo Marx would be about right, honking on his horn, a mad umpire arrived to throw him out. It seems I get to stay. All these years, such a roundabout route, and I finally fulfilled a dream my parents had for me. I look like a Republican.

13

CORRECTNESS WAS THE OVERRIDING QUALITY OF HIS affair with Ann Townsend. She held herself slightly apart from him sexually. She was not an unwilling partner. She was correct and did what was "expected." If they were at a social function during the week and sex would create a late evening, at these times he could feel her growing tense as they neared her apartment. He would kiss her, correctly, and arrange to see her on the weekend. They talked about events in the news, about people in New York, about their respective work, they did not spend much time in talking about themselves. He did not reveal truths about himself, nor did she. Somewhere behind the *House Beautiful* bedroom and the staff in service had to be fears, demons. When he tried to enter these corridors because he felt this was required for passage to another level in the relationship, she made it clear that she was not eager to be in that place. One time they were talking about marriage in general, and he offered, "It took me a long time to get over my marriage, longer than I ever thought it would. And you?'' ''Not long,'' she said. ''I was over it while we were still married. Both times—'' and she changed the subject, leaving no doubt that she considered such conversation incorrect. Her deepest personal revelation was when she said one night, ''I know my skills. They're limited. What I'm best at is being poised. Since I don't give a hoot about making money, that's always been men's work in my background, and since I have all the money I need, I try to use my poise to do some good.'' Then she quickly moved the subject to a general discussion about jobs for women in the business world, as if she had risked losing that poise by becoming too personal.

ONCE A WEEK DOUG AND MACKLIN MET FOR BREAKFAST at the Regency Hotel, where Doug gave a verbal report on his progress. The Regency at breakfast was dense with highly successful businessmen whose names were featured regularly in the financial media.

''Look at them,'' Macklin said, referring to the other businessmen in the room. ''We have an obligation to relieve them of some of their money legitimately, by providing services they can use and by charging them as much as the traffic will bear. That's how they get *their* money.''

''Steve, this has been on my mind. The suits my lawyer negotiated. I'm very embarrassed about that. Suits!''

''Note that many of the suits in this room hang with a minimum of wrinkling. Custom-made. Also, and on this you'll have to take my word, there is not a man in here who wouldn't have attempted to get the best possible deal for himself, and if it included suits, it would have been suits.''

''What did you think when Kleinman made the proposal?''

''I thought he was a good lawyer. He wasn't getting
187

anything out of me, so he took a wild flyer. But he didn't go far enough.''

''Oh, you would have gone for shirts, too?''

''You could have had an overcoat.''

''Steve—''

''Really. Now with the ten-thousand-dollar bonus I'm going to give you for the tennis and softball tie-ins, you can buy yourself your own overcoat.''

''Suits. An overcoat. A bonus. My life has become a game show.''

KAREN CAME TO THE APARTMENT WITH HER SAFARI PHO-tographs. Through judicious editing by Karen and/or Su-san, in only one picture appeared the Great White Bankroller. The trip looked like the standard spectacular edition, and the father of city zoos nodded his head and made appropriate remarks knowing that even if he could afford to take his daughter on a safari, and with this job it had become a possibility one day, she already had been on a safari with Broeden, grinning in his Banana Repub-lic hat.

DOUG RETURNED TO HIS PLACE ON A SATURDAY AFTER jogging with the dog, and Karen was on the phone talk-ing rapidly. She completed her conversation and came running to see Doug.

''I have the most stupendous news,'' she said.

A measure of the continual dread he lived with con-cerning Broeden, his first thought was that he had been outmaneuvered again—what's left, ballooning in the south of France?

''I was called into the office today. Lana Krupcek was there. She used to coach in Eastern Europe and now she works with American gymnasts. I've been chosen. I'm

188

one of three girls from our group, only twelve in the entire East. You go to a boarding school in Wilmington, Delaware, and that would start in the fall, but first in the summer there's a camp in Colorado. And you're trained for the U.S. National Championship and after that you can even try for the Olympics! If you're going to college, they get you into a college with a good gymnastics program and you can compete while you're in college. She said I had excellent skills and I need competition, but I'm exceptionally promising! Me, Dad. And she's a world-famous coach.''

"That's wonderful.''

"I have a few weeks to decide, but I have to let them know because of the school. Room and board is on scholarship. I would have gone to camp anyway, but this is a specialty camp.''

"Congratulations, darling.''

And I lose you now, two years before I expected to?

He phoned Susan after Karen had gone to sleep.

"What about this gymnastics?''

"She has a big decision to make.''

"Is that something?'' Broeden said, coming on the line. "That's our girl.''

"I thought we had another two years,'' Doug said, ignoring Broeden.

"I know.''

"A great girl,'' Broeden said, in his own sphere.

"We'll talk.'' And Doug ended the conversation.

She was just starting kindergarten. It seems like just a few years ago. Did I go with Nancy six months? It seems like a month. How do you slow this down? How much of all this am I actually getting?

DOUG AND ANN WERE SCHEDULED FOR TWO BLACK-TIE events in the same evening, the first a cocktail party at the Macklins', followed by a dinner party hosted by friends of Ann's. The cocktail party was for a sculptor from the Southwest Jane Macklin had discovered. Doug and Macklin were in a corner, Doug telling him about a presentation he was going to make for a tie-in with a sporting-goods company. The president of the company had been an investor in the North American Soccer League.

"The man is a shark," Macklin said. "I wouldn't mind an arrangement where I could pick his pockets a little bit."

"This is the street boy coming out in Steve," Jane Macklin responded, overhearing.

"Which street?" Doug asked.

"Twenty-ninth and Seventh," Steve Macklin answered.

"Really?" Doug said.

"I came from Twenty-sixth and Eighth," Jane Macklin volunteered.

"Jane and I may look like the other guys and live like the other guys, but we didn't start out like the other guys."

The dinner party at a town house in the East Seventies was for the benefit of Music Artists, a program to develop American recitalists. Ann was a patron. The hosts, Dr. and Mrs. Baldwin Fairly, a sophisticated-looking couple in their 60s, seated the guests at tables of eight throughout the house. Doug and Ann were seated when the latecomers to their table arrived, tan, smiling. Mrs. Fairly introduced them.

"Dr. and Mrs. Mitchell Breen, Paul and Elizabeth Dawson, Ann Townsend and Doug Gardner, I'd like you to meet Susan Brook and Jerry Broeden."

Broeden was surveying the room, presumably to see if he and Susan were being seated at a prominent table, and he missed the introductions. Doug and Susan acknowledged each other, and then Broeden, startled, saw Doug seated one couple away.

"How are you doing, folks?" Doug said to Susan and Broeden.

"Do you know each other?" Ann asked.

"Yes," Susan said.

"From where?"

"From marriage," Doug answered.

"Don't you just love these excruciatingly awkward situations?" Ann said.

"It is excruciatingly awkward. I'll grant you that," Doug replied, and he, Susan, and Ann were able to smile. Broeden did not. Doug sensed that Broeden was offended to see Doug there, that Broeden had put on the tuxedo, the dress shirt, the studs, had taken the trouble to get ready for this event, and had found Doug on his turf.

The Music Artists program occupied the conversation at the table, and in the middle of polite talk Broeden made a transition so grinding, that to Doug it was like hearing truck brakes screeching. The Dawsons said they had recently returned from a vacation to Japan where they attended several concerts, and suddenly Broeden was holding forth about Japan. He spoke about the difficulty of doing business with the Japanese, the time it takes while their customs are observed, but he showed *them*, opening three Flash stores in record speed.

"Japan is nothing much," Broeden stated.

"The entire nation?" Doug said.

"And their designers are supposed to be so great now," Broeden continued. "We can give them lessons."

"I thought the Japanese were in the forefront," one of the women said.

"My daughter is a young designer, a teenager, and she can design circles around them," Broeden declared.

Your daughter is a young designer?

191

Broeden rolled on, eventually giving up the spotlight to conversation about travel and terrorism, Broeden reentering with his opinion that no terrorist was going to restrict *his* right to travel, Doug imagining Karen being hauled by Broeden through an airport under siege so Broeden could argue his point personally with Iranian terrorists.

Ann and Susan talked briefly; Susan was also a patron of the music program. On the way home after the dinner, Ann said to Doug, "I liked her. She's very nice. She made a mistake with you."

"Thanks. But you're assuming it was only hers to make."

TWO DAYS LATER A STORY ABOUT THE DINNER APPEARED in *The New York Times*, listing the names of notable guests. After seeing so many column items about Susan and Broeden, Doug had reached an odd kind of parity with them. They were mentioned in the *Times* piece, but so were he and Ann.

"The man who used to come to the beach house with his clothes in a shopping bag gets on the style page of *The New York Times*?" Jeannie said to Doug on the phone.

"Would you like to do my publicity?" he said teasingly.

"You don't need me. Mister Chic. Well, you'll be my showpiece. I have a new friend. A widower, retired, grown children. A real gentleman. He buys his *underwear* at Bergdorf."

"That's beyond me."

"You never know. His name is David Whitley. I've been seeing him awhile. I didn't want to say anything before this because I was afraid I might jinx it."

"That's great, Jeannie."

192

"I have other news. Not so great, but also juicy. Last night, David and I were at a restaurant way downtown. And there was the beloved Jerry Broeden. With a girl, Doug. Probably a model. So young she'd make Brooke Shields look geriatric."

"It may have been a business dinner."

"Holding hands? I felt like walking over and saying, 'Excuse me Mr. Broeden. I'm in publicity. Would you like a column item out of this?'"

"Can we give him benefit of the doubt?"

"No way. Cutesy stuff. Giggling. *He* was giggling."

"It sounds about right for him."

"Did he really think if he goes to a restaurant nobody was going to see him?"

"Where does he get to be in my Karen's life, the bastard?"

He tapped the table with his fingers out of tension.

"What?"

"I guess a part of me still feels proprietary, because I was also thinking, What is he doing to my Susan?"

JEANNIE INVITED DOUG TO A BUFFET DINNER AT HER apartment, where David would be making his debut. Doug brought Ann, who was appearing for the first time before his friends. David Whitley was in his 60s, white-haired, trim. In his own honor he was wearing a tuxedo and when he smiled he had what Doug considered to be debonair teeth. About forty people were present. The Kleinmans arrived and were introduced to David and Ann. Sarah Kleinman began to physically shrink, to withdraw into her unfashionable skirt and sweater, looking at Ann in her exquisite tailored suit, and Doug sensing this, feeling for Sarah, hugged her and stood with his arm around her.

"I know how long some of you have known each

193

other," David said. "I feel you've kept Jeannie company until I could arrive in her life."

"Bob, you can go off your diet tonight," Jeannie said. Bob looked over at the lavish buffet.

"All due respect, the cholesterol at that table—I'd be one forkful away from death."

"They used to have court jesters," Doug explained to David and Ann. "Bob is our court depressive. No matter how depressed you might be, you feel cheerful around him, because he's even more depressed."

"Sarah, I have a special kosher meal for you tonight," Jeannie said. "I ordered it from El Al."

Sarah took the tease in good spirit, laughing with the others.

"Look," Jeannie said, turning around a diamond ring that had been concealed in her hand. "Engaged!"

People were congratulating her and she circulated among guests, showing the ring.

Bob came over to Doug at the side of the room.

"This Ann is a very rich lady, I understand. The kind who asks for a pre-nup. See me before you do anything big."

"You're going to get some suits out of her for me?"

"Doug, I've got to tell you something," he said sotto voce. "Yesterday I was with Connie after work. When I got home at night and took off my shirt, Sarah noticed my undershirt inside out, which it wasn't in the morning. Thinking fast, I told her you and I went to a steam room. So if she brings it up, cover for me, okay?"

"No. Don't enlist me in your affair."

"What do you mean?"

"What I mean is I consider Sarah my friend. She's been very loyal. And I suspect if I called her and said, 'I can't explain, but meet me in twenty minutes at Forty-second and Lex with three hundred dollars,' I'd like to think she'd be there."

"Would she do that for me? She would. Would Connie, though? This is a good test of trust, Doug. I find this very meaningful—" and he began to brood.

"You will never be found out in this affair from being so joyful in it."

Jeannie came over to them and said, "So what do you think of David?"

"He's very sweet," Doug answered. "The care he was taking to acknowledge us."

"Isn't he splendid?"

"He is. You're marrying Maurice Chevalier."

"Has he asked for a pre-nup?" Bob said.

"A what?" Jeannie replied.

"A pre-nuptial agreement. I'd better look into that for you."

"Bob, we're celebrating. We're not in court," she said.

"I'm very happy for you," Doug told her.

Jeannie put her arm through Doug's and said, "It was just dumb luck."

KAREN WAS STILL UNDECIDED ABOUT HOW A GYMNAS-tics commitment would affect her. She talked to Doug about her choices and he presumed if Karen was talking to him, she was also talking to Broeden. With what he knew of Broeden's values, he was concerned about the advice she would receive from that quarter. Doug offered to look into the matter for her and he researched it as if he were working on a story for a newspaper. He called people who worked with the American Olympic gymnastics teams, he spoke to athletes, college coaches, he compiled a listing of the best-regarded gymnastics programs on a college level, and then turned to the art side, making inquiries about art institutes and college art programs.

"It's a dilemma," he said to her a few days later.

195

"Athletes only have a few good years in gymnastics. If you're world class, that becomes your living, competitions, endorsements. Being on that level would have to affect your art training. But you can always go back to it later."

"And if I want to go to a college and do both?"

"The problem is, the colleges with the good arts programs aren't usually the ones with the good gymnastics teams. You'll probably have to decide between disciplines."

He handed her the file he had compiled for her, and she was momentarily startled by the attention to detail. She nodded in thanks and took it to her room.

DOUG RECEIVED A PHONE CALL FROM HIS MOTHER WHEN he was in the office. "It happened," she said grimly.

"What?"

"Your father. He had a heart attack."

"Oh, no."

"He's all right. He'll live."

"Where is he?"

"Roosevelt Hospital."

"I'm on my way. Does Marty know?"

"I just spoke to him. So it starts. Hospitals."

Frank Gardner lay in a ward that smelled of bedpans. Marty, Ellen, and Doug stood by his bed, Norma sat in a chair. Frank had experienced chest pains and, familiar with the signs from stories of his friends he had called for an ambulance.

"I wasn't in any danger. I could have taken a taxi."

"Sure, you might have walked, too," Doug said. "Next is to get you into a private room."

"I'll be home in a few days. I don't need a private room."

"We'll pay for it, Dad," Marty said.

196

"I don't have to have a private room. You want to argue with me and give me another heart attack?"

"That's a neat trick to get your way from now on," Doug teased.

"Like he didn't get it before?" Norma said.

They left his room after a while and convened in the hospital lobby.

"He really should think of retiring," Marty said.

"I told him," Norma replied. "He's sixty-nine. It's enough. I got news for him, Rockefeller he's never going to be."

"We'd like to get him into a decent room," Ellen said.

"Fine. But he'll be out soon. They don't keep them. If you live through the first heart attack, you're okay. A man I know, he made a career out of heart attacks. Six. He had them like you take out the garbage. His wife is the one it did in. *She* had a stroke. She died, and he lived and got married again."

"This is *Tales from the Crypt*," Doug said.

On the night before Frank was to be released from the hospital, Marty, Ellen, and Doug met at Norma's apartment and looked over brochures she had collected of Florida condominiums.

"This place has the best clubhouse," Norma said. "Pools, indoor and outdoor."

"Why don't we see if he wants to retire first, then we can fill in the rest?" Doug suggested.

"I want Florida. I want a suntan while I can still enjoy it. And no more New York winters. We can afford it."

"Can you?" Doug asked.

"Maybe not the apartment by the lake," she said, showing them a page in the brochure. "That's another six thousand dollars in the purchase price. But we can afford behind the lake in the less desirable area."

Doug and Marty looked at each other in agreement. They would upgrade them to the apartment by the lake.

"What am I going to do there all day?" Frank said when he returned home from the hospital.

"Stay alive," Norma answered.

"They have activities," Marty offered.

"I don't play golf. I don't swim. I don't make pots. What's there for me? What I do is fish."

"You don't think there's a fish in Florida?" Norma said. "Somewhere in all that water there's a fish."

"There's fine fishing," Marty said.

"This is true. I don't think I'm ready."

"Your heart recently attacked you," Norma said, "which is how ready you are."

Negotiations between Frank and Norma behind closed doors resulted in an announcement a few days later. They were moving to Palm Vista, a development north of Fort Lauderdale, the apartment by the lake.

Frank attempted to sell his business, making phone calls, placing ads in classified sections. Since he rented factory space for manufacturing and owned only his office furniture, what he had to sell, apart from his furniture, was his goodwill, the name "Norma Creations," and nobody wanted it. On a Saturday, Marty was working, and Frank asked Doug to accompany him to the factory to help clear out his belongings. Doug suggested they rent a car or borrow Marty's. Frank said it wasn't necessary, he had already shipped the paperwork to his accountant and wouldn't be bringing anything back. He preferred to travel there by subway as he had always traveled. The place was four blocks from the Hunts Point station in a commercial section of the South Bronx. The office was entered through a side door of a one-story manufacturing plant. Adjacent to the door was a square sign in blue with white lettering, "Norma Creations." The room, about ten by twelve, had been furnished with dark wood office furniture, not good enough to be antique, the room painted red for some reason, red walls, red ceiling.

"Did you and Mom paint this yourselves?"

"Sure. You don't have to pay good money to a painter."

Frank told Doug to push the furniture from the office to the sidewalk, where it was to be picked up later that day by a junk collector. Frank sat in a swivel chair giving instructions, and then the chair itself was pushed outside. Frank looked around, nodded his head with finality, and closed the door. He had a screwdriver in his pocket which he had apparently taken for this purpose and he pried the "Norma Creations" sign off the outside of the building. He walked to a trash bin and was about to toss the sign in.

"Wait, Dad, don't you want to keep that?"

"Why?" he said, taking the sign, which was made of thin metal, bending it in half and throwing it into the pile. "There's no Norma Creations anymore. What do I need a sign for?"

He turned for one more look at the building, nodded again, affirming that it was finished, and walked away.

"I came here without anything. I leave without anything," he said as they headed for the subway.

"You leave with a place in Florida."

"For all that? Fifty years of working?"

Doug tried to envision that span of time. Frank and Norma were married as teenagers, Frank was 18 when Marty was born, 19 for Doug—fifty years, many of those years paying bills for his family of four. Doug, who had been so bedeviled by bills in his life, found that to be an extraordinary effort, month after month of food and clothing and utilities for fifty years. I can't even grasp it. It's a time concept Carl Sagan would talk about. The goddamn perseverance, and in such a cause, Norma Creations. And out of it, to have paid all those bills. It's heroic. He turned and suddenly kissed his father.

DECLARING THEIR POSSESSIONS "JUNK," FRANK AND Norma Gardner left everything in the apartment for the Salvation Army. They bought a used car and set out for Florida.

Doug agreed with the appraisal that their possessions were junk. The economic distress that darkened his parents' lives would not be his. Aggressively he pursued a tie-in with Palton, manufacturers of athletic footwear, selling the vice-president for promotion on a series of specialty mile runs down the main shopping areas of major American cities. When the Palton tie-in was signed, he decided nobody he conducted business with lived in an apartment like his—this was workers' housing. After a day of Manhattan apartment seeking he learned he was still another year or so away in bonuses from moving up in the real-estate market. For the moment, though, at least he could get rid of the furniture he bought at the time of the divorce. He went to various stores and while in Lord and Taylor saw a display living room he liked, an eclectic combination of modern pieces and American crafts. He bought a sofa and two chairs shown in the display, and in antique stores located an antique oak chest to use as a coffee table, two patchwork American quilts, a Navajo rug as a wall hanging, and then, for sheer affluence, he bought a new stereo system.

He no longer had the time or the interest to prepare for a television appearance every Saturday afternoon. His mind was not on sports results or yesterday's heroes. Scouting locations in other cities for the latest tie-in, he was obliged to miss a television appearance, and he could anticipate this happening more often in the future. He called the general manager and informed him he was leaving the show.

Doug sat in his new living room sipping cognac with

the cast album of *Annie Get Your Gun* playing on his new stereo system. If he smoked cigars he would have been smoking cigars, like Red Auerbach lighting up on a victory. The dirty little secret was that the work he did before, writing three columns a week, and before that, covering a sports beat, was far more difficult than this and paid far less. He had cut all ties with sports journalism. He was purely an entrepreneur now, back on schedule for making it by 50, and with antiques, no junk in his apartment.

14

JOHN GANNON, RECENTLY THE SUBJECT OF A PIECE IN the *Wall Street Journal* on the profitability of his company, Gannon, Inc., manufacturers of timing mechanisms for industry, said to be a confidant of Ronald Reagan, was interested in meeting with Doug to discuss a possible sports tie-in. Mr. Gannon would be arriving at LaGuardia Airport at eight at night, Gannon's secretary told Doug, his limousine would take the men to a restaurant in Westchester, and after taking Mr. Gannon home, the limousine would bring Doug back to Manhattan. Doug was given instructions on where to meet the limousine. He and the driver waited until nearly nine, when John Gannon appeared. In his late 50s, tall, lean, his hair graying at the sides, he walked with long strides, carrying an attaché case and a squash racket. Doug was outside the limousine. As Gannon entered, he barely made eye contact with Doug.

"Mr. Gannon, I presume."

"Sir."

Doug followed Gannon into the car. Without speaking

to Doug, Gannon made six phone calls from his car phone. They were now well along on the highway.

"Saw President Reagan today," he said, finally directing his attention toward Doug. "Great guy. Ever met him?"

"I've seen him on TV."

"I have his confidence. That's a position of public trust, having the confidence of the President."

He proceeded to talk about his relationship with Ronald Reagan for fifteen minutes; Doug exhausted his "uh-uh"'s and just shook his head after a while.

"So, sports tie-ins. That's why you're here. What did you have in mind?"

"I read that you like golf and I was thinking of a golf event."

"I saw something in the paper about one of your tie-ins. But now, as I think about it, why would an industrial company like ours want that kind of publicity?"

"Let me do a little salesmanship—"

"No, no, it won't work out. We've had a change of plans here. Phil!" he called to the driver. "Take me to the house, then take Mr.—"

"—Gardner."

"To the train station."

"What are you doing?" Doug asked.

Ignoring Doug, Gannon picked up the phone and began to make a call.

"At the very least the arrangement was for the driver to take me back to the city," Doug said.

"The arrangement has been changed."

Gannon was on the phone until they arrived at his home in Mamaroneck, a large Colonial on heavily wooded property. The driver held the door for him, and, as Gannon left the limousine, Doug said, "Maybe we'll do this again sometime. We'll meet on the subway and I'll leave you stranded in Coney Island."

203

"Is that supposed to be funny?"

"This has been for me what they call in baseball the Instructional League. There are guys and then there are the other guys. I've got a way to go before I can be the other guys."

Not understanding, and with no interest in doing so, Gannon waved his hand dismissively and walked toward the entrance of his house.

"Sorry. I have to do this," the limousine driver said. He left him at the secluded railroad station. The next train was not scheduled to arrive for forty minutes. What would my father do in this situation? He'd sit. What would Reynolds do, Macklin, Broeden? Doug called a local service and hired a limousine to take him back to Manhattan. He still felt humiliated but discovered that it was easier to deal with humiliation in a limo.

He told Ann the story the next day. "A dreadful person," she said. "I'm going to put you together with Tom Daley. He's every bit as powerful as John Gannon, and very nice."

"I decided someone who needs to discard people like Kleenex is not basically a happy person," he said, trying to be light about it.

"Doug, you meet enough of these men and you realize he's probably blissfully happy."

JEANNIE ASKED DOUG TO JOIN HER FOR A DRINK AT THE Algonquin. She showed him a wedding ring. She and David had eloped and were married in Rome.

"I hope you're not hurt about the way we did it. When we started planning a wedding we decided, why go through it? We already had the party."

"It's great news. You're a married lady!"

"The other thing I have to tell you is we're going to leave New York."

"Oh—"

"David has a home in Scottsdale and he has real-estate interests out there. Even though he's retired he wants to oversee things, busy work."

"What will you do?"

"The boutique. Accessories, jewelry. I've had it with the publicity business. Bob is working on a marriage contract after all, so David's children don't feel I'm encroaching on their father's money. I'm not really offended. I like the idea that after working so hard for a living, I could be considered in the same category of woman as Jackie O."

"Bob is going to put an earthquake clause in it for sure."

"I gave him the details on the phone this morning, and when I was through he said, 'Scottsdale, Jeannie? Arizona? Stay out of the sun. You'll get cancer. And you can die.'"

"You'll be coming back to visit, right?"

"Absolutely. Buying trips. And if there's something good playing in the movies, just give me a call. That's what wealth and jet planes are for."

"Okay."

"You know, at the party, when David said that about your keeping me company until he could show up, it was true. You helped keep me sane. Having a pal for a hamburger and the movies, I wasn't all gnarled and crazy by the time he got here."

"You did that for me, too."

Outside on the sidewalk Jeannie put her arms around Doug tightly and pressed her head against his chest.

"Thank you, my pal, my good pal."

"Have fun with it, Jeannie."

"Right. They could use me out there. Doug—" She looked in his eyes. "Did we mess up in some terrible way? Would it have been different if we were lovers?"

205

"We ran through a lot of lovers, but not so many pals."

TOM DALEY'S OFFICE WAS LOCATED IN A BUILDING OVER-looking New York Harbor, the walls decorated with vintage maps and prints of New York City. A portly man in his 50s, he seemed informal and unconcerned with appearances. Rather than a business suit, he wore a tweed sports jacket and slacks, a striped shirt, and a knit tie. But when he came from behind his desk to shake hands with Doug, the little luxuries revealed themselves as if there was no way for the man to contain his affluence—the Rolex watch, the gold stickpin, the alligator loafers. The company of which he was chairman, Waldron Electronics, was a newly developed entity Daley had assembled from several electronics firms, the company manufacturing home-electronics products. Doug brought along a presentation book he was now able to offer prospective clients showing other tie-ins that were in progress.

"You're a friend of Ann Townsend's?"

"Yes."

"My wife and Ann were college roommates. We used to go out on dates together. It seems like a lifetime and a half ago."

"I know the feeling."

On Daley's desk was an array of family photographs with an attractive auburn-haired woman in her 40s and three young people in their 20s.

"Your wife and kids?"

"Kids grow up," he said wistfully.

"So I'm learning. I have a boy, a freshman in college, and a girl in high school."

"You're lucky they're still fairly young."

"I met John Gannon the other night. I can't imagine having this exchange with him. Do you know him?"

"We've been at some functions together. A blowhard. So—Ann said I should see you."

He opened a folder on his desk which had been prepared for him, a report on Doug's activities. "You apparently have a good thing going."

"This tells how we work—" and Doug began to offer the sales presentation.

"We can skip that. Do you have some ideas?"

"Oh, ideas. We've got good ideas, not-as-good ideas, good ideas that are expensive but worthwhile to do, ideas that aren't as expensive, but aren't as worthwhile."

"Everything's not equally fantastic?"

"No."

"I appreciate the honesty. Now when you say worthwhile, do you mean for my company or for the public good?"

"Worthwhile both ways."

"Well, we have a new ad campaign. It talks about American-made products, with everyday people using our products. So if I did anything with you, I wouldn't want polo or golf, not any country-club stuff. I *would* be interested in a promotion that increased our visibility and, as you put it, could be worthwhile both ways."

Doug appraised him, a man who was not John Gannon and who bothered even to think about the public good. He decided to tell him about the Street Olympics, which was foundering, he had learned in a recent conversation with Rosselli. It needed something like corporate sponsorship. Doug presented the idea, explaining how this could be of service in helping young people and would also give good exposure to the sponsor. He added that the creator of the event was an individual promoter and would have to be included in the project as a consultant. As Doug suspected he might, Daley liked the suggestion,

207

and they arranged for another meeting. Doug would bring Rosselli and Daley would have his advertising and promotion managers present.

Doug called Rosselli, who was eager for sponsorship by a corporation, having realized he couldn't handle this on his own.

"There *is* a problem," Doug said. "You're going to be meeting with high-level executives. I know you can sell them with enthusiasm. Unfortunately, appearances count."

"I'll get a shave and a haircut."

"You'll get more than that."

He told Rosselli to meet him at Brooks Brothers on Madison Avenue. Rosselli arrived wearing a shiny beige sharkskin suit and a black silk shirt. "I never was in here," he said to Doug. "This is not my kind of store."

"There are certain uniforms, and you, Tony, are out of uniform."

They entered Brooks Brothers and Rosselli was immediately ill at ease.

"I don't like it here, Doug. I want to go."

"It's for the good of the project."

Rosselli tried on jackets. The boxy Brooks Brothers cut was ill-matched to his wiry frame, and they went from the traditional men's department to the younger men's department, and still Rosselli looked like he was a boy wearing a grownup's clothing.

"We'll go to the boys' department. They probably have a thirty-six or thirty-seven for you, which you need."

"Not the boys' department," he moaned.

Standing rigidly in the boys' department, Rosselli tried on a double-breasted charcoal-gray suit, and it fit better than anything in the store. The pants were still slightly baggy, and the salesman suggested the tailor might take some material from the inseam.

"Doug!" Rosselli whispered desperately. "I'm not letting any fancy-store tailor touch my crotch!"

He took the suit, unaltered—he was going to bring it to his own tailor. Then Doug helped him with the purchase of conservative black shoes and a shirt and tie.

They met at Daley's office for the meeting. Daley's assistants were two men in their 40s, both also wearing Brooks Brothers suits. Doug was amused by his prescience. Rosselli looked like an executive. Rosselli talked with his passion for the project, and despite the rough edges in his speech, his sincerity was irresistible. Doug interjected information on how the project would be organized, Daley gave his approval to the tie-in, the assistants supported the decision, and they had an agreement. During the handshakes that concluded the meeting, Doug looked down, noticing a detail he had neglected in dressing Rosselli. Socks. Rosselli had worn his regular socks to the meeting and they were shiny electric blue.

On a Sunday Doug rented a car and drove to Wesleyan to have lunch with Andy. He told him about the Street Olympics and Rosselli and the socks.

"He's the one who had the wolf girl?"

"That's him. He's big time now. He's going to get prestige and a twenty-five-thousand-dollar consulting fee."

"So you like this new job?"

"That was a good thing to be able to do."

"And you're going out with somebody new, I hear."

"Yes, I am."

"Do you ever see Nancy?"

"It just couldn't work out with her," he said, feeling a rush of melancholy.

They strolled the grounds of the campus and Doug noticed even some of the faculty looked like kids. By the standard of his being nearly 50, they were kids. If you want to feel as old as Boris Karloff in *The Mummy*, walk around a college campus.

"WE'RE INTRODUCING A NEW LINE OF TVs NEXT week," Daley said to Doug on the phone. "Ice-cream colors. My PR people came up with the usual product publicity. But you have good ideas and I thought I'd ask you. I want to buy a good deed that will also sell the line."

"You want to buy a good deed?"

"That's what it amounts to. Not necessarily with sports. Something that can be in the media fast."

Doug had been pitched stories by so many publicists and Rossellis, he knew the elements required to get a story covered.

"If I were looking to 'buy a good deed' that also gets my company publicity, I'd do something for the homeless. I'd take a few thousand of your new television sets and donate them to every shelter for the homeless I could find. You'd be doing good and you might even get a press conference out of it."

"I like your thinking. I'm going to set it up. What can we send you in thanks? A CD player, a television set, a home computer?"

"That's all right. And I used to work in a field where buying a guy a beer was a big deal."

KAREN CAME TO DOUG'S APARTMENT ON A SUNDAY night with Harry. She was looking very somber. "Can I talk to you about something?" she said, and they sat in the living room.

"I've been thinking about what to do about the gymnastics. Do I want to go for it? Go for the gold, Jerry says. Do I want to keep up with my painting?''

"Big decisions."

"It's been hard. But you see, I have this father—" Suddenly, she started to cry, sobbing as he hadn't seen her do since she was little. He held her, she tried to speak, and she was sobbing between her words. "You gave me a file . . . to help me . . . a whole file . . . and everything I needed to make up my mind . . . was in it.''

"All right, darling, easy now."

She began to steady herself.

"You just handed it to me. Here's what you need to know. And you said, if you choose this, then that might happen. If you choose the other—Dad, I'm not going to try for gymnastics. I'm going to finish high school here. And then I'd like to get into a college with a good art program. And I'd like to be a good artist, I mean, as good as I have the talent to be.''

"That sounds great."

"Before I decided, I talked with Jerry and Mom. Mom said I have to try to listen to my heart. Jerry—he kept talking about Mary Lou Retton. How if I went for it maybe I could be on a cereal box one day and make a fortune in commercials. Go for the gold. Be Mary Lou Retton. He was so glitzy. And he never got into what you give up. What are the plusses and the minuses? But you gave me what I needed to help me decide . . .'' She was on the verge of crying again. "So I'm trying to listen to my heart and my heart tells me . . . I've been very mean.'' She was sobbing again. "I have this wonderful father who loves me and I love him . . . and he bought me my first paints. Do you remember? Mom was out of town and we spent a whole Saturday going from store to store. And—'' She couldn't speak. She was crying too hard.

211

"Easy, angel."

"And I don't even paint in your apartment anymore!" She was trembling, and he held her.

"Remember we used to watch *Sesame Street* and Kermit the Frog used to sing 'It's Not Easy Being Green'? Well, it's not easy being so talented. And it's not easy living in two homes. And it's not easy being you. But you must be doing all right. Why else do I love you so much?"

"I'm so sorry. Please say you forgive me."

"There's nothing to forgive. But personally I think you made the right decision," he said, getting her to smile. "Come. Let's take Harry out to sneak pizza crusts from us on the street. And then I think we need some Serious Chinese."

CBS Sports made a commitment to televise three preliminary trial events and the final championships of the Street Olympics. A television production company Macklin owned would produce the shows. Macklin suggested Doug reward himself and take a few days off, and Doug arranged to visit his parents and see their new place in Florida. Then he was going to link up with Ann, who was spending a long weekend at her house in St. Thomas.

Doug's parents met him at the Fort Lauderdale airport, their faces dark and leathery from the sun, Norma wearing an inexpensive print dress and plastic clogs, Frank in a cabana outfit with short pants that Doug thought went out with "The Miami Beach Rhumba."

Palm Vista was a development of stucco garden apartments with a screened porch for each residence. The streets carried the names of gems—Frank and Norma lived on Opal. The lake their apartment faced was a man-made body of water surrounded on all sides by other apartments. The lakefront section had the bonus of a small patio sitting area in front of each screened porch, and pleased with this luxury, Frank and Norma pointed out the feature and led Doug into the apartment from the patio side. The apartment contained a living room–dining room combination, a kitchen off the dining room, a master bedroom and a guest room. All the rooms were furnished with rattan, as if Frank and Norma had gone to a warehouse and in five minutes bought "a houseful of furniture, $399." He was in his parents' home, and it had no history.

"Very handsome," he said.

"We got a good deal on everything," Frank explained.

They were eager to show him the facilities and drove him past the outdoor swimming pool, the shuffleboard courts, and stopped at the main house, a large white-brick two-story building containing the indoor pool, hobby rooms, a theater. Air-conditioned, clean, and well maintained, this was an important feature of Palm Vista, and Frank and Norma were proud of the building.

Doug wanted to take them to dinner. They insisted on saving money for him with an early-bird special at a restaurant, and at 5:30 P.M., picking at a salad, he watched as they enthusiastically ate their beef goulash and noodle pudding.

After dinner he walked with his parents along a brick path that encircled the lake.

"How is the job?" Frank asked.

"Better than I would have thought."

"And your social life?" Norma said.

"I'm seeing someone. She works as a fund-raiser. When I leave here I'm going to spend time in her house on Saint Thomas."

"Saint Thomas?" Norma said. "This is not a person on food stamps."

Later, as he lay in the guest room, he heard Frank and

213

Norma talking softly in the kitchen, laughing together, a sound he did not associate with his parents.

He tried to spend time with them separately the next day, taking turns walking the grounds with each.

"The facilities here are first-rate," Doug said to his father.

"Also the medical assistance. You see more ambu-ances than taxicabs."

"Fishing much?"

"I fish. I found some fishing buddies. I've got enough fish in the freezer to open a fish store."

"But you're keeping busy."

"Busy here is not New York–busy. It's Florida-busy. I'll get adjusted. They have a workshop on getting ad-justed. They have workshops on everything. Bend down to tie your shoelace around here, they have a workshop on tying your shoelace."

"Is there anything you'd like, a VCR?"

"Your life doesn't change with a VCR. If I could be working, I'd be working. If I could be making big dol-lars, I'd be making big dollars. But I can't complain. It's a beautiful place. It's retirement."

A lady in her 60s with sagging breasts nearly falling out of her blouse passed by and nodded at Frank.

"Not my type," Frank said.

"Listen to this."

"You think nothing goes on in this place? Not by me. There's plenty of mufky-fufky."

"Honestly?"

"Virgins we don't have here."

Later in the day Doug took a walk with his mother.

"You and Dad seem to be getting along really well."

"We'd better. This is last gas before the highway."

"I'd like to know something. You had some difficult years—"

"I'll say difficult."

214

"What kept you together?"

"Nobody got divorced in the neighborhood. Hollywood stars got divorced. Myrna Loy got divorced. As far as I know, I was not Myrna Loy."

"People left each other."

"Not people we knew. You stayed. You had children, you stayed for the children. I'm not criticizing. You've done wonderful with my grandchildren, but you and your brother, no matter what, you had one roof over your head and two parents."

"True."

"You stayed. What you have is what you have. Who says it's going to be better somewhere else?"

His generation had sophisticated marriages and divorces, but he wondered, listening to his mother, if this older generation for all their lack of sophistication knew something his did not.

The following morning they went to the outdoor pool. People were competing to get the best spots, leaving sunglasses or a book on the poolside chairs, then coming back after breakfast to claim the chairs. Doug went in the water, then dried himself in the sun in a lounge chair, Frank and Norma in chairs on either side of him, sunning themselves.

"What do you call this?" he heard someone say angrily.

He turned to see a bony man of about 70 in a baggy bathing suit confronting a stout woman a few years younger in a one-piece suit that did not cover the folds of her fleshy body.

"This is my chair! It had my hat on it," he said.

"What hat? There's no hat."

The man bent to look under the chair and found a peaked cap lying nearby on the ground.

"It was on the chair. You threw it off."

"I didn't throw it off," she said, pulling the chair toward herself.

"Gimme my chair back," the man said, trying to pull it away from her. "You fat moose."

"You call me names? You old bonebag."

"Gimme. It was my chair. Gimme!"

They were both pulling on the chair, and Doug could see, the way they were doing this, if either lost a grip that person would fall backward and be hurt. People poolside were watching as though it were the morning program. Doug rose to intercede but before he could reach them the man yelled, "It's my chair, you fat robber!" He pulled with great effort and collapsed, a kite falling. He was grabbing his chest and gasping. The regulars knew the signs. People were rushing on all sides, one man ministering to him, someone else running to use the security guard's phone. The man lay on the ground next to his prized chair, and in a few minutes an ambulance came and took him away. People settled back to their places, late arrivals were told about what had happened, and in a while it was quiet at the pool again.

At night, Doug and his parents were sitting on the patio, looking out at the artificial lake.

"This is yours someday," Frank said. "Yours and Marty's."

"Incredible, isn't it?" Norma said of this small patch of space she owned. "To have something like this in your life."

The incident at the pool seemed to have no particular effect on them. They had learned to live with ambulances. Doug was shaken by the occurrence. Comparing himself to his children or to yuppies, he was not extraordinarily younger than some of these people at the pool. Was this next? Your life is about a place to sit and you can have a heart attack over a chair?

15

ANN TOWNSEND'S HOUSE OVERLOOKED THE HAR-
bor on a hill high above the town of Charlotte
Amalie in St. Thomas. A person could sit on her terrace,
scan the boats and cruise ships in the harbor, sip daiqui-
ris served by her houseboy, and congratulate oneself on
one's personal wonderfulness.

In the afternoon Doug drove a Jeep Ann kept at the
house and they went to a cove facing the island of St.
John. Ann was there for a meeting with Steve Clair, a
developer who was converting a former beach club into
a condominium complex. Ann's financial adviser had
made an investment for her in the development, and
Clair, whom she knew in New York, had asked her to
look at the site while she was on the island. Out of courtesy she came for a tour of the grounds. Clair was in his
40s, blond, tanned, six feet tall, casually dressed in a
work shirt and dungarees. He showed them the site while
referring to blueprints and drawings.

"Steve is a genius at real estate," Ann said to Doug.

"If you know how to get work done down here, you can come out very well," Clair said.

"All looks good to me. I gather I'm in it anyway," Ann said.

"You are. Incidentally," he said to Doug, "if you want to get in on this, have your lawyer call us in New York."

That was how it was done in certain circles. If you belong—have your lawyer call us. Clair went off to his Jaguar and Doug and Ann strolled along the secluded beach.

"We're going to make love right now, right here," Doug said.

"Not in public."

"This is not public. There's no one here."

"Doug, please."

"Even if someone saw us, they wouldn't quite believe what they were seeing," and playfully he started to pull her to the sand, but she resisted.

They made love that night, after cocktails, after dinner, after the houseboy left, at the correct end point of the evening. On a beach the next day Doug found a Frisbee half buried in the sand, and he tried to toss it with Ann, but she did not care to join in. He wanted to take her by the shoulders and shake her and say, "I like you, but I want you, just once, to throw a Frisbee, be spontaneous, sing 'On the Road to Mandalay' like Jerry Colonna." He started to sing "On the Road to Mandalay" and when he got to where the flying fishes play, a few sunbathers looked up and Ann asked him to stop. They stayed in St. Thomas for another two days and nights, reading, talking about what they were reading, making love at the appropriate moment, after dinner, before sleep, a time in the Caribbean without tropical passion, rather, with tropical correctness.

A few days later in New York a charity ball was held for the Red Cross at the Waldorf, Ann listed on the program as a member of the organizing committee, while Doug was a "friend of the ball" for five hundred dollars. Ann was busy with other members of the committee talking to the press, and Doug stood by himself observing the assemblage. Tom Daley was there with his wife, Mary, an attractive woman in a glittering silver gown, and he introduced her to Doug.

"This man's a quick thinker," Daley said. "What have you got for me fast? A modest good deed."

"Literacy. You manufacture computers. There's a relationship. A person has to read to use them. Give some money to literacy programs."

"See that?" Daley said. "I will, Doug."

Daley excused himself and led his wife to the dance floor. Doug watched the dancers while he sipped champagne. He knew several people on the floor and they waved to him, a few executives he had met in business, people he knew through Ann and the Macklins. God! This is *my* crowd. I've become *they*.

SUSAN PHONED DOUG TO HAVE A DRINK WITH HER AT the Pierre after work. She did not look well to him. Had he not been paying attention or was it that now, completely released from her, he saw her more clearly? He noticed wrinkles in the corners of her eyes, the faint beginnings of a redistribution of weight around her face and chin. No. I really don't want this to be. But you, too, Susan. You're looking older.

They talked about the children and Karen's decision to stay in New York. Susan was preoccupied while they spoke, nervous, fidgeting with her glass, folding and refolding a cocktail napkin. Then she said, "Doug, I have something to tell you. Jerry and I are getting a divorce."

"What?"

"We've brought in lawyers. We've told the children. I'm moving out this week."

"You are?"

"He was having affairs. Whether that's the symptom or the cause, I don't know. But he was having them—" her voice broke. "From the beginning. I didn't want to see it. Eventually the pattern was so evident, I couldn't deny it anymore."

"Are you all right?"

"I'm coping."

"How did the kids react?"

"They were upset. I had to give them a reason and I said, among other things, that Jerry and I were incompatible, and that didn't go over too well. Then I told them Jerry was a bit immature for marriage, and I imagine they understood it had something to do with other women. He had a long talk with them privately. He was crying. He said he cared for them very much and that they should continue to be friends. I wish I could believe him. Looking back, I think I was just another possession. We all were. He got me the way he would a new car."

"I'm very sorry for you."

"I've been seeing a shrink. We discussed the impact on the children. Apparently it's better than if they were little. She said it would be good if they didn't create any reconciliation fantasies about us."

"Right," he said, finally beyond those himself.

"So I talked to them about the new apartment I was going to take and about fixing it up with them."

"You're going to leave that palace?"

"I don't want to be there. I'm getting a smaller place on East Seventy-second Street. Poor Harry. I don't know how he's going to take it, sleeping in a hallway like other dogs."

"All those rooms in all your houses—"

"Jerry's going to keep the country house and sell the apartment. He'll make a profit. And I'll be all right. He's paying for my new apartment, which he should, and I own a piece of the Flash stores."

"Oh—"

"I thought of them. I planned them. I designed them. His imagination is limited to stories covering his tracks with women. Doug, I'm such a disaster. Two divorces!"

"Right now there are young girls going to schools and working in their first jobs trying to be you."

"Thank you for saying that. But maybe they'd want my bankbook—they wouldn't want the rest of it. My shrink said that Andy and Karen should come through this all right because they know that individually you and I have been 'rocklike.' "

"That's us, rocklike," he responded softly.

"Who would have known? As a couple we ended up better in divorce than we were in marriage."

HE WENT HOME, EXULTANT. THE GAMES WITH BROEDEN were over. Doug bought a bottle of chilled champagne and sat in his living room drinking adieu to Denim Jerry. He ordered a pizza, pizza and champagne, a goodbye Broeden party. About an hour later, having finished the bottle, tipsy, he went into the shower and tried to think of an appropriate song for the occasion, choosing to sing "I'm Gonna Wash That Man Right Out of My Hair," shouting, "I know it's a girl's song, neighbors, but the sentiment is right!"

Then the headache in the morning and the implications of the divorce. What view of love could Karen and Andy possibly take out of this, their parents divorced, their mother divorced twice? And Susan was going to have to begin all over. He wanted to believe that in Susan's marriage to him she had married for love, and with Broeden, perhaps in part, she had married for convenience. Either way it didn't work out for her.

Doug felt it was important to see the children soon to talk about the divorce. Andy was coming into New York to visit the new apartment, and Doug took Andy and Karen to lunch. They sat in a booth in the Blarney and the children tried to give him the impression that furnishing rooms in another new place was a positive experience, they were going to choose new art, new colors, but Doug could read the pain in their faces. We're doing this again. It didn't work out again. Humpty-Dumpty. He couldn't put together the pieces of these marriages or remake his own. The children talked on, too fast, too enthusiastically, about interior-decoration details, trying to conceal the pain from him and themselves. They stopped. Karen and Andy were still, seemingly exhausted from pretending interior decoration was the real concern.

"I want you to know," he said, "even though this marriage didn't work out, that doesn't mean love isn't possible."

"Your marriage didn't work out either," Andy said.

"I'm well aware of that fact, Eunice," he answered, quoting a line from a funny television commercial they all liked, and they smiled.

"Maybe when I'm older there'll be something invented beside marriage," Karen said.

"The important thing is for you not to decide from this that love can't happen. You've got to look at my marriage to Mom and Mom's to Jerry and say to yourselves that we don't speak for you. That you can fall in love and get married in spite of us. You've got to listen to the most old-fashioned, syrupy, June-moon sentiments about love and believe them for yourselves. And at your gloomiest, most cynical times—"

"—which may be right now," Andy said.

"Fair enough. And when you're older, I want you to think back on this moment, this very instant, and I want you to remember that I said to you, the most important thing in my life, what I care about more than anything, is being your father. And I wouldn't be your father, and you wouldn't be here, if once upon a time I hadn't fallen in love with your mother and she hadn't fallen in love with me."

DOUG WAS ON A LARGE POWERBOAT, POSSIBLY A YACHT, he couldn't tell the difference. The last boat he'd been on was a rowboat in Central Park. This boat was called *The Red Herring* and was owned by Sy Chapman of Chapman Realty. They were bursting through the waters of the Hudson on a tour of Manhattan Island so that Chapman could point out his real-estate holdings along the way. A crew of three were doing boat tasks while Doug and Chapman surveyed the skyline. Chapman was five feet six, in his late 50s, and so round his shape looked like it was created by someone rolling dough for a large pizza.

"You like it so far?" he asked Doug.

"It's sort of my own Circle Line Cruise."

"I'm one of the biggest owners of residential. Commercial there's bigger. Residential, I'm tops. Right in there, I got," he said pointing to the shore. "And there, I got."

"There" was an apartment house on Riverside Drive, the scene of a landlord-tenant dispute over alleged harassment by Chapman, which Doug had read about, the argument eventually ending in a compromise.

"You had some problems there."

"We settled. We're all friends. I'm for the tenant, I'm for the city. I came from the Lower East Side. I'm fair, 'The Fair Landlord.' That's our motto."

"I didn't know real-estate companies had mottos."

"I thought it up myself. Now how do we get it across?"

"We're talking about a sports tie-in principally in New York?"

"I don't own real estate in Chicago."

"I'm a little slow today. I'm not a water person."

"You want to go back?"

"Yes, to be truthful."

"Hey!" he yelled. "Back!"

"A nice event could be a walk race through the streets of the city, ending in Central Park. There haven't been many walk races. We could set this up in advance with classes, walk race clinics."

"The people, they would wear my T-shirts?"

"You could donate T-shirts to the walkers."

"And on the front would be my picture and it would say, 'Chapman, the Fair Landlord'?"

"You want your picture and your motto on the T-shirts?"

" 'The Fair Landlord.' I'm stressing that."

"I hear you. I don't think the public will go for it, Mr. Chapman. They may feel a little used, to become walking billboards for you."

"Why should I do this, then?"

"For general publicity, for goodwill."

"The finish line, there's a banner?"

"Yes."

"It could go there, too."

"These are not political campaigns."

"I'm going to have to think about it. But you try to get my picture in. I got a nice picture. Bachrach. Fancy photographers."

DOUG WAS INTERVIEWED IN HIS OFFICE THE FOLLOWING week by a reporter for *Business Times* magazine on the subject of sports tie-ins. The reporter was in her early 20s, a studious-looking brunette who used a tape recorder and constantly checked to see if it was recording. She asked questions from a prepared list in her notebook, so intent on her system and her tape recorder, Doug was not certain she was listening to the answers. When she asked if tie-ins weren't a vulgarization of sports, a question he had asked himself, he answered that they were not, as long as they were bona fide events, which he tried to maintain as a requirement.

"You're doing a tie-in with Sy Chapman, I understand."

"We talked. We don't have anything definite. How do you know that?"

"He hounds our office for publicity. Now—do you find any difficulty—" she read from her notes—"doing business with a man accused of harassing tenants and blocking the designation of a Greenwich Village apartment house as a landmark in order to demolish it for profit purposes?"

"A compromise was reached in the first instance and in the second he withdrew his plans. He's not guilty of any crimes, and we're talking about an event that will be good fun for the public."

"Do you think tennis tie-ins are saturated in the marketplace?" she said, briskly moving on.

As she pressed along with her questions, he was still thinking about the way he bluffed his way through the hard part—and that he'd probably succeeded. He was on the other side now, doing what people he had interviewed attempted to do—finesse the interview.

ANN WAS INTERESTED IN GOING TO AN ANTIQUES SHOW in Greenwich, Connecticut, and asked Doug to join her. She did not bother to own a car; she used a car service for herself in the city, and Doug rented a car for this excursion. At the show she bought a child's needlework sampler from 1840, exquisite and four thousand dollars. "I've been looking for one," she explained, and wrote a check. A few minutes later he saw a patchwork American quilt, red, white, and blue squares, which Ann pronounced "well executed," and he bought it for four hundred. I didn't need that, but this life-style is not about need, is it? What the hell. It's "well executed." Doug and Ann left the show with their purchases and Ann suggested, since they were so near, that they stop by to see her mother in Darien. Ann called, her mother was out, but was expected within the hour, and they drove to her house. He expected a house, not Versailles. Past thick, tree-height hedges, and through a locked gate, opened after communicating by phone with the main building, they entered a long circular driveway leading to a Georgian style red-brick structure that made John Gannon's Mamaroneck Colonial look like a bungalow.

"How many rooms?" he asked.

"Twenty or so," Ann replied.

"And who lives here?"

"Just my mother. And the staff."

"Is this where you grew up?"

"With my brothers."

An elderly uniformed butler greeted them at the door. "Miss Ann."

"Walter. This is Mr. Gardner."

"Your mother will be back soon."

"Where did she go?" Ann asked.

"OTB."

"Your mother went to the betting parlor?" Doug said.

"It's a hobby," she answered.

They strolled the beautifully landscaped grounds. A crew of grounds keepers were at work under the supervision of an old man in green work clothes whom Ann greeted, and he tipped his hat.

She showed Doug the inside of the house, bedrooms Ann and her brothers had occupied, a bedroom suite which had been her father's, who had died ten years earlier—her mother had her own bedroom suite—guest rooms for adults, guest rooms for children, a billiards room, a Ping-Pong room, dens, parlors, a servants' wing.

A vintage Cadillac limousine, high off the ground, with big fenders and large whitewall tires came into view, driven by a chauffeur so old and fragile he could barely see over the steering wheel. Moving stiffly, he came out to open the door for Ann's mother, Mrs. Grace Fielding, a small gray-haired woman in her 80s, stoop-shouldered, with a well-preserved face, probably once a beauty. She was in a pink dress, pink shoes, carrying *The Daily Racing Form*, and wearing a green eyeshade.

"A terrible morning," she said. "All my ponies were out of the money. How are you, Ann? Who is this?"

"Doug Gardner, a friend of mine."

"A new friend? What do you do?"

"I work in the sports field. I put together sports events which corporations can sponsor."

"I never heard of such a thing. Do you know the ponies?"

"It is not my strongest point."

"Doug used to be a sportswriter, Mother."

"Were you? Tell me about it over tea."

She moved slowly into the house, servants opening doors for her as she went.

"Fast start, slowing now toward the finish," she said to Doug on the way to the rear patio. "But don't count this filly out."

An elderly maid served tea and cookies at a wicker table and chairs. Except for the laborers in the garden, nobody on the staff looked under 70.

227

"Happy Banquet. Off at twelve-to-one and I had him. Led all the way and went into stud on the back stretch. Know the horse?" she asked Doug.

"Not personally."

"Not personally. Amusing. Did you ever know any horses personally?"

"I was introduced once to Dr. Fager."

"And?"

"He tried to bite me."

"He *was* a biter! That's true Ann." She opened the *Racing Form.* "Let's talk a little about the trotters."

"Mother, I don't think Doug wants to sit here and pick horses."

"Where did you do your writing?"

"*Sports Day*. The *New York Post.*"

"I used to buy the *Post* for the charts. Then I went over to the real horse sheets. Remember Native Dancer? Short odds, but I bet big. I furnished the bedrooms off that horse."

"Jimmy Cannon wrote a piece about him I'll never forget. It was nearly over the line of taste, how Native Dancer was a great horse, but a nicer guy."

"He wouldn't bite you, the Dancer." She turned to Ann. "I like him," she said about Doug. "Why don't you marry him?"

"Mother!"

"We can throw you a nice wedding on the grounds."

"I've been married on the grounds."

"But *he* hasn't."

Ann's mother announced she wanted to play croquet, Ann declined, and Doug went with her mother, taking instruction from her on how the game was played.

"You never played croquet? Where have you been? You should think about marrying Ann. Faded last two starts. Could surprise."

"I'm flattered."

228

"She's not the liveliest of women."

God, is this my future, too, muttering about sports and saying outrageous things?

"Ann is a good person," he said.

"Yes, she is. And she comes with the house. I left her the house. My boys don't need it. They have houses."

They played awhile and then she grew tired.

"I appreciate your doing this," she said, and they walked back to the patio where Ann was sitting.

"One of your best," she pronounced about Doug, and sat in a chair. "Impressive start. Could close well." Her head dropped down and she fell fast asleep.

"She is very colorful," Doug said.

"Less so when she's yours."

He could see himself sitting with the old lady on a Saturday, sipping tea at the wicker table and handicapping horses, drifting along in this convenient, slightly emotionally detached affair with Ann, accruing benefits, or one day even marrying her and being in this immense house on these elegant grounds. I played baseball. I could learn to play croquet.

16

THE EXECUTIVE DINING ROOM FOR TOM DALEY'S
company was in a glass-enclosed terrace on the top
floor of the office building overlooking the harbor, fresh
flowers on the table, two waiters serving wine and pâté.
Doug and Daley were joined for a drink by the advertising manager and the promotion manager. In two meetings with these associates of Daley's neither had said
anything Doug would have characterized as particularly
insightful or creative. They probably held well-paying
jobs and lived in nice homes in the suburbs, the kind of
men Doug saw illustrated in advertisements in *The Saturday Evening Post* in the 1950s and had aspired to be
when he enrolled in the business program at NYU. Now
in the room with them, he felt they were unexceptional.
Daley was sharper than his two executives. Doug did not
know if he could handle Daley's job. He was sure he
could match the other two.

"What would you like for dinner tonight?" Daley
asked Doug.

"What is on the menu?"

"There is no menu," Daley said, smiling. "Order whatever you feel like eating. My chef will send someone for the ingredients and prepare it."

"The Ultimate Take-Out Order."

Doug asked for poached salmon and a salad. Daley ordered the same. They talked about the Street Olympics, and other likely promotions. Dinner was ready in about an hour and on cue the two executives, who had not been invited by Daley to remain, excused themselves. Daley's mood changed when they left, he became more intense, now he could do the real talking.

"Doug, our company is moving to take on the Japanese in international markets. I see us getting involved in a sports tie-in on a grand scale, something global. And you're the guy who can put it together."

"It's what I do."

Daley opened a file folder that had been on the table and thumbed through copies of some columns and articles Doug had written.

"You're creative and you don't come up from the corporate ranks."

"I did get a B in Management, as I recall."

"Most of the people around me wouldn't say that. They're too frightened. I like that you didn't work your way along in the bureaucracy."

"I have paid my dues, Tom."

"But you're not all smoothed out from fitting in. You have a unique feel and I'd like it full time. Doug, I want you to come and work for me."

"Tom, the guys who were in here before, they were dismissed from the room. Basically you just dismissed them. I wouldn't want to be in that situation. I answer to Macklin in a loose sense, but I'm on my own."

"Let's talk about that. You've got to call on companies to make sales. You have competition. The competition could get tougher. What looks good now won't in a few years.''

"Once a tie-in is set, it goes on making money.''

"But you've got to keep selling tie-ins. Doug, I want you here very much. I see myself relying on you for the company's image, my public image, overseeing speeches and in other areas, too, in corporate decisions. I see you as an important right-hand man for me.''

"Looking at those guys skulk out of here—''

"You won't answer to anybody in the corporation but me, and I've got a feeling you won't be toadying up to me, either. We'll put you outside the organizational lines. Vice-president in charge of special promotions. This is the gold ring on the carousel.''

"You have that.''

"Yes, I do. But there's a smaller ring and it's still gold. Two hundred thousand a year to start. A three-year guaranteed contract. Fifty thousand a year automatic increases. Stock options, and we're growing. You'll never touch that kind of money with Macklin. And we'll throw in access to one of the corporate limos with a driver. This job doesn't exist, Doug. It's being created for you.''

"You're giving me quite a lot to think about.''

"From my standpoint, there's nothing to think about. You're moving from seller to buyer, doing interesting work, and getting rich. By the way, how's the salmon?''

"Excellent.''

"This room is yours. Only a few of us are permitted to use it. I'll make it available to you.''

"Amazing. The last perk was suits. Now it's personalized poached salmon.''

DOUG SPOKE TO BOB KLEINMAN THAT EVENING WHO said the job offer was "fabulous.'' His main concern was whether access to the limousine and driver extended to personal use.

"Incidentally, I'm not seeing Connie anymore," Bob said. "She started making demands like a wife. I have a wife. I figured out if I spent as much time on the marriage as I spent maintaining the affair, maybe I wouldn't need the affair."

"I think you made the right move, hot pants."

"I doubt if Sarah ever knew. But I got into the habit of doing the dishes at home, something I picked up when I was with Connie. And Sarah looked at me sort of suspiciously one night."

"Men are supposed to give themselves away in bed. You would have been the first to give yourself away in the kitchen."

Doug went to work the next day trying to compare his current job with Daley's proposal. His first call of the morning was from Sy Chapman asking if Doug would agree to having Chapman's picture and motto on all T-shirts and banners in return for sponsorship of the walk race. Doug offered a compromise to get the tie-in: the motto, but no pictures. They were concluding their conversation when they were interrupted by the operator who said there was an emergency call coming in. The call was from Doug's mother.

"It's about your father," she said.

"What?"

"He had another heart attack. He's alive. He's not dead yet."

"What do you mean, yet? How bad is it?"

"Worse than the last time."

"Where is he?"

"Broward General."

"Did you speak to Marty?"

"He was out. He'll be back soon, they told me."

"We'll be on the next plane."

They went down on the first available flight. At the hospital, Doug and Marty found Norma in a housedress sitting in the reception room.

"Mother, what's happening?" Doug asked.

"No visitors again for an hour."

"How is he?" Marty said.

"Critical."

Doug and Marty spoke with the cardiologist. They were going to run tests when Frank was stronger, to check the feasibility of a bypass. Visitors were permitted, a limit of two at a time, and since Norma had been there earlier, Doug and Marty went up together. Frank was tied to a system of tubing and connected to monitoring equipment. He looked white and waxen. In the room were two other men behind screens, also wired to technology.

"My guys. My guys have come to see me," Frank said, speaking with difficulty.

"Hello, Dad," Doug said.

"How are you feeling?" Marty asked.

"You gotta have heart. That's what we say at the condo. It's supposed to be funny. I still got heart."

"Sure you do, Dad," Doug said.

"How are the children?"

"They're fine," Doug answered.

"Everybody's good," Marty told him.

"We saw your doctor. He wants to run some tests," Doug said. "They can do amazing things these days."

"I want you two to make me a promise. When I go—"

"You're not going, Dad," Doug said.

"When I go, I don't want to be put in the ground where the worms can eat me. I want to be cremated."

"Dad—"

"Promise me you'll do this. You promise?"

"I promise."

"Marty, speak up."

234

"I promise."

"I want my ashes to be taken out to sea. And I want you to scatter them over the water, in the clean, beautiful water. But not in Florida," he said, his eyes going back and forth between them. "It can't be in Florida. I don't want my ashes out there with any southern fish. You take me to Sheepshead Bay and you go out and scatter me over the water, and my soul will rest with good New York flounder."

The effort of speaking drained him and he closed his eyes. Doug and Marty sat for a while watching him as he slept. They went down to the lobby and Norma went up for a half hour and returned, saying he was still sleeping. She checked again, he hadn't awakened, and they went back to the apartment. Doug and Marty stayed in the guest room that night, the brothers sharing a room together as they had when they were young, whispering in the dark, this time not of girls or plans, but medical talk about their father. The phone rang at five in the morning. Frank Gardner was dead.

"He would do this," Norma said, crying. "Just when it was getting good."

Doug and Marty handled the arrangements concerning cremation, tickets for people to fly down from New York, the planning of a memorial service. Doug raised the question about where the service should be held, in New York or Florida, Norma preferring to stay in Florida. On the night before the ceremony the family assembled at Norma's apartment and collectively wrote a eulogy. They decided the group effort would best be read by the rabbi. He was provided by a nearby synagogue, a suitably sympathetic man, but young, he looked no more than 30. The *rabbis* are now younger than I am.

The main house in the Palm Vista development contained a chapel, where the memorial service was held. A few of Frank and Norma's friends from New York who had moved to Florida were there, and two men introduced themselves as fishing friends of Frank's. The eulogy was an accumulation of details, Andy's recollections of card games with his grandfather, Karen's playing board games with him; Marty and Ellen's daughters contributed their memories of Frank helping them make snowmen, Marty and Ellen recalled Frank's visits to their country house, Norma remembered how hard he worked for so many years, and this touched on Doug's contribution, the sheer longevity, all those years of paying bills and staying solvent, which had come to seem, in time, a form of heroism.

Doug could not keep from thinking, One day this will be me. If they follow this script, I'll go out on a good song, something from *Guys and Dolls* or *Annie Get Your Gun*. Under instruction from Doug, the organist was concluding the service by playing a song Frank Gardner liked to hum, "When My Baby Smiles at Me."

Doug helped Karen and Andy through these few days, Karen frequently weeping openly, Andy fighting his tears. He reminded them their grandfather had lived a long life and they had been part of it. Both stayed close to Doug, always sitting near him. Andy with his manly gait—I'm in college, I'm not a child—and Karen with her burgeoning womanly carriage were unnerved by this lesson in human perishability. Doug sensed their need to be physically near him was to reassure themselves that *he* was all right. He saw, in his father's death, his own mortality, and so did his children.

After the ceremony people milled outside the building, everyone agreeing the service had gone well, but Doug was feeling something was not right here. His father's memorial service was held on a balmy day in Florida, people strolling outside in shorts, golfers and palm trees in the distance. This had nothing to do with his father. They should have been in Manhattan with cabs and cars going by, city textures, movement, noise. These were part of Frank's world and Doug wondered if coming to this place had actually accelerated the end and that Frank Gardner hadn't belonged here any more than he should have had his memorial service here.

DOUG AND MARTY CHARTERED A FISHING BOAT BY phone, and when they arrived in Sheepshead Bay without fishing equipment and with Doug carrying a briefcase which contained the urn, what they did not look like was fishermen. The boat owner was in his 30s, a tall, lanky man who viewed them suspiciously.

"Are you going to rent any stuff?"

"We won't be fishing," Doug answered.

"You won't be fishing. I guess I better just take you and not ask any more questions, huh?"

"Sounds good," Marty said.

"Poor guy," Doug said to Marty. "He's got to think we're with the Mob."

When they were out away from shore Doug opened the briefcase and removed the urn. Doug and Marty both held the urn, and as the boat cruised along they let the ashes trail into the water.

"Goodbye, Dad," Doug said. "You worked so hard. You did your best."

"I haven't anything to say," Marty told Doug. "Basically, he never liked me."

"What do you mean?"

"He didn't."

"That's not true."

"I was too short."

"Marty—"

"He wanted his son to be tall, and I wasn't much taller than he was. And he was disappointed in the way I turned out."

"He was very proud of you, of the stores, Ellen, the kids, the house in the country. You could see it in his face whenever he was around you. He was proud, Marty."

"Really?"

"Really. Ellen and the kids remembered that for the service. And the height thing, that's in your head. How tall was he? Neither of us was going to be Kareem Abdul Jabbar."

"Well, I would want to say to him—you *did* do your best, Dad. And I'm going to miss you."

The boat headed back to shore and they sat in silence, watching the water.

He was 69. In six weeks I'll be 50. If it seems like two minutes ago since I was 30, what do I have left, two more minutes? What difference does it make how I spend them, working for Macklin or working for Daley? Time is rushing by so fast, it's frightening.

Doug made no decision about Daley's offer in the period following his father's death. He went back to work. At night he watched movies on the video recorder. He did not read. He had all the information he needed. He was going to be 50.

The children called him at home from Susan's new apartment asking how they could celebrate his birthday. They wanted to give him a party.

"I don't want to do anything."

"Dad, your birthday is going to end in a forfeit," Andy said.

"You have to do something wonderful," Karen said. "Something you haven't done before. Like a helicopter ride over New York."

"Maybe I could overwhelm it with banality," Doug

238

answered. "Dinner at Burger King. Then you go to bed and it's over."

He had spoken to Ann when he was in Florida. She called wondering why she hadn't heard from him since.

"It's this birthday. It really is a myth that men should celebrate their fiftieth. What is there to celebrate?"

"Your achievements."

"Oh, is that it?"

"Doug, you have to get out of this. We'll have a fantastic party. We'll do it at the Fairlys' house. We'll get Lester Lanin. Do it black tie. Sumptuous. But I've got to work fast. I'll start calling people."

"I don't want it, Ann."

"Right now you don't know what's good for you."

"I agree."

"And what about tomorrow night?"

"Tomorrow night?"

"The Hilton. The awards dinner."

This was a banquet Ann had helped organize to honor major contributors to United Way.

"I totally forgot."

"Doug!"

"I know it's important to you. I'll be there."

He took her to the event, wearing his tuxedo, and made courteous small talk with various people in his new crowd. Tom Daley, who was one of the guests, came over to him. "Well?"

"I can't say yet."

"Doug, I'm going to Europe for a few weeks. When I get back I'd like to have you start working for us."

Among the people at the table where he and Ann were seated was a venture capitalist planning a luxury resort in New Jersey, which he talked about with religious zeal, and a retired general, who had been in service during the Vietnam war, attempting to rewrite history at dinner tables. Champagne was poured freely, and Doug interspersed the champagne with double Scotches to get though the speeches at the table and the podium. His head was spinning from the drinks and he sat uneasily in the cab back to Ann's apartment, worried that he might throw up. He kissed her goodnight at her door—this was a weekday night and he was not staying, and rather than take a cab home he thought it wiser to walk for a while. Unsteadily he headed down Fifth Avenue and turned west on Central Park South.

He started to think about his father, who had never gone to an event such as this evening's, or owned a tuxedo, who had never set foot in rooms such as Doug now passed through, a workingman about whom the summation was that he did his best. Doug had gone far beyond his father, they were not in the same social class. But the question he asked himself on this night was, Am *I* doing my best? Was working for Macklin his best? The job offered by Daley was probably a better version, but was work where he promoted a corporation his best? Was this relationship with Ann, businesslike and formal for mutual convenience, his best? Was going to her events, spending that much time at balls and parties his best? Would marrying Ann and playing croquet on the great lawn be his best? The marriage to Susan, was *that* his best? To be attracted to someone because of her style and then to resent it when she takes that style into the business world? So she began to work longer hours. You can't be attracted to a woman for her qualities and then resent where her qualities lead her. That was so pitifully second-rate. And what about Nancy? You let her get away and you settled for this—this tuxedo. The tuxedo suddenly became the embodiment of everything that was wrong. He was choking in these clothes. He pulled the bow tie from his collar, threw the jacket to the ground, pulled the cummerbund away from his body. No air. Choking. Can't breathe.

He was going to rest sitting against the wall of a building for only a moment to catch his breath. He passed out on the sidewalk. An ambulance came for him and Doug was revived by an orderly's slapping him on the face. He entered the ambulance on shaky legs. "Where are we going?" he asked. "Roosevelt Hospital." They took Dad to Roosevelt Hospital.

The doctor in the emergency room said to him, "Our medical analysis is you're drunk." Doug was released and he walked to his apartment in shirtsleeves, throwing up twice in the gutter along the way.

He took a hangover to work the following morning, canceled a lunch appointment, and managed to get through the day. He was not seeing Ann that night; he thought of himself as "off" for the evening. He noticed in the paper the Mets had a night game against the Philadelphia Phillies. It had been months since he had been to a ball game and he decided to go. He went by subway to Shea Stadium, bought a general-admission ticket and walked to the highest point of the ball park, the last seat in the last row in the right-field corner, so he could have the entire panorama in front of him. The sky grew darker, the lights in the stadium took effect, converting the playing field into deeper contrasts, the greens and whites more vivid, the field coming into sharper focus for him. The dimensions of the game were striking from that high up, the open expanses of baseball. The spaces were the beautiful aspect, the empty spaces between the players, between the bases, the fielders attempting to fill the spaces, the instant of not knowing whether the ball would drop, go fair, foul, into the seats. In that instant, in those spaces was the beauty of the game. He was reminded of that again, sitting at this distance.

The crowd did not reach all the way back to Doug, closest to him was a burly man of about 40 in a windbreaker drinking beer, three rows in front. He was a

241

grandstand manager, turning to make pronouncements to Doug, the only person in his vicinity.

"Third-base coaching, it can kill you," the man said. "It's a split-second thing, to send a guy, hold him. And who do they get for it, a lot of teams? Fat guys. Management. I'd have guys who were good base runners, that's who I'd get. Pennants been won and lost by third-base coaches but you don't hear about it."

When a pinch hitter came to bat for the Mets, he said to Doug, "I say, let the righties hit against the righties more and the lefties against the lefties. It's too much with the percentages. You follow my drift?"

"I do."

"You got to give them confidence instead of all this platooning, platooning. These are human people here. This is not computer baseball."

He kept up a running commentary, and at one point challenged Doug to prove he was worthy of his attention. He wanted Doug to call the Mets' strategy with a runner on base. Doug successfully predicted a hit-and-run, which satisfied him that Doug was a real fan. The Mets, behind 3–2, scored a run in the eighth.

"All right! We tied it!" the man yelled. "You want a beer? I'll buy you a beer."

"That's okay."

"No, no, for good luck."

He brought Doug a beer and returned to his seat, calling out instructions to the players. When the Mets won in the tenth on a Gary Carter home run, the man, beaming, walked back to shake hands with Doug.

"Nice game," he said.

"You, too."

"I'm Mike O'Brien. I'm here a lot. This is my spot."

"Doug Gardner."

"The sports guy?"

"The sports guy."

242

"No kidding? I used to read you at the *Post*. What ever happened to you?"

"I moved up."

Doug sat for a long time watching the crowd leave and the stadium become empty. I love it. I love the Mike O'Briens and the Tony Rossellis and the ball games. And I wasn't as good a writer as I could be. I hadn't done my best yet. I can be better.

THE NEXT DAY HE MADE CALLS TO EDITORS AT THE NEW York City newspapers looking for a job. As he had suspected during the conflicts with Reynolds, there weren't any openings for a columnist and the people of his prominence in the sports departments were all in place. The most encouraging response was from the *Daily News*. He knew the sports editor, Dave Goodman, for whom he had worked when they were both at the *New York Post*. Goodman said he was interested in Doug, but couldn't make a decision unilaterally, it would have to be discussed within the company.

Doug was scheduled for another black-tie event with Ann the following night, a dinner party at the Sutton Place apartment of Dr. and Mrs. Mitchell Breen—a night for his backup tuxedo. He contacted Ann and asked if he could stop by at her apartment. She dismissed the staff and they sat in the living room, where she served wine and a perfectly displayed assortment of cheese and crackers.

"We were supposed to go to that dinner tomorrow night," he said. "And I wanted to tell you, I can't go, Ann. I can't go to any more of these events."

"What are you saying?"

"It's not working out. And on top of everything, I realize I'm in love with someone else."

"Doug, this is very unlike you. To be so duplicitous. Carrying on with two women at the same time."

"I'm too monogamous for that."

"I don't follow."

"It's a woman I was seeing a while back, a prior commitment I have to renegotiate, if I can. I just felt with another dinner tomorrow and two more next week and more to follow after that, I couldn't go through with them anymore. In a sense, I'd be deceiving you."

"I see. My mother will be disappointed." And with a trace of a frown she added, "And I am, Doug."

"You're lovely, Ann. I'm really sorry."

"I suppose we won't be having your birthday party then?"

"No, we won't be having my party."

"Maybe I should have been, I don't know, what should I have been, looser, more frivolous? I can't be."

"That's the thing. We were ourselves. There's a sports expression, 'playing out of position,' when you're where you shouldn't be on the field. With this life-style I've been playing out of position."

"This life-style is all I know."

"I thank you for everything. You've been very generous, the contacts, Tom Daley—"

"That was part of the deal," she said softly.

HE TRIED SEVERAL TIMES TO REACH NANCY BY PHONE that night. The time was after eleven when she answered.

"Hello?"

"It's Doug. I have to see you. Nancy, I love you."

"Doug—"

"Can I come over right now?"

"Aren't you in a relationship with somebody?"

"I can honestly say I'm not. Are you with anyone?"

"No."

244

"I'll be there in ten minutes."

"Doug, I literally just came back from work. I'm completely exhausted. We'll have dinner one night."

"Tomorrow."

"I can't tomorrow. I'll call you. I'll let you know."

The exchange reminded him of what he might have sounded like putting off Tony Rosselli. Rosselli would not take an "I'll let you know." Rosselli would be standing in front of the woman's building the following morning at 7 A.M., waiting for her to leave for work, ready to sell, hoping she was not with a man, and prepared to deal with it if she were.

Doug was there at seven and when Nancy emerged at nine, alone, he approached her.

"How long have you been out here?"

"A couple of hours. I have a speech. It keeps getting shorter. I love you and I want to marry you."

"You said you didn't want children. You were very direct about your feelings."

"I'm not going to lose you over children. We'll have wonderful children."

"And what about not having the energy for it?"

"Well, it's not like I'm one of those guys trying to fight off old age with young kids. If I'm still thinking about my options, I'm not that old, am I?"

"No, you're not that old, Doug, which I was trying to get you to see. Why didn't you tell me all this before?"

"It took me a while to get here. Unfortunately, I took the scenic route."

Perplexed, she sat on the steps of the building.

"After we broke up, I had to think about the possibility that I'll never get married," she said. "And I thought, I have my work, and if that's my life, I can accept it. But if my work is important enough to sustain me, how could I throw it away to have a family?"

"You wouldn't have to."

245

"I don't know what you expect. What if we had children and I went back to work? I wouldn't work insane hours, but I might work full time."

"Fine. I'll arrange my time for our children. I'll make my tuna croquettes."

"Until you resented my working."

"I won't. Nancy, I offer my first marriage in evidence. It was messed up partly because I didn't accept then what I'm accepting now."

"You *say* that."

"I mean it. This is like the guy who wants to sleep with the girl and she says, 'Will you respect me?' and he says, 'I'll respect you like crazy.' I love how smart you are, and that you have a career, and I will *after* we're married. I'll respect you like crazy."

"Do you know how many two-career marriages fail?"

"*All* of mine. I can cut that ratio in half if we make it."

DOUG AND NANCY BEGAN SEEING EACH OTHER AGAIN. He was attentive whenever she talked about projects at work, trying to prove his good intentions. But he thought the only test of how he would react in a marriage to a working wife was to be in the marriage. She was still uncertain, though, and wanting to proceed cautiously she suggested they not get together every night. He was so happy to be with her, and she seemed to respond the same way, that not seeing her was maddening. He didn't think they could continue like this, a decision would have to be made.

DOUG WAS STILL AWAITING A RESPONSE FROM THE *DAILY News*, and two weeks after his inquiry, he was asked by Dave Goodman to meet at a coffee shop near the newspaper offices. Goodman was an amiable, balding man in his 50s with a round, cherubic face.

"Doug, this wasn't something I could do on my own. I had to talk to the higher-ups."

"I understand."

"I said this was an excellent opportunity for us and I definitely wanted you. Except everybody's in a slot. So we can't offer you that much. Fifty thousand is our limit."

"I see. That would be to start. One hopes it will get bigger."

"Obviously, later on."

"And if I want to do any TV or books on the side, I assume I can. I'd also like to retain syndication rights on my pieces."

He smiled at Doug's response. "Have you been negotiating lately? I'm sure we can work all that out. Look, Doug, basically we'd be making room for you because it's you. You'd have to cover a beat. With the season on now it would be baseball. And we'd give you a Sunday column for whatever you'd want to write."

"Great."

"But isn't this a comedown? It's like starting over."

"That's what I need."

"Then you've got a job, friend."

Goodman took Doug through the *Daily News* offices, Doug saying hello to people. He was jubilant to be at a newspaper again. Then he went to see Macklin and told him it had been an interesting experiment and he was grateful for the opportunity, but he was going back to sportswriting. He also sent a letter of explanation to Tom Daley.

When Doug spoke to Bob Kleinman, Bob started to stutter.

"You—you turned down that job? And—you're going to live on that?"

"I intend to increase the money."

"I should hope so. And what about the terms? We've got to find out if your services are exclusive, what rights you retain."

"That's already been discussed. And you won't have to negotiate clothes this time. This is not about clothes."

"Doug, is *this* what you want?"

"It's what I am."

ANDY WAS COMING TO NEW YORK FOR THE WEEKEND and Doug had plans to take the children to dinner on Friday night. He called Nancy and asked her to join them. The atmosphere at the Blarney when Karen, Andy and Nancy saw one another again was like a reunion. They accounted for the time that had passed since they were last together. Then Doug made his announcement.

"I have a new job. I'm on the sports desk of the *Daily News*. I'm back!"

Nancy threw her arms around him, the children were giving him high fives, low fives.

"This is so wonderful," Nancy said.

"We get good seats again," Karen teased.

"And we get to read you again," Andy said.

They were excited for Doug, he was excited, it was a victory dinner. At the end of the meal Doug asked Nancy if she would linger over coffee for a few minutes, and if Karen and Andy didn't mind, he would put them in a cab.

"I'm thrilled about the job," Nancy said when they were alone.

"Nancy, anything more you need to know about us you can only know after we're married. I have you on this point, Counselor. You have to marry me to know if you want to be married to me."

"I love you, Doug. It's the marriage I have doubts about."

"So do I."

"Then if we both have doubts—"

"The doubts are going to save us. They mean we're not naive, that we'll be watching out for the problems. As for me I'm going to get it right this time."

"I don't know."

"Let's give it a try."

She began to laugh. "With the entire body of romantic literature in the English language, do you think that ranks with the great ones? Let's give it a try. All right, Doug. Let's give it a try."

THE MARRIAGE CEREMONY WAS HELD AT THE HOME OF Nancy's parents three days before Doug Gardner's 50th birthday. Doug's mother came from Florida, Jeannie and her husband from Arizona, Nancy's relatives, friends, and business associates were there, as were Tony Rosselli, John McCarthy, Marty, Ellen, and their children, Sarah and Bob Kleinman. Karen was the maid of honor. Andy was the best man. Next to the wedding cake was a birthday cake for Doug with fifty candles. On the cake was an inscription Doug had asked for, the words of the sage Yogi Berra: "It ain't over till it's over."

ABOUT THE AUTHOR

AVERY CORMAN came into national prominence with his first novel, OH GOD!, which later became a George Burns motion picture. His next novel, KRAMER VERSUS KRAMER, was made into an award-winning motion picture starring Dustin Hoffman and Meryl Streep. His third novel, THE OLD NEIGHBORHOOD, was a hardcover bestseller. He lives in New York City with his wife and two children.